CHRISTMAS COWBOY

HOPE ETERNAL RANCH ROMANCE, BOOK 4

ELANA JOHNSON

ISBN-13: 978-1-953506-18-4

CHAPTER ONE

S late Sanders drove down the highway next to the Gulf of Mexico, the window down as the sun came up. The scent of the beach and seaweed touched his nose every so often, and he couldn't wipe the smile from his face.

He'd spent four years behind the fences and walls of River Bay Federal Correctional Facility. He hadn't had a girlfriend or a wife when he'd gone into prison, and he hadn't thought he wanted one now that he was out.

Images of Nate and Ginger walking hand-in-hand, their heads bent together, flowed through his mind. He then remembered the way Ted and Emma sat on the back porch of their cabin, the love between them real and infectious.

Maybe Slate had been bitten. Maybe he wanted to meet someone who would make his heart feel less like a black stone and more like a vital human organ. Maybe he could if he didn't literally run away from every female he laid eyes on.

He'd been at Hope Eternal Ranch for almost two months, and he still hadn't said more than hello to any of the women who worked there. A few women lived next door in the West Wing, but Slate never went there. More women worked out on the ranch, with the horseback riding lessons, or with other chores. He kept his head down and hadn't spoken to any of them either.

He wasn't sure why, other than he wasn't sure Hope Eternal was his final landing place. He couldn't go back to banking, but he wasn't as keen to grab onto the cowboy life-style with both hands the way Nate, Ted, and Dallas had.

The three of them never went anywhere without their cowboy hats and boots, and they fit right in on this ranch. Slate hadn't fit in anywhere, except with the other junkies.

"Can't go back there," he told himself. He absolutely would not go back to Austin, where he could easily slip back into the businessmen underground, where professionals worked their day jobs and then partied all night.

His phone rang, and Slate reached for it. Nate's name sat on the screen, and Slate slowed down to pull over. The truck he'd been able to get wasn't new or fancy, like the one Nate drove, and he couldn't talk without holding the phone to his ear.

"Hey," he answered as he pulled to the side of the road.

"Where are you?"

"Just driving."

"You're not going north, are you?"

Slate rolled his eyes, glad this wasn't a video call. "No, *Dad*," he said.

Nate didn't laugh, sigh, or otherwise make any noise. He did say, "Ted worries about you when you leave before dawn."

"Ted does, huh?"

"We all do," Nate said.

"I'm clean," Slate said. "I haven't touched drugs in over four years, Nate."

"I know that," he said. "I also know, as does Dallas, how loud the call of addictive substances can be. We love you, and we want you to be happy."

"I'm just driving by the water," Slate said, looking over to it. "I like the water."

"Yeah," Nate said. Several moments of silence went by, and then he added, "It's Sunday, and that means we'll have breakfast at the West Wing."

"Yeah, I know about it," Slate said.

"You've never come."

"No, I haven't." Slate didn't explain further. He'd only been twenty-nine when he'd gone into prison, and he'd only had a couple of girlfriends in his life at all. Once the drugs had taken center stage in his life, Slate didn't care about anything or anyone else.

He needed something else to focus on, but Slate had never felt so lost.

"I'll let you go," Nate said. "Just...call one of us if you need us, okay?"

"Okay," Slate said. He stayed still on the shoulder for another minute, and then he eased back onto the road and pulled over into a parking lot at a beach. One other car sat there, and Slate barely gave it a glance as he got out of his vehicle. The warmth of the sun never really went away in this part of Texas, but the morning was definitely the best time to find a whisper of cool air.

He went down the wooden steps to the sand, trying to remember who he was. Thinking about who he was five years ago, before everything had gone down at the bank, was like trying to think about someone else. Trying to live someone else's life, with memories that didn't fit who he was now. There was nothing to remember about who he was, because he wasn't that man anymore.

The wind picked up, and Slate ran one hand through his hair, thinking he'd like to grow it out as long as he could stand it. Then, and only then, would he cut it. Since he'd been out for a couple of months now, his hair had grown quite a bit, but Slate still didn't feel the need to cut it.

He went all the way to the water's edge, the horizon made only of waves and sunshine. He bent down and touched the gulf, feeling the power of the earth and the water all at the same time. In that moment, he knew he should get a job where he got to work outside, and another heartbeat later, he realized he already had a job like that if he wanted to keep it.

A sense of peace and serenity washed over him, and while he didn't have all the answers for his future, he at least felt like he could start making new memories for the new man he was.

A woman screamed, startling him and breaking into his little bubble of reflection. He stood and looked left, toward the sound.

A woman ran toward the water dozens of yards down the beach, and another primal yell ripped from her throat as she threw something into the water.

Slate wasn't sure if he should go make sure she was okay or just walk away. He watched as she bent and picked up something else from the beach. She screamed as she hurled it into the ocean too.

Without thinking too hard about it, Slate started walking toward her. She seemed like she could use a friend —or at least someone to help her if she threw herself into the ocean next.

As he got closer, she started yelling, and while Slate couldn't catch all of the words, he got the general idea. Someone in her family was very sick, and she'd come to the beach to release her frustrations at the injustices of the world.

Slate slowed, suddenly not wanting to intrude. He knew exactly how she felt, though he'd learned to control and contain the rage and irritation while behind bars. He could box up everything and keep it silent. He could stare at the bottom of a bunk bed and let his thoughts run until he fell asleep, never saying anything to anyone.

Only Nate knew what Slate really thought. Then when he'd left, Ted. Dallas. Luke.

He needed to get back to the ranch.

The woman turned toward him, and Slate froze. He knew her, and his stomach dropped to his shoes before it rebounded back to its proper place. "Jill?" he asked.

She sobbed and flew toward him so quickly that Slate barely had time to open his arms before she latched onto him. He wrapped her up tight, her anguish seeping right into the fleshy parts of his heart and making him close his eyes and pray for her relief.

TWENTY MINUTES LATER, HE HELPED JILL INTO THE front seat of his truck with a, "There you go. Yep, you're good." He met her eye again and closed the door before going around to get behind the wheel.

"I'm sorry," she said, wiping her eyes again. "I was just on my way back to the ranch, and I started crying, and...." Her voice trailed off, and she shook her head.

"You don't owe me any explanations," he said quietly.

"What did you hear on the beach?"

"Nothing much," he said. "Combined with the waves, it was just noise."

Jill nodded, the longer front pieces of her hair flopping a

little bit. She sniffed as she pushed it off her forehead and tucked her hair behind her ears. "My mother is very sick," she said. "I'm very angry at God about it."

Pure surprise flowed through Slate, and his eyebrows went up as their eyes met. "I can imagine," he said. "In fact, I don't have to imagine." He looked back out the windshield. "I've been very angry at God about things before." By the time he finished speaking, his voice was at whisper level. "Very angry at myself too."

Jill nodded and wiped her face again.

"I think there are some napkins in the glove box," he said.

She opened it and pulled out a couple of the scratchy, brown napkins Slate had gotten at some fast food restaurant. "Thanks." She wiped her nose and eyes and drew in a long, deep breath. She held it for so long that Slate thought he might have to perform some sort of rescue procedure this morning after all.

She finally released it and said, "I think I can drive back now."

"Okay," he said, flipping the truck into reverse.

"No, I meant I can drive myself."

"That's not happening," he said. "I've been precisely where you are, and you're just on the top of the roller coaster right now. There's another dip coming, unfortunately." He glanced at her as he pulled up to the highway. "How long have you known about your mother?"

"I just found out this weekend," she said, her voice

pitching up on the last word. "She's a fighter. She's going to be okay."

Slate liked the optimism, but he also knew that sometimes things were not okay. He said nothing, though, because Jill deserved to cling to that hope and positivity if she chose to.

After a couple of minutes, he said, "I can bring someone to get your car any time."

"Thank you, Slate," she said, and he did like the way his name rolled out of her mouth.

"How long have you worked at the ranch?" he asked.

"Seven or eight years," she said. "Are you going to stay? Ginger has mentioned that you're up in the air."

"Yeah," Slate said. "That about sums up my whole life right now." It had all gotten tossed up into the air, and he had no idea where all the pieces would end up falling. He looked at her and found her with her head leaned back against the rest, turned toward him.

She had pretty blue eyes, even watery as they were, and her hair was a messy kind of short style she could muss up with her fingers and it would look better than before.

"Have you ever felt like that?" he asked, looking out the windshield again so he didn't drive them into the gulf.

"Like what?"

"Up in the air."

"No," she said quietly. "That's probably why I'm handling this diagnosis so badly." She half scoffed and half sobbed. "That's what my sister says, at least."

"How old is your sister?"

"The oldest one is forty, and she's, you know, perfect. Perfect husband, with the perfect job. Two perfect kids, perfectly balanced with a boy and a girl." She exhaled and wiped her face with the napkin again.

"I know the type," he said, seeing the family perfectly in his mind's eye. "That was my family growing up."

Jill sucked in a tight breath. "Oh."

"I'm not offended," Slate assured her quickly. "I just... know the type." He looked out his window at the gulf again, wishing he had the guts to call his parents and let them know he was out. The fact that they didn't know spoke volumes about their relationship, but Slate wondered if the new version of himself could try again to be the son they wanted.

The miles passed in silence after that, and after a few minutes, Slate looked over to find Jill leaning against the window, fast asleep. His heart went out to her, because he understood what it felt like to go through trauma and the sheer exhaustion that caused.

He wanted to protect her from the tumultuous times ahead, but he knew he couldn't. He'd learned to release the things he couldn't control in prison, and he couldn't control her mother's health.

When he turned onto the ranch and bumped from a smooth road to a dirt one, Jill jostled and woke.

"We're back," he said softly. "I'm sure they still have breakfast going in the West Wing if you want to eat."

Jill wiped her hair back again and glanced around. "I'm sorry I fell asleep."

"Don't be." He pulled into the gravel lot and parked. Neither of them got out of the truck. "You should probably eat something."

She looked at him, and Slate turned his head toward her. She was a beautiful woman, and his pulse performed a weird flip in his chest. He had no idea what it meant, only that he couldn't look away from Jill, almost like her gaze had become a tractor beam, and he'd gotten stuck in it.

"Will you come with me?" she asked. "I don't want to go in alone."

Slate didn't understand why. She'd lived here for years, and with one look at her, all of her friends would rally around her. They'd provide the support she needed, and Slate would disappear into the background.

He knew, because he'd seen the women here at Hope Eternal Ranch do that for each other several times in the short time he'd been there.

"Okay," he said anyway. "But I can't stay long. I have to get out to the...." He let his sentence die, because it was Sunday, and he didn't have to get out to the fields that day. He had no reason why he couldn't accompany Jill to breakfast and then spend the rest of the day with her too.

No reason except the fear pounding through his bloodstream at the very thought of walking into the West Wing and eating breakfast with everyone on the ranch.

CHAPTER TWO

J ill Kyle shimmied into the pale blue bridesmaid dress, frustrated at herself for the extra few pounds she carried. A month ago, she hadn't had the extra curve in her hip, but she'd had a very trying couple of weeks, and she'd been coping with her stress by eating.

Her kryptonite was ice cream and potato chips, and she'd been drinking a protein shake for lunch while carrying a bag of chips at the same time.

"You're stunning," Hannah said, and Jill turned toward her.

"You're joking," she said, taking in Hannah's much taller frame and much trimmer waistline. "I can't even zip this thing up."

"I can." Hannah stepped over to her, bringing the soft scent of a rosy perfume that Bill had given her. The zipper went right up, and Jill could still breathe. That was a win in her book, and she had something to put in her gratitude journal that night.

Jess and Dallas were getting married today, so she should probably put something like, *I got to watch one of my best friends marry the man she loves*, in her gratitude journal. She was grateful for that, and she decided to save the zipper for a day when she literally couldn't find anything to express her gratitude.

Hannah wrapped her in a hug, and Jill turned to return the embrace. "How are you today?" Hannah asked.

She searched her emotions, and thankfully, she'd found some stable ground. "I'm okay," Jill said honestly. She wasn't alone, and that helped immensely. She lived about twenty-five minutes away from where her parents did, and Ginger had been more than accommodating with Jill's requests to be there when her mom went to her doctor's appointments, and when she got home from the first round of chemotherapy.

Daddy was taking good care of her, and Jill's youngest sibling, McKenna, lived in Sugar Hill, so she'd been able to help a lot too. Haven, the oldest, lived thirty minutes in the opposite direction of Jill, and she'd been present at everything Jill was. Probably more, because Haven was the most perfect at everything.

Their brother had come to what he could, but he lived in Oklahoma now, and he had a wife and family there, along with an important job he couldn't just leave whenever he wanted.

"We better get going," Hannah said. "We don't want to be late." She slipped out of Jill's bedroom and down the hall to hers while Jill moved over to the closet to find her shoes.

Jess and Dallas were getting married in their back yard, and they were having the most traditional ceremony of anyone who'd been married in the past year. Jess was still going to ride her horse down the aisle, but then they'd have a traditional wedding dinner and dance following the nuptials.

Her parents had been in town for a week, and Jill already missed her sassy and strong presence around the ranch while she'd been off entertaining them and finalizing details for the wedding. She and her dad had come to the West Wing yesterday, and together, the two of them had cleaned out the bedroom where she'd lived for twice as long as Jill had been at the ranch.

Jess was still going to work at Hope Eternal Ranch, so Jill would get to see her. She knew it wouldn't be the same, because when change happened, things simply weren't the same anymore.

She put on her shoes, wishing it was as easy to slip on a smile. Stopping in front of the mirror mounted to the back of her closet door, Jill tried on her smile. It looked surprisingly real, and she paid attention to how it pulled, and how her muscles in her face felt. If she could just get through the next few hours with this smile in place, she could retreat to the safety of her bedroom and text her father to find out how Mama was doing.

She met Hannah and Michelle in the hallway, and the three of them walked into the kitchen one after the other. Jill remembered she couldn't go anywhere without Chapstick and detoured over to the drawer beneath the microwave, where they kept several tubes of the stuff. She slathered up her lips and tucked the tube into her bra before following the other girls out the door that led into the garage.

Michelle almost always parked in the garage, because she only lived at the homestead part-time. She came to the ranch about once a week to meet with Ginger, talk about the prisoners they had there, and offer other legal advice to keep the ranch in the clear. She had a bedroom here, because there was enough room—especially now that Emma, Ginger, and Jess had all vacated their rooms—and because she often came in the evenings after she finished her work in San Antonio, which was a two-hour drive from Sweet Water Falls.

She'd come on Thursday night and stay until Sunday, and Jill had been crossing her path at odd hours as she left the ranch when Michelle was arriving.

Her sleek, dark eggplant SUV sat just steps away from the entrance to the West Wing, and Jill rounded the hood to get in the passenger seat. She glanced to the back deck that extended off the Annex, and she found Slate leaning against the railing, looking out over the ranch.

He wore a dark suit that fit him like a glove, and

coupled with that cowboy hat...Jill's pulse went crazy. She'd vowed not to date anyone for a while after her last boyfriend—a man she'd met at Nate and Ginger's wedding —had cited the reason for their break-up to be the distance between them.

Physical distance, he'd meant, and the drive was eighteen minutes.

Jill knew it was something else, but Mike had refused to say what. She'd decided she'd had enough of flirting and flitting from man to man. She was thirty-three years old now, and she was going to take her relationships more seriously. That way, maybe the men she dated would take her more seriously.

"Slate," she called, though she hadn't expressly told herself to speak. The faux cowboy turned toward her, his face a stoic mask until he recognized her. Then he lit up, and Jill wondered if that meant something.

It doesn't, she told herself.

He'd been extremely kind to her a couple of weeks ago, and Jill had not forgotten it. She'd been a complete mess, about to launch herself into the ocean waves and tell God to take her instead of her mother. Slate had been there, and he'd calmed her enough to get her into his truck. He'd spoken to her like her feelings and actions were normal, that she wasn't the only one who felt the way she did, and that she didn't need to apologize for the emotions raging through her.

Haven had scolded Jill about "falling apart" in front of

their mother, and to "have more faith" to see them all through this crisis.

Jill wasn't even sure what that meant. All she knew was that she'd had plenty of faith about a lot of things in her life, and God did what He wanted to do anyway. What was the point of pouring her heart out to Him? Why should she kneel beside the bed and beg, plead, and cry, only to do it again the next night? And then the next. And the next.

She felt abandoned, and that morning at the beach had been the worst bout of abandonment of all.

Then Slate Sanders had been here, and while Jill had met him once and seen him around the ranch a couple of times, she didn't know him.

"Hey," he said easily, coming toward her though he remained on the deck. His smile was hitched in place too. Jill wondered if he'd looked in the mirror and memorized how it should feel on his face the way she had. "You ladies heading out for the wedding?"

"Yeah." Jill indicated the car. "Do you need a ride?"

"Nah," he said. "I'm waiting for Luke and Ted. We're going together."

Jill frowned, a conversation from last night's dinner tickling her memory. "You sure? Ted said he was going with Nate, I thought."

Slate frowned and looked toward the back door. "I guess I better find out."

"Do you want us to wait?" She knew the rules with the men who came to Hope Eternal Ranch in the Residential

Reentry Program. Slate wasn't in that program; his sentence was complete. But Luke was, and that meant that he couldn't leave the ranch by himself. He had to be with a ranch employee, and Jill wondered if Slate counted.

He just likes to drive by the beach. Nate's words moved through her head. He'd been worried about Slate the past few weeks—worried that he'd get in his truck, start driving, and never come back.

"Maybe," Slate said. "Give me a minute, okay?" He strode away, and Jill could admit she liked the breadth of his shoulders in that suit coat. *Wow*, she thought. Tall, trim, tan Slate Sanders. A month ago, had she seen him like this, she'd have sidled up to him at the wedding and tried to get to know him better.

Now, her heart resisted what would come so naturally to her.

Jill loved people, and she'd always enjoyed talking to them, getting to know them, and spending time with them. She was no good alone, and she was usually the last one to go to bed, as she stayed up with whoever was willing to sit with her so she didn't have to be alone.

"Jill," Michelle said. "We don't want to be late."

"I'm not sure Slate and Luke have a ride," she said. "He said he needed a minute." She looked back to the deck, but Slate had gone inside the Annex, and he hadn't returned yet. "You guys can go. I can drive them in a ranch truck."

"Are you sure?" Hannah asked, getting out of the back seat. She looked at Michelle and then back to Jill.

"Yeah, sure," Jill said easily, and her pulse started an increased rhythm.

"They won't start without Luke and Slate," Hannah reasoned. "They're two of Dallas's best friends."

"We can wait," Michelle said. "Because she has a point."

"You can ride in the front," Jill said to Hannah.

"I'm fine." Their eyes met, and Jill had never had to spell out much for Hannah. She must've been able to say she had some sort of insane crush on Slate, because Hannah just nodded. "I do need to fix my mascara, and I can use the mirror in the front." She went around the back of the car and got in the front seat.

Slate came out onto the deck. "Can we ride with you guys? Ted left a while ago." He didn't look happy about it either, and Jill didn't blame him.

"Sure," she said. "We have room."

Luke came outside too, and Jill seriously doubted they'd fit in the back seat of Michelle's SUV. They had shoulders Jill had never seen, and she knew all the River Bay men met in the equipment shed at six-thirty to lift weights, something they'd apparently done together in prison.

Slate arrived at her side, and Jill smiled at him. "I'll ride on the hump in the middle. You scoot on over, cowboy."

He grinned and reached up to touch his hat. "Do you really think I look like a cowboy?"

"You certainly do," she said. "I'm not sure if you are one, but you look the part."

"Good," he said, and he slid all the way over behind

Michelle. Jill gathered up her skirt and got in the car too, sliding over into the middle spot. Luke managed to cram himself in next to her and close the door, and that alone was a miracle.

"All right," Michelle said. "Are we all in?"

"Yes," Luke said, and Jill looked at him. He was a handsome man too, and he'd started to grow a beard the same way Slate had. She smiled at him, and he smiled back at her before looking out his window.

Her pulse didn't react, and she knew he wasn't the one she'd spend her time with at this wedding. She didn't even dare look at Slate, because her hip was pressed into his, and her thigh too, and the entire left side of her body tingled with his touch.

He cleared his throat, and Jill glanced at him. "Do you have enough room?" he asked, moving his right leg over a little. "You can put your foot over here."

"Thanks," she said, and she did adjust her leg so it wasn't so tightly crammed into the back of the console between Hannah and Michelle. She smoothed down her skirt so her legs were properly covered and listened as Hannah and Michelle started talking about the cooking show they'd watched last night.

With the radio playing, and conversations happening, Jill looked at Slate again. "Have you decided if you're going to stay at Hope Eternal?"

He shook his head, his slate-gray eyes still sparkling under that cowboy hat. "What do you think? Should I?"

"Do you hate it?"

"No."

"Do you like it?"

"You know what? I actually do."

Jill looked up at the charcoal-colored cowboy hat. "I mean, the hat fits, right?" She smiled, and it was easier than the one she'd practiced in the bedroom. The smile she could give him felt as easy as the flirty ones she'd doled out at the previous weddings she'd attended.

"So you're saying if the boot fits, wear it?"

"Sure," she said. "You have a nice room here. The Annex is big and air conditioned. You like the job. You look the part." She reached over and smoothed down his tie from where it had stuck on his lapel. Something hot and charged zinged through her, and her eyes immediately went back to Slate's.

He'd felt that, Jill could tell. She could no longer hear Hannah and Michelle talking, and if there was music playing, it wasn't reaching her ears.

"Okay," Slate said. "I'll stay." He shifted his shoulders so he could lean his head closer to hers. She actually leaned into him too, ducking her head so he could whisper in her ear. His hand landed on her knee, and Jill pulled in a breath as sparks shot up her leg and down to her toes.

"For you, Jill," he said. "I'll stay for you." He took her hand in his then, and his was so much bigger than hers. Warm, and large, and everything a cowboy's hand should be. Jill *loved* holding hands with a cowboy, and she smiled to herself as he settled their joined hands on his leg and looked out his window, the conversation obviously done.

The conversation her heart was pounding out to her brain wasn't done, but Jill didn't even listen to the two of them. She closed her eyes and leaned against Slate's shoulder, her fingers twined nice and tight with his.

CHAPTER THREE

Slate wasn't sure what in the heck he was doing. Whispering sweet things in a woman's ear and holding her hand. He could admit that when Jill laid her head against his arm that he'd felt mighty fine.

He felt like perhaps he was worth something, and somehow, Jill Kyle could see it.

Slate knew he couldn't. Nate and Ted and Dallas had told him to keep looking, because he'd eventually discover how amazing he was, but Slate only nodded while they talked. Luke hadn't seemed to have a problem finding his role on the ranch and in his new life.

He has it easier than you, Slate thought. Luke himself had admitted that because he was still in the Residential Reentry Program, and his life was not entirely his to live yet, that his transition from prison to ranch had been easier than Slate's.

His phone buzzed, and Slate glanced down at the armrest where he'd stowed his phone. Luke's name sat there, the message flipping up as well, then disappearing before Slate could read it.

He used his left hand—as his right was still firmly clasped in Jill's—to pick up his phone and swipe. His left thumb stumbled a bit, but he got the job done.

What are you doing? Are you and Jill a thing now?

Slate pulled in a breath and looked at Luke. He lifted his eyebrows so high, Slate thought they might go right off his face. He wore darkness in his expression too, and he actually frowned as if he wasn't happy with the very idea of Slate and Jill being "a thing."

Slate looked back at his phone, more confusion running through him. Luke knew him better than anyone on the planet. He'd heard all of Slate's deepest, darkest secrets, his greatest fears, and what made him wish for things he never thought would happen.

Another text came in, and Luke said, *I mean, it's fine if you are. I just didn't realize. You never said anything.*

I don't know what I'm doing. Slate pecked out the sentence one painful letter at a time. He really wasn't very ambidextrous, and it took several long seconds before he sent the message five feet to his right.

Jill sat up and drew in a deep breath. She removed her hand from Slate's with a quick glance at him that he didn't meet. Relief ran through him at the same time disappointment cut into his chest.

He really had no idea what any of it meant. The ride to Dallas's house blinked by, and before he knew it, he was getting out of the luxury SUV and turning back to help Jill. The skirt on her blue bridesmaid's dress hitched up a little, revealing a few inches of skin above her knee.

"Oops," she said, sliding the rest of the way out quickly and pulling it down. She flicked her eyes in his direction and looked away again.

Slate closed the door behind her, his eyes following the trail of people leading around the garage to the right, where a bunch of balloons in pink, white, blue, and yellow floated lazily above the milk can they'd been anchored to.

There was something quaint and calming about it, and Slate took a long breath that seared the inside of his nose, down his throat, and into his lugs. He coughed, and Jill laughed lightly. "Yeah, you really can't breathe that deeply in June," she drawled. "It's like breathing in fire."

"Yeah," Slate said, his throat suddenly so dry.

"I don't get a proper breath of air until at least November." She kicked a smile in his direction and started walking toward the balloons. Hannah came to her side almost instantly, and the two of them struck up a conversation.

Slate watched Jill go, his mind running through all the possible scenarios that would bring her back to him.

"Come on," Luke said, turning to call to Slate. "Don't just stand there staring."

That got Slate to move—and a healthy dose of heat to fill

his face—and he joined Luke. "I don't want to talk about it," he said.

"You were holding her hand," Luke practically hissed. "You're going to talk about it."

"It's not a crime," Slate said, glaring at his friend. "I'm allowed to hold a woman's hand."

"Yeah, but." Luke glanced around as if there might be federal agents about to burst from behind fences and take them back to River Bay. He was definitely the most paranoid of the men in the group, and Slate usually got a rise from Luke's rants about government conspiracies and that he'd seen a guy at the grocery store that looked just like one of their Unit Managers.

Today, though, he really didn't want to hear what Luke was going to say next. The sidewalk along the side of the garage wasn't very wide, and he fell back to walk behind Luke. That didn't stop him from saying, "I didn't even know you were staying at Hope Eternal. I only have six more weeks, and I thought we were going to go see what else the world had to offer."

"Yeah," Slate said, though he knew what the world had to offer. Heartache. Disappointment. Tragedy.

The same things he'd experienced before the decisions that had led to his incarceration, and the same things that existed in the world now.

Just look at Jill's mom, he thought. She was only sixty-one and dealing with a terrible, life-threatening disease. He knew Jill's heart ached for her mother. He knew she was disappointed her mom might not be able to see her get married or have kids. Her mother's death would be a tragedy for Jill.

Life was hard, Slate knew that.

"Has the plan changed?" Luke demanded once they reached the back yard.

"I don't have a plan," Slate said. Once, he'd lived his life according to a plan. He'd had to in order to cover up the drug use.

Now, he woke each day with new possibilities on the horizon. No two days were the same at Hope Eternal, and Slate thrived on that.

He glanced around the back yard while Luke continued to mutter about the plans he'd been making for the both of them. Slate had been to Dallas's house previously, but it had been transformed with flowers, antique jars and cans, stumps of wood, strings of lights, and miles and miles of ribbons and flowing fabric.

The large patio that extended from the back of the house had been covered by an enormous, free-standing pergola made of a light-colored wood. The sides let in the breeze, but the top had been latticed, and then white, gauzy fabric had been woven through the holes to create the shade on the patio.

Ribbons of fabric hung down in the corners, and flowers sat on every table surrounding the patio. Right now, rows and rows of chairs took up the patio, and Slate started toward the row where Ted sat with Emma and Nate sat with Ginger.

He took a spot next to Nate, who looked over at him. "There you are. Dallas was just starting to get twitchy."

"Yes, well," Slate said, leaning over to look past Nate to Ted. "*Someone* told us we were riding with him."

Ted met Slate's eye, and Slate challenged him by raising his eyebrows. "I had to come help set up."

"I heard that too," Slate said. "It's fine. Whatever. We got a ride with the women."

"Yeah," Luke said, taking the end seat next to Slate. "He—"

"Stop it," Slate said, practically growling the words at Luke. To his surprise, Luke cut off and didn't say anything else.

"I'm sorry, Slate," Ted said. "I wasn't thinking clearly when I said I'd give you guys a ride."

Slate felt Nate's gaze on the side of his face, and he didn't appreciate it. The man had a way of seeing things and knowing things he shouldn't possibly know. "I said it was okay," he said. "We got here, and we're not late."

"I'll text Dallas," Nate said. "Then he'll know."

"We have to go line up in a minute anyway," Ted said.

A tiny part of Slate died. He'd forgotten that he had to walk in the wedding. A couple of rows up, Jill sat down next to Hannah and Michelle, and Slate thought if he could walk down the aisle beside her, it might not be so bad.

"Yeah," Nate said. "Let's go check with him. They

should be ready to start soon." He stood, and that meant everyone had to. He held Ginger's hand as he went past Slate and Luke, and they followed him.

Inside the house, Slate could take that deep breath without searing his lungs, and a few seconds later, the back door opened again, and several women wearing the same blue dress Jill had on spilled into the house too.

"Okay," Dallas said, and Slate looked away from the short-haired blonde to the groom. Dallas wore a black tuxedo, and Slate had never seen him look so sophisticated. Nerves rode in his eyes too, and Slate couldn't even imagine the turmoil in Dallas's soul.

"We're five minutes out," he said. "It's a simple procedure. You line up and walk out. Jess and her dad will come last. We don't want anyone up at the altar with us, so you'll circle back to your seats." He glanced around at the small crowd that had gathered around the dining room table just inside the back door. "You all have seats, right?"

Murmurs of assent went through the crowd, but Slate said nothing.

"And that's it," Dallas said. "After the ceremony, we'll have lunch, and we should all be out of here by two o'clock." He nodded like this wedding was just one of his many tasks on his to-do list that day.

Slate didn't believe that for a single moment, though. He'd seen Dallas with Jess, and they were obviously very much in love.

"Kids first," Dallas said. "Come on, Thomas. Remmy."

He glanced around when only his son came forward out of the crowd. "Where's Remmy?"

"She wants to walk with Jess," Dallas's mother said, her voice very quiet.

"Well, she can't." Dallas set his mouth into a firm line and went down the hall. "Nate and the other boys right after the kids. Get lined up," he called over his shoulder.

Nate, who always seemed to know where to go and exactly what to do, led Ginger to the front of the line, right behind Thomas. He spoke easily to the boy while Ted and Emma lined up behind them. Slate supposed he could go third, though Luke could've just as easily. He took the spot, though, with Luke behind him. The other cowboys from the ranch move into position behind him.

Slate wasn't sure if the women in the bridal party had been assigned a spot or not, and he only looked over when someone came to stand next to him.

Jill smiled at him, a gesture which lit up her pretty face, and said, "Do you have a partner?"

"No, ma'am," he said, reaching for the brim of his cowboy hat. He wasn't even sure why. He tipped his hat at her and smiled when she laughed and shook her head.

"So Texan," she said, linking her arm through his. She was very good at flirting, which only amped up Slate's nerves. He hadn't had a reason to flirt with another human being in many long years. "Did you grow up in Texas?"

"Yes, ma'am," he said. "My family lives on the outskirts of Austin. My daddy owns a barbecue joint in the city."

"Oh, that's amazing," she said. "I'm from just up the road. Sugar Hill?"

There were probably a million small towns in Texas, just like Sweet Water Falls. He said, "I don't know it, but it sounds nice."

"It is nice," she said. "Rolling, green hills, blue sky, big sunflowers in my mom's yard." She smiled at something in her mind's eye, but Slate liked the relaxed, happy look on her face. "There's this pond we used to swim in. And big water towers. And sometimes, I swear when you go to Sugar Hill—there's an actual hill there named Sugar Hill too—it smells like freshly baked cupcakes."

"Wow," Slate said, his smile genuine now. "That really does sound amazing. I can always go for a cupcake."

"Right?" Jill laughed again and sighed. "I love weddings."

"Yeah?" he asked. "Why's that?"

"They're just so happy," she said. "There's so much love in the air. You can just *feel* it."

Slate could feel something, he could admit that. He wasn't sure if he'd classify it at love. The air held a definitely crackle in it, like something amazing was about to happen.

"You're up front," Dallas said, marching his daughter to the spot next to Thomas. He turned and took in the others who'd lined up, and some of the tension fell off his face. "Okay," he said. "I guess everyone's just waiting on me then."

"That's right," Nate said. "So get out there so we can get started. It's not getting any cooler."

"You got married in the middle of the afternoon in September," Dallas quipped, reaching for his cowboy hat. He settled the black-as-midnight hat on his head and ducked out the door. He left it open, but Slate stood back far enough to still be bathed in air conditioning.

The wedding march started, and he pressed his arm closer to his side, bringing Jill closer. "Here we go," he said. "I hope I don't fall down."

"I was just going to say that," Jill said. "And ask you to catch me if I did."

Slate grinned at her, their eyes truly meeting for the first time in several minutes. "I'll do my best," he said. "But it is dang hot out there, and I hate it when people are watching me."

"We'll make it," she said, and before he knew it, it was their turn to step out of the house and head down the aisle.

He made the trip without making a fool of himself, and he made it all the way back to his seat. He didn't sit though, but stayed standing and turned to watch Jess coming down the aisle.

She rode a magnificent white horse with flowers in its mane and along its ears. Her bear of a father led the horse with loose reins in his hand. He was tall and broad, and he wore a cowboy hat as well.

At the altar, he helped Jess glide gracefully to the ground, and Slate saw more flowers and ribbons braided into the horse's tail. He smiled, because that was an amazing way to get down the aisle.

Jess hugged her dad and kissed his cheek before stepping beside Dallas. Her father hugged them both again—one big squishy sandwich that had a few people laughing—and turned to lead the horse away.

"Please be seated," the pastor said, smiling. He waited while all the scuffling and moving happened, and then he focused on Jess and Dallas. "Marriage is such a wonderful blessing," he said. "To have found someone you can share your life with is indeed something to be grateful for. I encourage you to find the good in one another every day, because there will be trying times ahead."

Slate seized onto those words, because they felt so true. There would be trying times ahead—for everyone. He wanted to have loved ones at his side to help him during those times. As the ceremony continued, he allowed himself to feel some of that happy buzz he and Jill had been talking about, but in the back of his mind he knew he needed to call his parents and make things right between them.

Dallas read his vows to Jess, which were sweet and loving. "I won't be perfect," he said. "I'm going to try my best every day. I think that's all either of us can ask. I love you, and I'm grateful you love me too."

Short, sweet, and totally Dallas.

"I love you too," Jess said. "I appreciate that you appreciate who I am, and that you give me the rope I need to be who I am. I know we will build a beautiful life together."

Even better, in Slate's opinion. The pastor did the official business, finally concluding with, "You may now kiss your bride."

Slate blinked as Dallas and Jess laughed and then kissed, and he cheered and clapped with everyone else at the wedding.

Dallas and Jess faced the crowd, both of them grinning for all they were worth. Slate's emotions swelled, and he whistled through his teeth to try to release it. He identified it as so much joy, and he simply couldn't contain it.

The cheering died down, and Nate turned to Slate. "Okay, lunch."

Slate shook his head and rolled his eyes. "You have such a one-track mind."

Nate smiled, and a moment later, he nodded behind Slate. He turned, thinking Luke had stepped out of the row to go find a table. Instead, he found Jill standing next to the chair on the end, her blue eyes sparkling.

"Want to sit by me, Slate?" she asked.

He wasn't going to say no, so he nodded and moved out of the row to go with her. He didn't want to say no, but he also wasn't sure he was ready to say yes to a woman like Jill.

Probably shouldn't have held her hand in the car then, he told himself.

CHAPTER FOUR

J ill's thirst burned in her throat, and she considered
jogging the last hundred yards to the homestead.
She didn't, because she had far too many curves to
run with. Things bounced that shouldn't, and she
settled for walking as quickly as she could.

Inside, the cool kiss of air conditioning met her skin. The
homestead was quiet, and for once, Jill soaked in it. She
hurried into the kitchen and opened the fridge, finding the
top shelf fully stocked with bottled water, as usual.

Her hands shook as she twisted the lid, and she couldn't
drink fast enough. This heat wave that had hit Texas was no
joke. Jill had lived in the state her whole life, but this was a
new level of heat she hadn't experienced before.

She exhaled heavily and set the half-empty bottle on the
counter. She sucked at the air now, trying to get her head to

stop swimming. "Can't pass out," she said to herself, her voice far too breathy. "You can't. Go sit down."

She couldn't seem to get her body to move though. If she just stayed here, the lightheadedness would pass, and she'd be fine. She took breath after breath, trying to slow them. They wouldn't listen, and she reached up and touched her forehead, finding it clammy.

"Emma," she called as loud as she could. Emma worked in the office just around the corner from the kitchen. Maybe she could help get Jill to the couch. "Emma."

"Jill?"

She turned toward the man's voice, not expecting Slate to be in the homestead. Her mind blanked at the glorious sight of him. Maybe she was hallucinating now too. She needed to tell him she was going to pass out, but her voice had gone on vacation.

"Okay, let's get you over to the couch," Slate said. He approached her quickly, putting one hand on her back and taking her arm with the other. He led her across the cavernous kitchen and into the living room. "There you go."

Humiliation filled her, because this was the second time he'd helped her. She groaned as she lay down, and Slate knelt next to the couch. "What's going on?" he asked. "Do I need to call an ambulance?"

"No," she rasped. "I just got a little heat stroke. I just needed a drink."

"Did you get a drink?" He stood up, the sound of his

boots against the tile moving away from her and then coming back. "Drink more, Jill."

She'd closed her eyes at some point, and she opened them again. "I'm okay," she said.

"Drink it all," he said. "I'm going to go tell Emma what I'm doing." He handed her the bottle and supervised while she finished it. "Be right back."

Jill looked up at the ceiling, her mind catching up to his words. "Emma?" she asked. What was he doing here with Emma?

"Jill?" Emma's face appeared from over the back of the couch. "If you have heat stroke, we should definitely go to the hospital."

"I'm okay," Jill said. She sat up, and the world stayed still. "I am."

"You didn't eat breakfast." Emma looked at Slate, who wore a frown between his eyebrows. "Go find her something to eat, would you, Slate?"

"Sure." He moved away again, and Jill wanted to protest. She didn't though, because she hadn't eaten breakfast. Ginger would be upset with her; Jill was upset with herself, because she knew better than to go out to work on the ranch without eating, especially in heat like this.

"I don't like breakfast," Jill said.

"Drink a protein shake, then," Emma said as she came around the couch. "That's what I've been doing. Nothing sounds good to me either, but I have to have something to combat the morning sickness."

Slate arrived, sandwiching Jill on the couch. "I found string cheese and salami."

"You're pregnant?" Jill asked, her eyes never leaving Emma's.

Her friend smiled, a completely new glow about her. "Yes," she said. "That's why I'm showing Slate all the financial stuff for the ranch. He's going to help out when I'm not feeling well and after I have the baby."

Tears welled in Jill's eyes, and she leaned over and hugged Emma. "Congratulations."

"Eat," Emma said after breaking the embrace. She nodded toward Slate.

Jill took the food from him with a murmured, "Thanks," and unwrapped the string cheese. "I really am okay."

Emma looked toward the office. "My phone is ringing."

"I'll sit with her," Slate said, and Emma nodded and bustled away.

Jill didn't dare look at Slate as she ate. She took small bites and ate slowly, because she didn't want Slate to leave. She also had no idea what to say to him. The wedding had been beautiful, and she'd enjoyed eating lunch with him. There'd been dancing after that, but Slate had disappeared for that part.

She hadn't known where he'd gone, but Luke had disappeared too. They'd come back to the ranch with Ted and Emma, and Jill couldn't help feeling like Slate had slighted her. She'd been trying to tell herself he hadn't, but her mind tended to wander down self-loathing paths when she was alone—which was why she didn't like being alone.

"Feeling better?" he asked, and Jill nodded, her eyes still on the salami.

"Listen, I wanted to talk to you about something," he said.

She glanced up and met his eyes for a moment. He looked real serious, and Jill didn't like that. *Yes, you do*, she told herself. She was tired of playing the fun, flirty blonde. That woman got a lot of dates, but she didn't settle down. Jill was ready to settle down.

"I shouldn't have held your hand the other day," he said. "Luke said it wasn't very fair, and he's right. I just want to apologize."

"It's fine," she said, her throat narrowing. She looked away, but her food was gone, and she didn't know what to focus on.

"I, uh, haven't done a lot of dating in my life, and I didn't get, ahem, much physical contact in prison, and it was just sort of this..." He blew his breath out. "I did like holding your hand, because I just needed the human touch."

She looked at him again, and he was so vulnerable and so real in that moment. "Thanks for letting me know."

Slate nodded and focused on his hands in his lap. "I was thinking I'd like to get to know you better." He looked at her for a microsecond and back at those hands. "But maybe we could start with something like lunch or dinner."

"I eat lunch and dinner," she said.

"Just not breakfast," he said.

"Just not breakfast." Jill smiled. "Though I'm going to from now on, because I don't want to repeat what just happened." She hadn't even dealt with Ginger yet, and she knew she'd have to.

"How's your mom?" Slate asked several seconds later.

"She's doing good," Jill said, her voice pitching up on the last word. "My daddy's doing a good job with her. The chemo treatments aren't as severe anymore, so she's doing good." She realized she'd said the same thing twice, but she couldn't take it back now.

Emma came back into the living room. "It was Ginger."

"Great," Jill said, though she didn't think it was great. "She's upset with me, right?"

"I had to tell her," Emma said. "I'm sorry. She's on her way in, and she wants to talk to you." She switched her gaze to Slate. "I just need another half-hour with you."

He stood. "Sure."

Emma left, and Slate paused. "So...I'll...we'll...go out sometime."

"Yes," Jill said.

"Okay." Slate left, and Jill laid back down on the couch. She'd have to face Ginger, and she still didn't have Slate's phone number, but right now she just wanted to breathe in and out.

Sometime later, Jill opened her eyes when she heard the door close. Footsteps came into the house, and she groaned as she pulled herself to a seated position. Her head swam, and she blinked. After the third time, everything settled, and Jill met the disapproving yet concerned eyes of her boss.

"Jill," Ginger said, quickly coming to her side and looking into her eyes. She lifted her hand and touched her fingertips to Jill's forehead, exactly the way Jill's mother would've done.

Her heart squeezed, the strings connecting it to her body so tender these days, especially when she thought about her mom.

"I'm okay," Jill said. "I just need to eat in the morning and drink throughout my chores."

"I sent a memo about it two days ago," Ginger said. She didn't wear makeup and her auburn hair was pulled into a pony tail beneath her cowgirl hat. She was gorgeous anyway, and Jill smiled at her.

"I know," Jill said. "I was just..." She didn't want to admit that she had so much on her mind that she'd simply forgotten. Ginger managed everything at Hope Eternal, though she had plenty of women to help her. She still oversaw everything and held meetings every Friday afternoon with her supervisors over school programs, finances, construction, equipment, maintenance, animals, and agriculture.

Jill attended the meetings, as she worked exclusively with their honeybee program with schools around the Coastal Bend area of Texas, all of their honey production and sales, and the budget for that tiny arm of the ranch. Her pulse sent out an extra beat when she realized Slate would probably start attending the meetings too, just to see what Emma did.

She shouldn't be so excited about that prospect. The man had let more than a week go by before even speaking to her again. He clearly wasn't in a place where he was ready to date a woman, and Jill knew better than to push a man to do that.

She did. She did know better, and she wasn't going to put any pressure on Slate whatsoever. In fact, she might even dust off the old dating app she'd used in the past and get herself another cowboy to date completely.

Even as she thought it, she knew she wouldn't. With her mother's illness, she could barely keep up with her job on the ranch and going home to check on her family.

"Jill," Ginger said gently, and Jill blinked her way back to the present conversation. "Have you heard anything I've said?"

Jill dropped her gaze to her hands. "No," she said. "I'm just tired."

"I know," Ginger said. "That's why I said you should stay in this afternoon. Take off early to go see your mother, if you'd like."

She shook her head. "Haven's going to be there today." She didn't have to explain more than that, not to Ginger. Ginger had sisters too, one of which seemed to be even more perfect than Haven, though Jill had witnessed Brooke using the wrong bucket to feed the horses. If Jess saw her, there'd be an exchange, and Jill smiled just thinking about her fiery friend.

"Okay, well, then put a movie on," Ginger said, brushing Jill's hair off her forehead again. "Go sit with Emma. She's going to be in the office all afternoon. Hannah will be in about three. Our meeting is at four, but if you can't—"

"I can," Jill said. "I don't want to be alone. I have work to do at the hives this afternoon. I'll be okay."

Ginger cocked her head and studied Jill with those keen eyes. "I can send someone out with you," she said. "I don't want you to be alone either, not until I'm sure you're really fine."

Jill pressed her lips together. "I don't need a babysitter."

"It's either that or you sit in here with Emma," Ginger said firmly. "She's done with Slate now, and she won't care what you put on your tablet."

Jill shook her head. "I already take too much time off." She looked at Ginger, begging her to understand. Jill needed to feel useful, and bedding up in the air conditioned office with her favorite movie wasn't what she needed right now.

"I'll text Slate," Ginger said, looking at her phone. "He was going to help with the construction this afternoon, but they weren't counting on him."

Jill opened her mouth to protest. She really didn't want Slate as a babysitter. How humiliating. But Ginger's fingers flew like wildfire spread in the dry, June heat, and she looked up before Jill could even formulate the sentence in her head. "He's on his way back in."

Jill clamped her mouth shut and nodded. "I'm going to fill up my water bottle." She got to her feet, feeling a teensy bit unsteady but determined not to let anyone know. On her fourth step, she felt normal, and she filled a large water bottle with ice and water, drank until she felt like her stomach would pop, and then refilled it.

The back door opened again, and this time, Slate rounded the corner from the hallway leading to the garage. He searched Jill's face before looking at Ginger. "Honeybees?"

"You're going to work the afternoon with Jill," Ginger said, all business again. "I don't want her to be alone, and she has work to do at the hives."

"All right," Slate said, flicking his gaze to Jill and back to Ginger in less time than it took to breathe.

"You'll be done by four," Ginger said. "That's when we meet for the administration weekly."

"Right." Slate stuck his hands in his pockets, and he had to know how handsome and striking he was. How adorable and soft with his hands hidden.

Ginger stepped over to Jill, who cleared her throat and looked away from Slate. She'd been staring, and someone as smart as Ginger—who literally saw and knew everything that happened on the ranch—would've seen it. She didn't say anything though. She just got out a couple of water bottles and paused next to Jill. "Okay?" she asked, her voice barely registering in Jill's ears.

"Yes," Jill said. "I'm good."

"Good," Ginger said, putting one arm around Jill and giving her a squeeze. "He's cute, right?"

Jill didn't acknowledge that Slate was beyond cute. He was drop-dead gorgeous, and the flirty, fun woman she'd been for so long knew exactly how to act around a man like him to get his number and get her first date.

The problem was, men as serious as Slate might ask her out once or twice, but they didn't really want a flirt for a girlfriend or a wife. He likely didn't want a woman who screamed at the ocean and almost passed out either.

"Okay, see you at four," Ginger said, and she left the kitchen, where Jill and Slate still stood, staring at one another.

CHAPTER FIVE

S late had no idea how to maintain a beehive. Jill did, though, and she ordered him around in a strong, sure voice for most of the afternoon. He did whatever she said, asking a few questions along the way. Nothing he really wanted to know, though, and as she prepped the last hive for the relocation of part of the swarm they housed at Hope Eternal, he asked, "How'd you learn how to do this?"

"My grandmother raised bees," Jill said, grinning at him from behind the headgear she wore to protect herself. It was hot and stuffy in the hood, but Slate hadn't dared to remove his. He wasn't allergic to bees, but he didn't want to get stung either.

Energy buzzed through his veins, the same way the low drone of buzzing bees had been in the air for the past couple of hours.

"She raised everything," Jill continued. "She'd plant different flowers in different patches just to see if the honey would taste different. She had chickens and turkeys she'd raise. I can't remember a Thanksgiving where we didn't have one of the toms she raised." Her voice took on a wistful, bygone tone, and Slate sure did like it.

"Is she still alive?" he asked.

"Yes," Jill said, turning away from him to slide in one of the trays. "She doesn't do much anymore. Just putters around in her yard—which is still beautiful. And she's still got her dogs."

"I want a dog," Slate said. "What kind does she have?"

"She's got little lap dogs," Jill said. "Bichon Frise's. Three of 'em." She shook her head as she turned around, and her smile really was gorgeous. "One time, I asked her if it made her sad she couldn't keep her bees and her chickens anymore. If she couldn't keep up with canning the peaches and making applesauce and shucking all the corn. She has an acre-big garden she'd plant, cultivate, and harvest every year—and that didn't include the orchards surrounding her house."

"And?" Slate asked when Jill paused for several moments.

"Bring that one over," Jill said, and Slate did what she said. Not a whisper of wind disturbed the air, and Slate felt like he was suffocating—especially when he got close to Jill. With their bee suits, he wasn't anywhere able to touch her, but just being with her made him feel something he hadn't in so long.

He needed to talk to Luke tonight, because he didn't want to hurt Jill needlessly. He also didn't want to lose part of himself just when he'd finally gotten everything back. *Not quite everything*, he thought, but he pushed the thought away.

Listening to Jill talk about her family made him think about his, and the fond memories of his childhood kept surging in his mind.

"She said she's not too sad," Jill said, picking up the story again. "She said when you get old, or if you get injured or whatever, and you can't do what you used to be able to, you only do what's absolutely necessary."

"That's her dogs," he said. "And doing a little yard work."

Jill nodded. "She misses my grampa terribly." She sounded like she did too. "She reads the Bible every day too, and she never misses church."

"Wow," Slate said. "Only doing what's absolutely necessary."

"Mm." Jill slid his tray into the hive and looked up at him. "Now we need to move the queen, and all her drones will follow her."

"What about the other hive?" he asked. "Won't they be just as crowded in this one as that one?"

"No," Jill said, stepping over to the old hive. "This one is full of honey, and we'll harvest it while they work on making more. So it's definitely bigger."

"Okay," Slate said, but he didn't really get it. Jill did, though, and he liked watching her work with such sure movements. The bee activity in the air increased as she moved the queen, and a few minutes later, she pronounced the job done.

"And we're going to be late for the meeting," she said. "So let's get out of these suits and back to the West Wing."

Slate did what she said, and he rode in her truck along the bumpy dirt road that led to a better one that went to the homestead. He drank a lot and pointed the air conditioning vents right on himself, the same way Jill did for herself.

As she approached the homestead, he glanced at her. "What's your weekend like?" he asked.

"I'm sticking around here tomorrow," Jill said. "I've been taking too much time off, and I have a ton of email to go through for our summer programs. Then I'm going to see my parents on Sunday."

He nodded and looked away as she focused on him. "Do you, uh, go to church if you're in town?"

"Sometimes," she hedged. "I can tell you where the chapel is, and Hannah almost always goes. Ted and Emma have been too. Sometimes Ginger or Nate will, but they still work a lot on Sundays."

"I think I'd like to try going." Slate shifted in his seat. "I've—" He cleared his throat. "Never really been to church, at least on the outside. There were services in River Bay, and I went to those pretty regularly."

He could feel the weight of Jill's gaze on his face, but he couldn't get himself to turn toward her. She came to a stop in the gravel lot in front of the homestead, and Slate's heartbeat raced the same way it had on the first day he'd been admitted to the prison.

"Sounds like lunch might have to be during the week?" he asked.

"We could try for Monday," she said. "I have a half-day camp that starts that morning, and then in the afternoon, I'll be in the stables. But I can definitely take a lunch."

Slate nodded, though he had no idea what Monday held for him. "Ginger just has me doing all kinds of different things," he said. "So I'm not sure what I'll be doing Monday. I'll see if I can pin it down this weekend, though."

"Okay." With that, Jill opened her door and slipped from the truck. Slate followed her, and she smiled up at him as they walked toward the house. "I'd love to know more about your family," she said. "Are your grandparents still alive?"

"Yeah," he said with a sigh. "My father's parents actually don't live too far from here."

"Maybe you could go see them after church on Sunday," Jill suggested, and Slate nearly stumbled.

"You know what?" he asked. "That's a great idea." Part of him felt frozen at the very idea of it, but the other part warmed instantly. He needed to reconnect with his family, and it wasn't going to happen if he didn't make an effort.

"Where do they live?" she asked.

"Short Tail?" He phrased it as a question, asking her if she knew it.

"You're kidding." She paused in the shade of the garage before going up the steps. "You know that's maybe ten minutes from Sugar Hill, right?"

"I didn't know that," he said. "We didn't visit super often. My dad—uh—he's not the easiest person to get along with."

Jill sobered, but the brightness in those blue eyes didn't go out. "Short Tail is about ten minutes due west of Sugar Hill," she said. "You wouldn't have made it to Sugar Hill if you went to visit them."

Slate nodded, his throat suddenly too tight. Everything about Jill was so *shiny*, and he wasn't sure how to handle her. He was dull, and rough, and he'd seen and done things she couldn't even imagine. Once she knew, she wouldn't want anything to do with him.

He shouldn't go to lunch with her. He shouldn't tell her anything about his life, his family, or his past. He didn't want to relive a lot of what he'd done and who he'd been in Austin, and he felt like he had when he'd graduated from high school—scared and worried about what he should do with his life.

At the same time, he recognized that he'd been given a second chance. He wasn't going to waste that. *I'm not*, he promised to himself and to the Lord. He'd made the same promise to his Unit Manager, and to Nate, Dallas, Ted, and Luke.

Some people who'd used substances the way he had didn't get a second chance. He did, and he wasn't going to blow it.

"Are you coming?" Jill asked, and he realized she'd moved up the steps.

"Yes," he said, following her. He didn't have to decide right then about a relationship with Jill. Perhaps he could just see how things went between them, and he could make a decision with more information later.

SUNDAY MORNING, SLATE WOKE UP WHEN THE SHOWER that connected his room to Luke's turned on. He wasn't used to sleeping in such absolute darkness, nor was he accustomed to sleeping in a room all by himself quite yet, so both he and Luke left their bedroom doors open. They had to get up and get going at the same time every day anyway, and it was usually Slate calling into Luke's bedroom after he'd showered with a, "Get up, Luke, or we'll be late."

The only good thing Slate had going for him was his friendships with Luke, Nate, Ted, and Dallas. If he didn't have them, he knew where he'd be right now—and it wasn't lying in a comfortable, queen-sized bed, with clean sheets and the sound of a hot shower running nearby.

He opened his eyes and looked up to the ceiling. He'd mentioned church to Luke yesterday morning, and after they'd finished working on the roof of one of the new cabins going in at the ranch, they'd stolen Ted and Nate from their wives and gone to town for dinner and a quick trip to get Slate a white shirt and tie. Luke had gotten one too, and he'd said he go with Slate, if that was okay.

It was more than okay with Slate, as he now didn't have to walk into the Sabbath-day meeting alone. He'd gotten Jill's number after the administration meeting on Friday afternoon, but he hadn't used it yet. She hadn't texted him either, and Slate found himself completely blank as to what to tell her. So much of his past was covered in wax paper, and he could barely see the shapes and remember the things that had happened.

"Your turn," Luke called into Slate, and he pushed his blanket down and swung his feet over the side of the bed. Everything would be better in that moment if he had a dog to greet him in the morning. A big dog, with a wet nose, who would lay on his feet at night, and then jump down, stretch, and come wagging his tail so Slate would let him outside once morning came.

He hadn't mentioned getting a dog to anyone, and he really only needed to clear it with Ginger. She owned the house where he and a lot of the other cowboys who worked full-time on the ranch lived. Ursula, her German shepherd, came in and out of the Annex at will, so Slate didn't think there were any allergies he needed to be aware of.

With a towel wrapped around his waist, Luke stood in front of the mirror, most of which had defogged. He held a razor in his hand, and Slate paused to meet his eyes. "You're shaving?"

"I think it's time," Luke said. "I mean, my beard's not growing in great anyway, and it definitely needs to be trimmed on the sides." He tilted his head up to see along his lower jaw and neck.

"Maybe just trim it then." Slate reached up and ran his hand along his jawline. "I'm not shaving."

"There's going to be little old ladies at church judging you," Luke said with a grin.

Slate shook his head and smiled. "Let 'em," he said. He already felt like a long-tailed cat in a room full of rocking chairs thinking he could even go to church. But the chaplain at River Bay had said good things, and he'd spoken of redemption, and making a better life, and taking time to listen to the Lord before big decisions—or any decisions at all—were made.

Twenty minutes later, he and Luke wore their slacks, white shirts, and ties when Connor came running into the kitchen. "Hey, Uncle Luke," he said to Luke, who'd already sat down at the dining room table with his cup of coffee.

"Hey, bud," Luke said, but Connor didn't slow down. The kid skipped or ran everywhere he went, and Slate wondered what it would be like to have that kind of energy.

"Uncle Slate," Connor said, coming to a skidding halt in front of him.

Slate stirred another spoonful of sugar into his coffee and grinned at Connor. "What, Connor?" He loved being called Uncle Slate by the kid, because he'd never really had that before. His older sister had been married before Slate had gone to prison, and she and her husband had two kids. But they were little when he'd been arrested, and he hadn't heard the words "Uncle Slate" until Connor said them.

"Dad says you're goin' to Short Tail today." Connor looked at him with such a brightness of hope that Slate suspected something was up.

"That's right." He lifted his coffee mug to his lips. "Why?"

"Well, Dad and Ginger can't take me, but they said if I could get a ride with you, then I could go see my grandparents this afternoon."

Surprise hit Slate right behind the lungs. He looked at Luke, who just shrugged. "They're in White Lake, right?" Slate asked. "I'm pretty sure I'm gonna be driving right through there."

"So can I go?"

"I don't see why not," Slate said. "I'm going to visit my grandparents too." A beating of nerves stole through his stomach that even the hottest coffee couldn't tame. "I don't know what time I'll be done," he added. "Maybe I should call them to find out if there's a time you need me to pick you up."

"They said I could sleep over if I had to," Connor said, a huge smile splitting his face. "So anytime's fine, Uncle

Slate." He spoke with the cutest Texas twang, really drawing out the I in *fine*, and Slate nodded at him as he moved toward the table and Luke.

"All right, then," he said. "I'm leavin' right after church." He sat down at the table and picked up one of the toaster pastries Luke had heated up.

"I'll be ready," Connor said, dashing for the door. He had his hand on the knob when he turned back. "Oh, thanks, Uncle Slate." He skipped over to him and wrapped both skinny arms around Slate's neck and part of one shoulder.

"Oh, sure, bud," Slate said, not quite sure how to interact with kids. Connor would be seven years old in a couple of months, but he'd already been through a lot in his short life. He left the Annex, singing something at the top of his lungs once he hit the deck.

"He probably misses them," Luke said, nodding toward the back door. "I don't think Nate gets out to see his parents much."

"I don't think he does either," Slate said. In Nate's case, it was a matter of being busy, not that he didn't speak to his parents. He'd gone to his brother's funeral an hour after getting released from River Bay, and according to the stories Slate had heard, Nate had been received well.

Slate couldn't take another drink of his coffee. He hoped he'd be received well this afternoon. He'd called his grandmother yesterday about lunchtime, and she'd said she and his grandfather would be home and they'd love to see him.

That would be mighty nice were the actual words she'd used, and Slate let them swell and grow in his head and heart. This was going to be a great day, Slate just knew it. At least he hoped it would be, and his confidence faltered when Ted knocked on the back door and said, "Let's go, guys. Church starts in thirty minutes."

CHAPTER SIX

"Let me get it, Mama," Jill said, jumping to her feet. Thankfully, she'd figured out how to lay off the chips and ice cream in the past couple of weeks, and with all her work on the ranch, she'd lost the five pounds she'd gained. She wouldn't lose any more, she knew that. Jill had come to simply accept the extra twenty pounds she carried, and if she were being honest, it was probably thirty.

She bustled into the kitchen where she'd grown up, though her mother had redone it several times since then. Mama couldn't stand sitting still, and she replaced furniture before it could even be deemed slightly used. The walls in here had been painted light gray, and the cabinets white. Daddy had put new hardware on the cabinets in the shape of roosters, tractors, and cowboy hats.

Jill didn't hate it—the pulls fit the farm where the house sat—she just wouldn't want them in her kitchen.

She stood at the sink and filled a glass with water, then added ice cubes to it from the tray in the freezer. "You guys need to get a new fridge," she said as she took the ice water to Mama. "That ice machine has been broken for years."

"But the fridge still works," Mama said, her smile thin and her eyes a bit too watery for Jill's liking. She supposed that her mother had just woken up, and she needed a few minutes to come back to full life.

"We just put stuff in there to get cold," she said, sipping her water a moment later. "There's bottled water in there that's more pH balanced."

"Oh, I'll get it." Jill got to her feet again.

"This is fine," her mom said, almost yelling the words. "Sit down, Jilly." Her smile broadened then, and Jill did what Mama said. She reached up and stroked Jill's hair. "I love this short cut on you," she said. "When my hair grows back in, I'm going to do something funky like that."

Jill smiled, her heartbeat barely squeezing through her veins. "Not going to grow it out, huh?"

"Heavens, no," Mama said with a light laugh. "I'm going to stop coloring it too. It's time to embrace the silver."

"Hey, I know women my age trying to get their hair the color of yours," Jill said.

Mama laughed then, and she hadn't lost any of her spunk. "Hand me that magazine, would you?"

Jill picked up the *Country Living* magazine on the coffee table in front of the couch where Mama had taken her afternoon nap. She'd been right tuckered out from a busy morning with Haven and her family, and then lunch with everyone. Daddy said she napped most afternoons, and Jill had volunteered to stay with her so Daddy could go get things done around the farm that needed doing.

McKenna and her boyfriend, Reece, had gone with him.

"There's this new peach pie recipe I want to try," Mama said. "Will you help me?" She flipped to a page in the back of the magazine, where a picture of a delectable peach pie gleamed.

"If I help, it's not going to look like that," Jill said.

"Nonsense," Mama said, which was what she always said when Jill claimed not to have inherited her culinary skills. Haven had, of course. Haven had the long, beautiful blonde hair too. Jill had only told one person why she'd cut her hair—Hannah—but it was to show that hair could be beautiful short too. Haven had brought her two kids to the farm that morning, and they'd brought Mama flowers from their garden and cards they'd made.

Jill had only had herself to bring, though she had stopped for the loaf of French bread her mother wanted to serve with dinner.

Jill rose with her mom and steadied her until she wasn't wobbling on her feet. She moved into the kitchen, only straightening fully after four or five steps. Jill hated seeing the age in Mama's stature, in the way she sighed as she reached to open the cupboard above the stove, and the way her hair had started to grow back in gray. It was wispy too, barely the fuzz on a baby chick.

"Get out the flour now," Mama said, and Jill followed her directions. Mama put the pie dough together before she grew too tired to keep standing. "Wrap it in plastic wrap," she said as she moved to the kitchen table and lowered herself into a seat. "Put it in the fridge. Then we'll get the filling made."

"How's the ranch?" Mama asked, and Jill concentrated on slicing the peaches while she talked. She told her mom about the honeybees, which brought a glow to Mama's face. "Oh, and Jess got married a couple of weeks ago. Remember that blue dress I showed you?"

"Of course," Mama said, her voice vibrant though her face looked gray and a bit sunken. "Make sure you add the lemon zest to those peaches, dear."

Jill did and returned her attention to the recipe. Brown sugar, sugar, and cornstarch.

"You're gonna let those peaches sit now," Mama said.

"Yep," Jill said, wondering how her mother knew exactly what the recipe said. She'd probably read it a hundred times while lying on the couch, and Jill's heart went out to her mom. "Anyway, the wedding was beautiful. They had this huge pergola that kept everything in the shade, and all these ribbons, and fabric, and lights." Jill sighed. "Jess rode her horse—her big dream, you know?—and now they're on a cruise. Well." She stirred the peaches and the sugars together. "It ended yesterday, but they're not back yet."

"Are they livin' at the ranch?" Mama asked.

"No, Dallas has a nice house in town," Jill said,

returning to the recipe. Cinnamon and nutmeg, though she couldn't do much until the peaches had released some of their juice. She got out the spices anyway and measured out what she needed.

"Are you gonna get married here at the farm?" Mama asked.

Jill dropped her teaspoons. "I...I'm not even really seeing anyone."

"I thought you met a man last fall," Mama said, and Jill watched her closely. Daddy had mentioned that her memory wasn't great while on the chemotherapy treatments. "Mike or Mickey or something."

"It was Mike," Jill said, her voice a touch cooler now. "We broke up, Mama. A few months ago. Remember I came over and you made me that chocolate mousse that soothes broken hearts?" She grinned at her mother, kidding though she did believe in the soothing power of all things chocolate.

"Oh, that's right," Mama said, some color coming back into her face now.

"Do you need something to eat, Mama? Maybe you should try having one of those shakes." Since she had a hard time keeping food down, she'd been drinking shakes with all the essential vitamins and minerals and nutrients in them.

"I'm feeling like another bowl of that macaroni salad," she said with a grin. "Did Haven take it all?"

"I don't think she took any of it," Jill said, grinning too. She retrieved the bowl from the fridge and didn't bother with individual bowls. She got two spoons out of the silverware drawer and joined her mom at the table. "I did meet a new man, Mama. His name's Slate."

"Oh? Tell me about him."

"Well..." Jill removed the aluminum foil from the large serving bowl and handed her mother a spoon. "He's new to the ranch. He's not really a cowboy, and he's got a background in finance...or something." In that moment, Jill realized how very little she knew about Slate. When they'd spoken in the past, he'd kept the conversation on her. Her family. Her time on the ranch. How she knew about honeybees.

"He's helping Emma a little bit, and Ginger assigns him to whatever needs to be done around the ranch." She scooped up a spoonful of mac salad and put it in her mouth.

"How are Emma and Ginger?"

"Mm." Jill's eyes widened as she chewed quickly. "Emma's going to have a baby."

"My, that's wonderful." Mama genuinely sounded like it was too. Jill had invited her parents to Hope Eternal Ranch several times over the years she'd lived and worked there, and they'd come for holiday meals, Sunday brunches, and big parties. They'd been there for Ginger's wedding, as well as Emma's. Mama hadn't come for Jess's, because she hadn't been feeling well, and Jill pasted a smile on her face as she thought about the past few weeks since Mama's diagnosis.

"Tell her congratulations from me. In fact." Mama started to stand, and she waved away any help Jill might have given her. "I've got baby blankets and bibs in the closet here."

Of course she did. Jill could only smile as her mother went down the hall and came back with a large, clear, plastic bin in her hands. She set it on the table and unlatched the lid. "She probably doesn't know if it's a boy or a girl." Mama looked at Jill for confirmation.

"She hasn't even told the whole ranch yet," Jill said, remembering the administration weekly on Friday. Everyone in the room had been surprised and offered congratulations when Emma had told them why Slate was there. Only Jill and Ginger had known before then. "She's not due until February."

"Maybe I'll wait then." Mama placed the bundles she'd started to pull out of the bin back inside. "It's nice to get a gender-specific set."

Jill stood and looked down into the bin. "Mama," she said when she saw how many baby blankets and bibs there were. "How many of these do you have?"

"Oh, I don't know. I just make them when I find some cute fabric." Mama looked up at her, hope shining on her face. "Besides, maybe you'll have a lot of babies, and you'll need them."

Jill gaped at her mother and then looked at the bin again. "Mama, Kenna and I would have to have a dozen each to use this many blankets."

"Oh, that's not so unreasonable, is it?"

"Yes," Jill said, starting to laugh. "It is, Mama. I'm thirty-three. I'm not going to have twelve babies in the next twelve years." She shook her head and went back to the island and the peach pie recipe.

"Maybe Haven will have more children," Mama mused.

"Mama," Jill said, her tone sobering. "She won't. She's told you that already."

"I know." Mama sighed, and a measure of guilt punched Jill in the chest. Her mother did love her grandchildren, and as Jill started to drain the peaches and thicken the juice with the spices and the cornstarch, she imagined a world where her own mother didn't get to see her get married. Where Mama wouldn't be able to hold Jill's children and fuss over them and tell them how wonderful and beautiful they were.

She could barely breathe by the time the sauce was thickened, and when she turned around to get the peaches, her mother stood right there. "Now, don't you be worried about anything," Mama said, her bright blue eyes shooting lasers the way Jill's felt like hers did when she got angry.

Jill didn't have to speak. She just grabbed onto her mother and held her tight while she tried to hold back the tears. She mostly achieved that, only letting out a few lung-fuls of air that shook like the wind and one tear that slid down her face before she could wipe it away.

"I'm going to be around for a long time," Mama said. "It's only stage two, dear. I'm responding well to the chemo-therapy. Before you know it, I'm going to be back on that tractor, mowing down the corn for the pigs."

Jill laughed then, though it mostly sounded like a sob. "I

know, Mama." She stepped back and wiped her face. "I'm trying to get married and have grandbabies for you. I am."

"Maybe this Slate fellow then," Mama said with a kind smile.

Jill didn't agree or disagree. She reached for the bowl of peaches and mixed them with the thickened, spiced juice. "We haven't even really gone out yet. He's just asked."

"You will," Mama said, opening the fridge and taking out the chilled pie dough. "Now, tell me where he's from and what he did before he came to the ranch."

Jill's voice stuck in her throat, and her first instinct was to deflect the question. Instead, she said. "Uh, he was in the River Bay Federal Correctional Facility. You know, with Nate, and Ted, and Dallas."

Mama's movements barely hitched, but Jill saw them. Thankfully, McKenna came through the back door at that moment, laughing at the top of her lungs. "Jilly, Mama, you have to come see what a mess Daddy made with the wheelbarrow."

"Oh, dear," Mama said, abandoning the dough. She hurried as fast as she could to the back door, where Kenna was still cackling. Jill followed, because she could use a good laugh to drive her reservations about her mother's current health condition—along with Slate—out of her mind.

A few hours later, Jill made the final turn that pointed her toward an old, white farmhouse at the end of the driveway. Slate's truck sat there, so she knew she'd found the right place. Her heartbeat hammered out of control, but she couldn't back out now. Literally, as another truck pulled into the driveway the moment she put her car in park.

She watched in her rearview mirror as Slate pulled around her and parked next to his truck, a smile on his face. They got out of their vehicles at the same time, and he said, "Hey, Jill," before turning back to open the back door of the truck. Two dogs spilled out, one already barking. They came trotting around her car to greet her, both of them jumping up on her legs.

She giggled at the pups, their faces flat just like a shih tzus. "You guys look so good," she said. "Did you get baths today?"

"Just got 'em from the groomer," Slate said, rounding the back of her car too. "Go on, girls. Go find Granny."

The dogs listened to him, and Jill looked up and into his dark eyes. He still wore his black slacks from church that morning, but he'd replaced the white shirt and tie with a yellow polo that was so light, it was the color of freshly churned butter.

"You don't look like you've been here all afternoon," she teased, taking in the spotless quality of his shirt.

"Well, I have," he said with a smile. He glanced toward the house as a screeching noise came from the screen door. "My grandparents have aged since I've last seen them." He wore concern in the line between his eyebrows, and his voice had dropped in volume. "Come meet them, and then I'll show you the farm."

"Okay," Jill said, feeling like she and Slate were all over the place. They technically hadn't even gone on a first date yet. But he'd held her hand, and now she was meeting his grandparents. It all felt rushed and out of order, but as she walked behind him up the narrow sidewalk to the wide front steps, it also felt right.

He'd called that afternoon and asked if she'd like to come see his grandparents' farm, but the peach pie had just come out of the oven. Jill had said yes, and she'd made a graceful exit from her parents' while McKenna and Reece had been setting the table for a light dinner of sandwiches and pie.

"Granny," Slate said, barely a Texan note in his voice. "This is Jill Kyle. She works at the ranch with me." He smiled at the elderly woman and then back at Jill. "Her parents live right over in Sugar Hill." That sounded more Texan, and Jill fastened a smile to her face. "Jill, this is my grandmother, Edith."

"Right nice to meet you, ma'am," she said, perhaps pouring her accent on a bit thick. She shook the older woman's hand, and while her skin was papery and soft, she had a firm grip. Her hair was nearly white and cut short, almost like Jill's.

"You too," she said with a smile. "Are you and Slate an item?" She shot a look at Slate, who lowered his head, effectively hiding his face with the brim of that cowboy hat he seemed to never take off.

Slate chuckled and shook his head. "Granny, I told you this story already."

"I'd like to hear it," Jill said, glancing from him to his grandmother.

She grinned and folded her arms. "I like her, Slate."

Slate lifted his head, a full smile on that gorgeous face. "Me too, Granny, and you're embarrassing me."

"Oh, what good am I if I'm not embarrassing someone?" she asked. "Come in, Jill. It's way too hot to stand out here. I'll tell you that story..."

"Granny," Slate said, practically jumping between Jill and his grandmother. "It's not your story to tell."

"She wants to know."

They continued to bicker as they went through the living room and into the kitchen, where Edith poured sweet tea for everyone and got out a box of cookies. For some reason, Jill couldn't stop smiling. Maybe because of how relaxed Slate seemed. He strung together more than a few words, and even a few sentences. He was natural, and fun, and he clearly adored his granny.

When he glanced at her and found her grinning, he asked, "What are you smilin' about?" in a falsely gruff voice.

"Just you," she said, feeling her face starting to stretch too far. She pulled back on the smile and accepted the glass of sweet tea from Edith, though she wasn't very thirsty. She lifted the glass and took a sip, and wow. "This is amazing," she said, the tartness of the tea bursting through her mouth.

"Oh, don't say that," Slate said with a smile. "She already thinks her sweet tea is the stuff Texas runs on."

"It is," Edith said, drawing her shoulders forward. "I've won four county fairs with this tea, I'll have you know."

"I know, Granny." He took his glass and the whole box of cookies. "We don't have long before the sun sets. I'll come say goodbye before I go."

"You better," Edith said, but Jill only had eyes for Slate. She watched him nod with his cowboy hat toward the back door, and she hopped right to following him, her glass of sweet tea firmly clenched in her fingers.

She didn't care that it was still hot outside, despite the sun being almost all the way down. She took a drink of her tea and was instantly refreshed.

"Here's the farm," he said, using the box of cookies to sweep the landscape in front of him.

"Where's your grandfather?" she asked.

"He wasn't feeling well," Slate said, that frown appearing between his eyes again. "You'll have to meet him another time."

"Did you...?" She paused but decided that she had to ask. "Did you have a good visit this afternoon?"

"Yeah," he said, blowing out his breath. "You know? It wasn't bad." He looked at her, everything tense in his face softening. "There's a great place to watch the sun set on the other side of that barn. You want to brave the walk in this heat?"

"To that barn?" Jill indicated the one probably fifty yards away. "I think I can do it." In her flirtier days, she'd have dared him to beat her there, and then she would've raced him, giggling and flirting until they jostled for a spot to watch the sun go down. Hopefully, he would've grabbed onto her at some point, and then she'd end up holding his hand and leaning into his side as another day went to sleep.

Today, though, she just went down the steps from the back porch and started along the cobbled path that led out to the farm. The grass grew in between the stones, and Jill found the whole scene before her full of charm and small-town goodness.

She paused when she got to the barn, which was painted red and white, just like the happily-ever-after movies she watched at Christmastime. She smiled at Slate as he opened the door, and she didn't let him take more than a few steps before she joined him. She couldn't hold his hand as he carried his tea and the cookies, but the moment she could, she was going to try. Oh, yes, she was going to hold this handsome cowboy's hand again tonight if it was the last thing she did.

CHAPTER SEVEN

Slate had eaten two cheeseburgers on the way home from the pet salon. Fine, maybe only one and a half by the time he finished sharing with Granny's dogs. He'd sworn them to secrecy though, as Granny didn't like it when the dogs ate anything other than dry dog food.

He was stuffed full, but he did manage to find room for a couple of cookies and all of his sweet tea. Nothing was better than a sunset and Granny's sweet tea, Slate decided.

Then Jill slipped her fingers into his, and everything in the whole world aligned. Holding Jill's hand was definitely better than the cookies, the tea, and the sunset. Maybe the combination of all of it was just what was amazing.

"Is this okay?" she asked.

"Fine with me," he said, his voice grinding in his throat

"I'm not leading you on," she said. "And I don't really crave human touch. I just want to hold your hand."

Slate nodded, his mind firing through questions. "Why?" he asked.

"Why do I want to hold your hand?"

"Yeah." He looked at her, their seat of a bale of straw so country he finally felt like he belonged on this farm, wearing the cowboy hat, watching the sun go down with a beautiful woman at his side.

"Let's start with the obvious," Jill said. "You're super good-looking."

For some reason, that reason made Slate burst out laughing. Jill joined him, her lighter, more feminine laugh so welcome in his ears. "Wow," he said, still chuckling. "I wasn't expecting that."

"Come on," she said with some measure of sarcasm. "You know you're good-looking."

"Honestly?" He shook his head as the sun went down another degree. "I've never been told that."

"Well, you've been surrounded by blind women for your whole life then," Jill said, and he didn't detect any sarcasm from her this time.

Slate cleared his throat, the magic of the evening suddenly fading like the sunlight. "Actually, I need to tell you something."

"Okay," she said. "Then I can go on about why I want to hold your hand."

Slate wanted to smile, but the gesture only lasted for a blip of a second. How did he phrase this? Did he start slow or just spit it all out? What would she think of him?

Would he ruin this tiny relationship they'd started to build?

"Do you know why I went to prison?" he asked, his voice surprisingly calm for how much his stomach had clenched.

"Not really," she said. "I mean, Jess said something about some bank transactions from a mall, but I didn't ask any questions."

"I did process a bunch of fraudulent charges from multiple stores at a mall in Austin," he said. "I didn't know they were fraudulent, but there are policies and procedures in place to catch that kind of thing." He told himself not to clear his throat or shift as he did both. "I didn't follow them, because I was so far outside of my head."

"What do you mean?"

"I was high," he said. "I was a junkie." Now that he'd started talking, he couldn't seem to stop himself. "I lived for the next fix, and I took it anywhere I could get it. I stole from my parents, my brother, anyone I had to in order to get the money I needed for the next round." He nodded like that was that. The secret was out, and in a lot of ways, that *was* that.

There was a lot of other fallout from those decisions, including the fact that he hadn't spoken to his parents yet. Granny said they'd be kind, and that Slate just needed to dig down deep and find his courage to make the call.

He'd just used his whole store of it to tell Jill about his addiction. "I've been clean for over four years," he said. "Fifty-two months and four days, to be exact." He watched the sun sink below the horizon, amplifying the reds and oranges already in the sky.

Jill said nothing, and Slate couldn't decide if that was a good sign or not. He let the silence permeate his soul, because the pastor he'd listened to that morning had said there was a lot to hear when things were silent. God often spoke to the heart when there weren't other distractions or media in his eyes and ears.

"I don't know what to say," Jill said, all of her previous flirt gone. Her fingers in his tightened though. "I think it's pretty amazing to be able to overcome something like that, though."

"I had to," Slate said. "I was in jail before the trial, and then I got transported from the courthouse to River Bay once I was convicted." He did not want to go through the detoxification process ever again. He wouldn't wish that on his worst enemy.

"You've been out for over two months," she said. "You haven't gone back to that lifestyle."

Slate didn't want any accolades for what he'd done since he'd gotten out of prison. The truth was, every day was a struggle. Every day, he thought about how all the troublesome thoughts in his head would disappear if he could find the right person who could supply him with the right stuff. He didn't say any of that, though.

"Everyone has a past, Slate," she said.

"Yeah?" he asked, maybe a little too challenging. "What's something in yours you don't want anyone to know?" He felt her tense next to him, and regret filled him. "I'm sorry. I didn't mean that to sound so combative."

"Well, I dropped out of college," she said. "My dad wasn't too happy about that. I literally keep bees for a living on a ranch I don't own. I don't own or live in my own house, and I can barely afford to keep gas in my car, because I have a ton of debt from what my grandmother calls my 'wild years.'"

Slate hated this conversation. "Okay," he said. "I don't want to talk about this. Look at the sunset. It's real nice tonight."

Jill sighed, and he couldn't tell if she was frustrated with him or not. She relaxed next to him and he released her hand and lifted his arm around her shoulders. She settled into his side and put both of her arms around him.

"Yeah," he said quietly, dipping his head to take a deep breath of her hair. She smelled like peaches and cinnamon, and Slate could hold her for hours and be happy. "Real nice."

"I think so too," she whispered, and they stayed that way until the last of the light left the sky.

Only then did Slate stand up and collect his glass and the box of cookies. He took her glass from her too and balanced it all in one arm and hand so he could hold hers on the way back to Granny's house. "Lunch tomorrow?" he asked, eyeing the square of light that was the kitchen window.

"Yes," Jill said. "Did you figure out where you'll be?"

"Yeah, I'm on construction with Luke."

"I'll text you when I'm coming in from camp?" she asked.

"Sure." He paused just outside of the reach of the light spilling from the house. "That works."

"You don't want me to come in and say goodbye to your granny." She reached up and played with the buttons near his collar. Heat rushed through his body, because this was a new kind of human touch he hadn't experienced in a while.

"It'll be better if you don't," he said. "Trust me on that." He cast a look toward the window and saw the curtains flutter. Kissing Jill was out of the question, though Slate had already started thinking about it.

Ridiculous, he told himself. They hadn't even been out yet. Maybe asking her to come to the farm was a date, though. Slate had been out of the game for so long, he wasn't sure. He wasn't going to ask Jill either, who obviously had way more experience with dating than he did.

"Okay." Jill tipped up onto her toes and kissed his cheek, letting her lips linger against his skin for a couple of long seconds. "See you tomorrow." With utmost confidence, she smiled at him as she settled back onto her feet, and then she turned and walked away.

"Wait," he blurted. "I'll walk you out before I go say good-bye."

"If you want," Jill called, nearly around the corner of the house already.

Slate cursed himself as he hurried to set the glasses and

cookies on the back steps and go after her. He caught her near the front of the house, where the porch lights bathed the driveway and part of the front lawn in light.

He tucked his hands in his pockets, his default for when he didn't know what to do with them. He also had no idea what to say, as it seemed like her mouth had branded him and rendered his thoughts dormant.

"Thanks for having me out to your grandparents' farm," she said. "We'll have to come again when you can actually show me around."

"Oh, there's a couple of cows and horses," he said, though he loved this place. "But sure. I think Granny likes you."

"Most grandmothers do like me," Jill said with a teasing glint in her eyes.

The moment stretched, and Slate decided to just act. He'd kissed a couple of other women in the past, and it hadn't been this hard. He reached for her, glad when she stepped into his embrace. "Thank you for not judging me," he said, running one hand up her back.

"I didn't even finish all of my failures," she said.

"Another time." He dipped his head as if he'd kiss her goodnight, which he fully intended to do.

"Slate," Granny barked. "Come inside, and bring those cookies."

Slate sighed, his mouth maybe three inches away from Jill's.

"Another time," she whispered, her fingers clenched in

the fabric on both sides of his collar. She released him and fell back, and she stepped out from behind him. "Good-night, Edith," she called.

"Oh, dear," Granny said, and Slate wished his troubles could be summed up as nicely.

"Bye, Slate," Jill said, throwing him a flirtatious smile before she got behind the wheel of her car and started it. He watched her back down the driveway, and only then did he turn toward the front porch. Granny had gone inside, and Slate would have to as well.

"Bring in the cookies," he grumbled as he went around the house to the back yard to get the box of sweets that had cost him a kiss with Jill Kyle.

"THANKS FOR TAKING CONNOR TO WHITE LAKE," NATE said the next morning when Slate arrived in the equipment shed.

"Yeah, no problem," Slate said. He'd picked the boy up after saying goodnight to Granny, and they'd had a great drive back to the ranch. Connor talked and talked, telling Slate about all the things he'd done that day with his grand-parents, and Slate just liked listening to the joy in the little boy's voice. "He's a great kid."

"His dad was great," Nate said, turning away from Slate.

Ted exchanged a glance with Slate, and pulled on his

weight-lifting gloves. "I think you've had him about as long as Ward now, right?"

Nate grunted, and that was all he'd say on the matter. Slate had known him in prison for long enough to know. The truth was, he'd been very lucky to be taken under the wing of Nathaniel Mulbury, and he wouldn't do anything to hurt Nate, ever.

"He can go with me anytime," Slate said.

"Yeah?" Ted asked. "Good visit then?"

Slate started to smile, his afternoon at the farm he hadn't seen in a while made of sunshine and forgiveness and cookies. *And Jill*, he thought. "Yeah," he said.

"He invited Jill to the farm, and she went," Luke said.

"Hey," Slate said, a whip of betrayal lashing against his heart. "I told you that in confidence."

"Yeah, to get my advice about her," Luke said. "And I suck at advice. These guys know what they're doing."

Nate had turned around and he looked at Ted, who looked at him with an equally blank expression. "I think he's talking about you," Nate said.

"No," Ted said, drawling out the word. "He definitely meant you." Ted looked at Luke and then Slate. "I have no idea what I'm doing and I'm the last person you should be asking for advice."

"What he said," Nate said, clapping his hands together. "Except I mean me."

"Oh, come on." Luke rolled his eyes. "You two are married. You're doing something right."

"I'm not sure what," Nate said. "I think I just got lucky."

Slate didn't believe that for a second. He went to the back of the shed and picked up the barbells he wanted to use. He wasn't looking to get ripped the way Luke was, but he was glad to be able to continue his weight-lifting regimen now that he was out of River Bay.

"You and Jill?" Ted asked, sidling up to Slate.

He tried the grunting technique Nate had used, but he knew that wouldn't fly for long. Not with Big-Mouth Luke there.

"He likes her," Luke said. "He said he doesn't want to hurt her needlessly, but he's not sure what he's doing."

No one said anything, and Slate put plenty of thunder in the glare he sent Luke's way. Luke frowned and raised his eyebrows. "What?" he asked. "You said you wanted help. We can all help you."

Slate shook his head, a measure of humiliation filling him.

"There's no shame in liking a beautiful woman like Jill," Nate finally said.

"He told her about the drug use," Luke said. "And she didn't freak out."

Slate was infinitely glad he hadn't mentioned a word about the hand-holding, or the kissing and near-kissing that had happened. He did want advice, and he did trust Nate and Ted as much as Luke. He just hadn't realized it would be a group discussion this morning.

He sat on the bench and began his bicep curls, timing

his breathing with the movement. Ted finished his warm-up and turned to Slate. "Are you going to ask her out?"

"I did already," Slate said.

"Oh, wow. Nice. When are you going?"

"Today," Slate said. "Lunch."

"Go to this ravioli place," Nate said. "Dallas told me about it, and it's amazing."

"I don't think they're open for lunch," Ted said. "Besides, lunch is casual. It should be pizza or pasta or something fast and easy." He snapped his fingers. "You know where you should go? Mama's and Papa's. They're lightning-fast, so if things aren't going well, you won't be stuck there forever."

Slate hadn't thought it wasn't going to go well before, but now the worry ate at him.

"Don't listen to him," Nate said, stepping between Slate and Ted. "He doesn't know what he's talking about." He turned his phone toward Slate. "The ravioli place is open for lunch."

"And you have nothing to worry about with Jill," Luke said. "It's not going to go badly."

"No?" Slate asked, putting the weights down. He wasn't focused this morning anyway. "Maybe it will."

"If you've already told her about the drugs, I don't see how anything else would cause a problem," Nate said.

"That's because you're good at talking to people," Slate said.

Nate blinked at him and then burst out laughing. "Come on."

"You come on," Slate said. "None of the rest of us worked in the Unit Office."

Nate stared at him. "I worked in the Unit Office because I *didn't* talk. Not the other way around." He scoffed and stepped over to the weight bench to spot Ted while he did the bench press. "If you ask Ginger if she'd like me to talk more or less, she'd said more before you even finished the question."

"I don't know what to say to her," Slate said. "I'm going to screw it up."

"We all screw it up," Ted said. "Just be yourself. If that's not good enough." He shrugged and laid down on the bench. "Okay, Nathaniel. What have you got on this?"

"Just enough for you, Teddy." Nate said, smiling at Luke. Slate looked at Luke too, who held a jump rope in his hand.

"I'm not tellin' you anything else, *Lucas*," Slate said, and that made everyone in the room smile—except for Luke, who hated being called Lucas.

"Come on," Luke said. "I was just trying to help."

"And who can we help you with?" Ted asked in a burst of air as he lifted the barbell with weights on both ends.

"Who what?" Luke asked, and Slate saw something in his eyes before he turned and started jumping rope.

"Oh, my stars," he said. "You like someone here on the

ranch." Slate took his weights over to Luke, who refused to look at him.

"Nope," Luke said. "Some of us are keeping are heads on straight so when the time comes, we can find out what the world has to offer us."

"You're still planning on leaving?" Nate asked from behind them.

"Yes," Luke said, locking eyes with Slate. "Five more weeks, and I'm going to leave Hope Eternal Ranch."

Slate frowned, because he didn't want to be left behind. He also didn't want Luke to have to go out into the wide unknown alone. He felt just as stuck now as he had in River Bay, and he once again questioned whether or not he should even take Jill to lunch that day.

CHAPTER EIGHT

J ill didn't care where Slate took her for lunch. She didn't have to drive, and she didn't have to think, and that was what she needed right now.

"You okay?" Slate asked, glancing at her. He was a completely different kind of cowboy with the cool Hollywood shades on, and Jill couldn't help the fantasies that had started when she'd met him in front of the homestead. Her own happily-ever-after loomed before her, just like the women got in the romantic movies she watched.

"Yeah," she said. "This morning's camp was just a beast. There was a little girl who didn't want to be there, and whose mother just drove away while she literally screamed for her to come back."

"Oh, so that was that noise we could hear from the construction site." He grinned at her.

Jill smiled back. "Might've been me screeching into a megaphone to be heard over her."

"That too," Slate said. "Since Luke and I haven't been here for Camp Honeybee before, we weren't sure what was going on."

"Camp Honeybee." Jill laughed, and that lightened her mood as well as the weight on her shoulders. Her mother had texted her that morning, and Jill could admit to herself that the message had contributed to her more contemplative mood.

I'm concerned about you dating someone who's been in prison. Can we please talk more about Slate next time you come visit?

Jill couldn't refuse having a simple conversation, though she knew there'd be nothing simple about it.

"Other than that, it went okay?" Slate asked.

"Oh, yeah," Jill said, looking out the window at the fields flying by. "Another mother had stayed for her anxious daughter, and she helped the screaming girl. She calmed down, and things were okay."

"I'm glad." Slate drove with both hands on the steering wheel, his message absolutely clear—there would be no hand-holding while driving. He'd bought a newer truck since his release from prison, and it had bucket seats, so she couldn't slide over and sit next to him on the bench either.

She'd grown up watching Haven, who was seven years older than her, go out with cute cowboys. When they'd come to the door and get her, Jill would admire them from the kitchen. She'd run to the front windows once Haven left for her date and watch as her teenage sister got in the truck and slid *all* the way over to sit right next to the driver. One time, Jill could've sworn she'd sat on the lap of one of her boyfriends, right there in the front driveway.

Haven had been a big flirt too, and she'd still managed to find a cowboy to settle down with. Jill had to hold onto hope that she could too.

She cut a glance out of the corner of her eye to Slate, who seemed utterly at ease with everything. She wondered if that was a façade, or if he was really just chill about things. He hadn't seemed to mind having her at his grandparents' farm last night either, though he did get a little uptight when his granny said she'd tell his story.

"What are you smilin' about?" he asked, a new smile on his face too.

"Am I?" Jill asked, just realizing it. "I was just thinking about your granny."

"Here we go," Slate said.

"What?"

"I suppose you want me to tell you the story, is that right?"

"Maybe," she said. "I told my mother about you too."

His eyebrows shot up underneath his cowboy hat. "You did?"

Jill sighed, and it sounded heavy to her own ears. "Yeah."

"That doesn't sound good."

"My sister interrupted us, and my mom texted this morning. She wants to talk more about our relationship."

"Why?"

"Um." Jill didn't know how to say what the issue was without hurting his feelings. "I don't know. Just that we didn't have much time for me to give her all the proper details."

Slate's fingers tightened and released on the steering wheel, and Jill's guilt crept through her for not telling the complete truth. "Actually," she said. "She's worried about you being...about you...uh..."

"About me being an ex-con," he said. "You can say it. I know what I am."

"It doesn't matter to me," Jill said quickly. "Honestly, Slate, it doesn't."

He pressed his lips together and nodded, but he wouldn't look at her. "I know it'll matter to a lot of people." He spoke at half the volume he'd been previously. "What did you tell her?"

"I said as long as she didn't make me bake a peach pie, I'd tell her anything she wanted to know about me and you." She turned toward him in her seat. "I've told my mother about all of my boyfriends. I don't usually hide things from her."

"Do you—so it's important to you what she thinks."

"Sure," Jill said, making her voice light. "But, Slate, I'm thirty-three years old. I make my own decisions."

"Hey, I'm thirty-three too," he said. "My birthday is in a couple of weeks, actually. So I won't be for much longer."

Jill watched him, really wanting to look into the dark depths of his eyes and reassure him that she really didn't care about his time in prison. She'd known a lot of the men who'd come through the ranch as part of the prison re-entry program, and they all seemed to be ready to make the right changes in their lives.

"What day?" she asked.

"July eleventh," he said. "You?"

"I just had a birthday in March."

He nodded, and the conversation lulled again. Jill didn't mind. She'd tell her mother whatever she wanted to know, and she'd keep dating Slate until something happened to break them up.

A pinch stole through her, and she realized she'd just thought that a relationship with Slate wouldn't be long-lasting. She frowned at herself, hoping he wouldn't ask what she was thinking now. He seemed lost inside his own head, and Jill turned to look out her window so he couldn't see her face.

Haven had told her once that she wore everything she was feeling and thinking in her eyes, and she really needed to learn how to mask over it. Jill had ignored her sister on that one, something that had become easier and easier as their lives diverged and went different ways.

Slate pulled up to a restaurant Jill hadn't tried before. "Dallas and Nate say this is a good place," he said, peering up at the sign. Red Light Ravioli bore a semi-cartoonish sign, and Jill did love good pasta.

"I'm sure it is, then," she said, reaching to unbuckle her seat belt. She dropped her phone on the floor just as Slate slid out of the truck, and she took a few extra seconds to feel around for it before she found it.

In the console next to her, his phone chimed, and Jill reached for it too. Surely he wouldn't want to leave it in the truck, which would be close to the temperature of the sun by the time they finished lunch. A text from Luke sat on the screen, which wasn't locked.

I've found an amazing cabinetmaker looking for apprentices. I have a call scheduled with him at six-thirty tonight. He's willing to talk to you too.

As Jill read and tried to absorb what the message meant, another one came in.

He's out of Lubbock, but he sells to furniture stores and general contractors all over Texas. This could be HUGE, Slate.

She dropped his phone back into the cupholder as he opened the door. "Are you coming?"

"Yeah," she said quickly, averting her eyes. "I just dropped my phone."

"Oh, my phone." He patted his pockets, front and back, before reaching for the device in the cupholder.

Jill got out of the truck, her legs shaking slightly. He wasn't going to stay at Hope Eternal Ranch. He and Luke were making plans to leave, to find other opportunities, to move on.

Of course he is, she told herself. Until Nate, every single man who'd come to the ranch from the re-entry program moved on. None of them stayed.

Foolishness raced through her, making the sunshine almost cold. Slate reached for her hand, and she barely felt his skin against hers. He said something, but the sound warbled and warped.

He opened the door ahead of her and waited for her to go in. She looked at him, trying to find the truth on his face. "Something's wrong," he said.

She shook her head. "I'm fine." She marched ahead of him, her nerves buzzing and her stomach vibrating. It was a couple of texts, taken out of context. Surely he'd tell her if he was planning to leave the ranch in a few weeks.

Don't accuse him, she coached herself. His words from the day of the wedding ran through her mind. *For you, Jill. I'll stay.*

He'd probably just been hormonal. Reacting to that human touch he hadn't had in such a long time. Something. Because now, a little over a week later, he was talking to Luke about leaving.

"Two, please," he said to the hostess, and she took them to a table in the corner. It was dark inside, and cool, and if Jill hadn't seen those texts, she'd be enthralled with the place. She put on a good show of saying how cozy it was, and looking at the menu with all the different types of ravioli.

"Ooh, I love butternut squash ravioli," she said. "Did you see that one?"

"I'm not a squash fan," he said.

"Why's that?"

He lowered his menu, which was just an oversized sheet of laminated paper, with options on both sides. "My family is pretty poor, I guess. My mother grew zucchini and squash from here to Georgia, it seemed. We ate a ton of it growing up, in every way you can imagine." He gave her a small smile. "Now that I'm an adult, and I don't have to clean my plate or get the belt, I don't have to eat squash."

Jill's surprise pulled at her eyes, widening them. "Your dad hit you if you didn't eat?"

"My daddy hit us for everything," Slate said quietly.

Jill didn't even know what to say. She hated feeling like that, and she'd experienced the stunned, sympathetic emotion powerfully twice in the past two days.

He cleared his throat and looked up. "Let's talk about something else."

"I still haven't told you all of my failures," she said, smiling.

"Nope, not that either." He didn't return her smile. "Let's start with easy stuff. Do you color your hair?"

Jill blinked, not having expected that question at all.

"I'm going to take that stunned look on your face as a no," Slate said. "I'm really bad at this, aren't I?" He smiled but dropped his chin so she didn't get to see it for long.

"No, you're not," she said. "I just wasn't expecting that."

She reached up and patted her hair. "No, I don't color my hair. Do you?"

"No, ma'am," he said.

"What do you want for your birthday?" she asked.

He met her eye then, something electric in his. "Dinner with you," he said. "That's all I need."

Heat rushed through her, and Jill smiled and reached for his hand. He allowed her to thread her fingers through his, and he sighed. "Sorry for whatever is happening here," he said. "You're sure you're okay?"

"Yeah," she said, determined not to bring up the texts she'd seen on his phone. He got to text his friends and make plans for his life.

"Do you ever see yourself leaving Hope Eternal?" he asked.

Jill shrugged one shoulder, though she felt like they'd just stepped out onto very thin ice. "I don't know. I've never thought about it. I mean, I'm happy there, and it's close to my family, so..." She let the sentence hang there, not sure what else to say. She hadn't absolutely said she would never leave the ranch. She really hadn't thought about it.

In her mind, she knew people moved all the time. They moved themselves and their families across the country. They took new jobs. They started businesses and moved away from family and then closer again.

A waitress arrived and took their drink orders, and Jill focused on Slate again. "Do you think we're too different to make a relationship work?"

"We're too different?" he asked.

"I mean, I don't know. I want lots of gifts for my birthday. You're happy with a dinner. I'm content running honeybee programs, and I think you have bigger dreams for you life. I'm close to my family; you don't talk to yours." She shrugged again, though a thread of misery had started to cloud her mind. "Maybe we're just playing at something here that isn't going to be real."

He nodded and took several long seconds before he spoke. "I think we're just barely starting, Jill," he said quietly. He absolutely could not say her name again, not in that soft, thoughtful voice anyway. Her whole heart had melted with a four-letter word.

"So I think we don't really know if we're opposites or the same. I love the country, and I think you do too. I don't want to live in the city."

"I don't either."

"See?" A ghost of a smile touched his mouth. "Something we have in common."

"I liked your granny too," she said. "We have that in common."

The waitress arrived with their drinks, and Jill put in her order for the butternut squash ravioli. Slate opted for the sausage, spinach, and cheese filled pasta, with plenty of pesto sauce. Jill could admit that his order sounded good, and she wondered why she'd thought they were so different.

He lifted his sweet tea to his lips and grimaced after he'd

taken a sip. "We both like Granny's tea better than whatever this is," he said, putting the glass back down.

Jill giggled and reached for it. "Let me try." She took a small sip too and shook her head. "You're right. We can agree that Granny's sweet tea is far superior to that."

He chuckled, and before she knew it, they were both laughing. She told herself that not everything had to be worked out on the first date, and the conversation moved to easier things. The construction around the ranch. If Slate could take a horseback riding lesson or two. What he did in the equipment shed in the mornings with his friends.

On the way back to the ranch, Jill reminded herself that she'd never set an end date on her boyfriends before. She'd never been in a rush for that first kiss, and she'd never worried too much about when she'd see them again. Slate lived next door, for crying out loud. She was definitely going to see him again.

"I'm wondering if you can help me with a problem," Slate said as he went over the bridge to the ranch.

"A problem?"

"Yeah," Slate said. "It's Luke. I'm pretty sure he likes someone here on the ranch, but he won't say who. I need more eyes and ears on the situation..." He grinned as he went under the gate marking the entrance to the ranch. "What do you say?"

"I love a good P.I. situation," she said, giddiness filling her. "I don't see Luke much, though."

"No, but you have access to the women," Slate said.

"Oh, I see where this is going. You want me to find out if any of them have been chatting it up with Luke when you weren't watching."

"I knew you'd get it." He laughed again and came to a stop on the gravel pad in front of the homestead. He sobered and looked at Jill. "Thanks for going to lunch with me today. I had a real nice time."

"I did too," Jill said, even though not every question had been comfortable.

He grinned at her, and Jill really wanted to lean toward him and kiss him. In fact, she started to do that. He shook his head almost imperceptibly. "I can read your cues, Jill, but we have an audience." He smashed his cowboy hat lower onto his head and reached to open his door.

Jill looked out the windshield and found Ted, Nate, and Dallas all coming across the lawn toward the truck. "Men," she muttered as she too got out of the truck. Didn't they know they shouldn't converge at the end of a date? Did they see any women out here, clamoring for her attention?

No. No, they did not. Because women knew to give privacy at the end of a date, just in case someone wanted to kiss someone else. Luckily, Jill knew who to talk to in order to make sure Slate's friends would leave him alone next time they went out.

And if Dallas was here, that meant Jess was back, and Jill couldn't wait to see her.

CHAPTER NINE

S late watched Jill hurry away from the front yard and disappear into the garage. Ted was talking about something already, but Slate hadn't heard a word yet.

"...and we just need to know if you want to do it," he finished.

"I'm sorry." Slate shook his head. "Do what?"

"I told you we should give him a few minutes," Dallas said.

"We need an answer," Ted said, a frown on his face. His beard was getting totally out of control, but Slate supposed the same argument could be made about his hair and facial hair.

"Tell me again," Slate said. "I was thinking about something else."

"Yeah, that blonde woman you ate lunch with," Nate said.

"Exactly." Slate pinned him with a look. "You guys gave me less than five seconds to switch over, so cut me some slack."

"We needed an answer," Ted repeated.

"Tell me the question again," Slate said, annoyance starting to eat at him. Plus, it was too hot to be standing out here having this conversation. He started for the Annex, because he needed to wash his hands and put on sunscreen before he went back out to the construction site.

"There's an opportunity to get season tickets for the Dallas Cowboys," Ted said. "We could get a pair and split up who goes, or we can get a quad and do the same thing. Nate's going to pay up front, because he has a ton of money —not sure if you knew that—and we can pay him back over time."

"Or not at all," Nate said. "Ward can buy us the tickets."

"It's through Ward that we'd get them anyway," Ted said, and he seemed so excited about this prospect.

"I didn't even know you liked the NFL," Slate said.

"Well, we're all different men out here," Ted said. "But the window is closing, and we want you to be included if you want to be included."

Slate's thoughts went immediately to Luke.

"Before you ask," Dallas said. "Luke said he was in. He wasn't sure how much he'd use them, because he doesn't know where he's going to land, but he said he'd like to consider the option to stay here or at least come back and visit, even just to go to a game together."

"Can we get five of them?" Slate asked. "Because if not, then we'll never get to go to a game together."

"They sell them in pairs," Nate said. "We could get six." He raised his eyebrows and looked at Ted, who strode along at his side.

"You've got kids," Slate said. "You could take Connor or Thomas to a game. Missy or Remmy. Whoever."

"So is that a yes?" Ted asked.

Slate took a deep breath and went up the steps to the front door of the Annex. Inside, the cool kiss of air conditioning met him. "Yeah," he said. "I don't know where I'm going to be either, but I don't want to be left out."

"That's my man." Ted whooped and turned to Nate. The two of them went into the kitchen, jabbering about making the call and getting the tickets paid for.

Slate turned to Dallas and shook his head. Dallas grinned and shrugged. "I leave for a week to go on a honeymoon, and you're dating Jill Kyle?"

Slate couldn't help smiling. "It was *one* date. Is that dating?"

"Yes," Dallas said with a laugh. "Around here it is."

"Good to know," Slate muttered, and he followed the others into the kitchen to get washed up and ready to get back to work.

His thoughts ran around the texts Luke had sent just before he and Jill had gone into the restaurant. Luke loved working with his hands. It was why he'd gone into boxing—which had ultimately landed him in prison.

He'd taken every available class or workshop offered at River Bay, and he'd liked Dallas's mechanic classes and his construction classes the best. Now that Ginger had put him to work on building cabins, it sure seemed like that was what Luke wanted to do with his life.

Custom cabinetry, Slate thought. It was about as far from banking as a man could get, that was for sure. But so was working on a ranch.

The truth was, Slate didn't know what he wanted his life to be. He didn't know how he wanted to spend his time. It sure would be nice if someone would just tell him what to do.

He let the cold water run over his hands as he closed his eyes. *Just tell me what to do,* he prayed. *Lead me in the right direction. I'll follow what Thou wants me to do.*

His thoughts didn't double or triple. If anything, they slowed, and all the chatter about the football tickets behind him vanished. He could only hear the running water and feel the chill of it start to seep into his muscles and bones.

One thought emerged out of the sound, and it made Slate frown.

Call your parents.

He realized in that moment, that his inability to clear the air with his parents was blocking him in every other way.

He couldn't make a decision about his life moving forward until the past was taken care of.

Glancing at the clock, he saw he still had plenty of time before he had to be back on the construction site. He slipped away from Nate, Ted, and Dallas at the kitchen table and down the hall to his bedroom.

The door leading to the bathroom was open, and he went to close it. Soft snores came from the other side of the doorway, and Slate walked through the bathroom to find Luke sleeping on top of his made bed. He looked peaceful in his sleep, and Slate knew what it was like to finally be able to sleep without worrying about going too deep. If he slept too deeply in prison, danger could be upon him without a moment's notice.

River Bay hadn't been a very violent place, but there were a few scary characters in there. Dallas had been beaten nearly to death on his first night there. Just because it was a low-security facility didn't mean it was a picnic.

Slate quietly closed the door to Luke's bedroom, then the one to his. He locked both entrances to his room and sat on his bed. His chest rose and fell with each breath. Granny had given him his parents' numbers, as he'd gotten a whole new phone, and no one memorized cell phone numbers anymore.

His parents were so old-school—and frugal—that they had one cell phone between the two of them. It acted as their landline for the house, as well as a way to text and call their friends and family on the go.

Slate had labeled the number Mom and Daddy in his phone, and he stared at the letters for what felt like a very long time. He finally took a deep breath and tapped on the name. The option to text or call came up, and he let his fingertip touch the phone icon.

The screen blipped, and the line began to ring. Slate jumped to his feet, his nervous energy far too high to stay sitting down.

"Hello?" his mother answered, and Slate's emotion welled in his throat. He couldn't speak, and he tried to clear his throat.

"Yes, there's someone there," his mom said. "I know how to answer a phone, Sterling." Her exasperation made Slate smile, and that loosened something inside his chest. "Hello?" she asked again. "Are you there?"

"Yes," he said, but his voice sure didn't sound like his. His mom wouldn't recognize it, he was sure.

But she sucked in an audible breath and let out a little screech. "Slate?" she asked, the word made of hope and air. "Slate Robinson Sanders, is that you?"

"Yes, Momma," he said, everything—including his voice —coming back to normal for him. He'd forgotten that she loved to use middle names when she wanted to get a point across or make sure she knew who she was talking to. "It's me."

She started to cry, which made Slate tip his head back and blink back his own tears as he studied the ceiling. "I'm out, Momma," he said. "I'm done with my prison term, and I wanted to...let you know, I guess."

She started speaking, but it wasn't to him. Her voice bore excitement as she told Daddy who was on the phone, and that Slate was out of prison. He didn't expect a parade or streamers from his father, that was for sure.

He also didn't expect the scuffling as something happened on their end of the line, nor his father to say, "Slate, is it really you?" with so much of that dang hope in his voice.

"Yes, Daddy," he said. "It's really me."

A couple of beats of silence went by, and Slate didn't know what to say. He'd already apologized a bunch of times for his behavior. The family name meant so much to his father, though Slate wasn't sure why. The barbecue joint which bore the Sanders name had been blasted in a public review for poor customer service, because Daddy was so hard to get along with.

"Why are you callin'?" he asked. "Because we don't have money."

"I know that," Slate said. "I'm not calling for money. I have a job on a ranch." His defenses flew right back into place. He wanted to ask the Lord if this was really what he should've done. *Call my parents?* he questioned. *Why? So I can be attacked and told how worthless I am?*

He took a deep breath. "I'm calling, because I haven't seen you guys in a long time, and I'd like to come spend an afternoon with you."

Where the words had come from, Slate didn't know. But they felt right, and best of all, they'd rendered his father mute.

More scuffling came through the line, then some murmured talking. His mother got back on the line with, "Slate? Come anytime, son. Daddy will put a pig in the ground, and we'll have Cindi and Win come."

Slate had to swallow to get himself to speak again. "Okay, Momma," he said. "I'll need to talk to my boss and work out a date, okay?"

"Of course, of course," she said. "I'm just so glad it's you. I love you, Slate."

He pressed his eyes closed, the burning sensation in them more than he could take. "I love you too, Momma." He cleared his throat. "Tell Daddy I love him too."

"I will, baby. I will."

Slate wrapped up the call and collapsed back onto his bed. His chest rose and fell like it always did, but he knew he'd just done something great. He'd done something hard. He'd done something the Lord had prompted him to, and while he'd wondered what in the world was happening there for a moment, he had to believe God wouldn't lead him astray.

"Thank you," he whispered. "Now, if you could tell me what to do about Jill, that would be amazing. Oh, and Luke too. The cabinetry. All of it. I could use help with all of it."

Nothing else came to him though, and before he knew

it, Luke was banging on the bathroom door and saying they had to get back to work.

Slate got up and answered the door. He looked right into the eyes of his best friend.

"Did you get my texts about the cabinetry call?" Luke asked. He was harsh in so many ways. He always said what was on his mind, and Slate had appreciated that in prison. Out in the real world though, he thought Luke could use some etiquette lessons.

"I got them," Slate said. "I was at lunch with Jill."

"Oh, right," Luke said, as if he'd forgotten. He frowned and pushed his long hair back so he could properly seat his cowboy hat. "Well? What do you think?"

"I think..." Slate sighed. "I think you're the one who likes building stuff."

"You do too," Luke said, his eyes wide. He looked at Slate again, the fear in his gaze right there. "I don't want to go to Lubbock alone."

"I know that," Slate said. "So let's talk to the guy tonight before we make any decisions, okay? It might not even be something you want to do."

"It looks great online," Luke argued.

Slate sighed and picked up his cowboy hat from the bed. He led the way out into the hallway, with Luke still detailing how "great" everything looked about the custom cabinetry apprenticeship online. Luke tended to get carried away with things he didn't know much about, and he'd pull back once all the real details came out.

So Slate let him talk, and he said he'd join the call at six-thirty that night. Meanwhile, he needed to talk to Ginger about some time off to go see his parents. He needed to ask Jill out again. He needed to talk to Granddaddy about why he hadn't wanted to meet Jill. And he needed a firm, fool-proof strategy for going to Austin and *not* contacting anyone he'd known in his previous life.

CHAPTER TEN

Jill dashed over to the stable, scanning for Jess along the way. She was supposed to have the horses ready for the sunrise ride Jill had planned for Slate's birthday. It wasn't exactly a surprise, though Slate didn't know exactly why he needed to meet her on the back deck at the Annex at six o'clock either. She'd asked him to be there, and he'd said he would be.

The past couple of weeks since their first date had been easy and casual with him. He'd asked her out to dinner for his birthday, and they had a date that night. She wanted to be the first person to see him in the morning, and the last to see him at night, for his birthday. That was part of her gift for him, actually.

He'd said going to dinner with him would be the best gift, but Jill had done a little investigative work. She'd put

Hannah on the task of learning Slate's favorite treat, and she'd done that by cozying up to Luke.

Jill had thought perhaps Luke's crush was on Hannah too, as his face lit up whenever she took him a bottle of lemonade. Hannah had dismissed the idea with a laugh, saying that Luke glowed like a Christmas tree whenever anyone came around with food of any kind.

She hadn't reported anything to Slate about that, and Luke was set to meet with his parole officer for the last time next week.

She hadn't heard anything more about the cabinetry apprenticeship in Lubbock—from anyone. Not Luke. Not Slate. It was like those texts didn't exist, and she was eternally grateful that she hadn't said anything to Slate and ruined their first date.

Luke had told Ginger he'd stay on at the ranch until the cabin construction was done, and that was a few more months. After that, he hadn't made any promises. For some reason, Jill considered Luke and Slate a pair, and she suspected if Luke left the ranch, Slate would too. She'd lain awake for far too long at night worrying about it, actually.

They approached the stable, and Jill put the thoughts of Slate leaving the ranch from her mind. He was still there right now, and she had the pan of cinnamon rolls she'd asked her mother to make in her hand. She just needed the horses.

"Jess?" she called, trying to remember who Jess had said she'd saddle that morning and what row of the stable they lived in.

"Row seven," Jess called, appearing a few seconds later at the end of the row. "I have Scalloped Potato and Aladdin ready for you." She breamed like a shining star, and Jill couldn't help smiling at her.

"Thank you." She broke into a jog and followed Jess down the row.

"He's going to love it," Jess said. "Don't worry."

Jill didn't say anything. Jess had a way of knowing how Jill felt without her saying anything, and she had been worried that this was all stupid. She could just send him a text and drop off the cinnamon rolls at a decent hour.

She simply wanted to do more than that. She wanted to make him feel special, because Jill believed everyone should feel special on their birthday.

Not only that, but she still hadn't kissed him yet, and she was really hoping for that to happen today. Maybe this morning. Maybe tonight. But today.

"You get Aladdin," Jess said. "He's ready for you."

"Thanks," Jill said again. She handed Jess the pan of rolls and swung into the saddle.

"I need to go see your mom," Jess said, looking up. "These look amazing."

"She's doing so much better now too," Jill said, taking the baked goods. "We should go while Slate and Dallas and Luke are in Austin."

"That's a great idea." Jess's face lit up. "But I'll have the kids, and Ginger will be down three cowboys."

"Hmm, yeah." Jill frowned as she thought. "We could

take the kids. My mom won't care as long as they wash real good before they go inside. She's still a little compromised in her immune system, but she won't be on chemo then."

"And we go on Sunday, just for a couple of hours. We don't work all day Sunday anyway." Jess wore hope in her eyes. "Do you think she'll make those apple fritters if I ask her?"

Jill laughed and reached for the reins Jess lifted toward her. "Yes, Jess. She will."

"Let's do it," Jess said. "The kids and I are going to stay in the Annex while everyone's gone anyway. It'll be fun."

"Deal." An alarm went off on Jill's phone, and she quickly silenced it. "I have to go. Wish me luck."

"You don't need it, but good luck," Jess said, waving as Jill nudged Aladdin to get him to go. The horses plodded along, and sunlight had started to fill the sky already. It was still on the gray side of golden though, and there would be plenty of sunrise left to see in only five minutes.

She thought about her chat with her mama the last time she'd been there. She'd texted to ask her to make cinnamon rolls for Slate, and they'd talked about him.

Her mother was concerned about his past, as Jill supposed she should be. Jill had simply told her that even good people make mistakes, and all people can change. She believed Slate to be one of the good men and someone who could change.

Mama had said, "I trust your instincts, Jill. Be smart with him, though."

Jill had been trying to be smart with Slate, but the man ignited something inside her that sometimes made her brain go on the fritz.

She spotted Slate on the back deck the moment she had a clear view of it, and he saw her only a few seconds later. She grinned from ear to ear, hoping she could pull that back by the time she got to him. She was already making a fool of herself, as she didn't ride horses everyday the way he did.

He'd been taking lessons for a few weeks now, and he made it a point to practice every day so he could get better. She rode a horse as necessity on the ranch called for it, and that wasn't very often in her role at Hope Eternal.

"Look at you," he called as he came down the steps and started to walk toward her.

"Happy birthday," she called back.

"What are we doing?"

"You said you love watching the sunrise and the sunset. So today, we're watching the sunrise from atop a horse." She grinned at him as he took the reins for Scalloped Potato and swung into the saddle like he'd been doing it all his life. He really was the sexiest man Jill had ever dated, and everything seemed so easy for him.

She only knew it wasn't because he told her of his internal struggles. Extending out the pan of cinnamon rolls, she said, "I asked my mother to bake these for you. I heard through the grapevine that they're your favorite."

"Cinnamon rolls?" He looked at her with pure delight in his eyes. "They are. Thank you so much."

Jill swelled under his praise. "Come on," she said, turning away before she leaned toward him and fell off the blasted horse. "There's a great place here on the ranch to watch the sunrise, but it's a ten-minute ride, and we don't want to miss too much."

She led him east as he rode with the reins looped around the saddle horn so he could take out a cinnamon roll. "No raisins," he said. "Which grapevine told you this?"

"I put Hannah on Luke," Jill admitted. "And my mother was happy to make them. She loves to bake, and since she's feeling better now, she said yes before I even finished asking." She glanced at him and caught him with a bit of frosting in the corner of his mouth. He licked it away and smiled at her. With the golden rays of the sun, and the horse, and the cowboy hat, and the cinnamon roll, Jill thought she might have fallen in love with him right then.

Too soon, she told herself. They'd had some good conversations over the past couple of weeks, but at least half of them had been through texts. She knew better than to think a person was exactly what they presented themselves to be through a message. But she knew Slate in person too, and he was as real as they came.

"I'm glad your mother is feeling better," he said.

"Me too," Jill said. "Though now I feel pretty stupid for yelling at the ocean and throwing rocks out into the water—like that really did anything."

"Hey," he said, his voice calm and perfect. She looked at

him on the next step Aladdin took. "It did. At that moment, that's what you needed, and it helped."

"What do you do when you need a release like that?"

He gazed at the horizon, where the sun was just starting to make an appearance. "I drive."

"That's what you were doing that same day," she said, just now getting it.

"Yes," he said. "It was an amazing thing to be able to get in my truck and drive wherever I wanted." He smiled and tucked the last of his first cinnamon roll in his mouth. After he finished eating it, he added, "It still is."

"I bet," Jill said. She didn't understand having her freedoms restricted by that, but she understood helplessness. And loneliness. And feeling like she was never good enough. "It's right past these trees," she said. "There's a wide river here, but it's cut down into the earth a little bit. Feels like you're on the edge of a cliff."

She urged Aladdin to go past the tree line, and the horse stopped almost immediately after that. "Here we are." She slid from the saddle, stumbling forward a couple of steps as she wasn't all that graceful with dismounting. An embarrassed giggle came out of her mouth as she tossed the reins over a post that had been erected there.

"You guys must come out here a lot,' he said, putting Potato's reins around the bar too. The horses started grazing, and Jill stood on the edge of the river and gazed at the sun.

"Yeah," she said. "I think Ginger's father did. He put the post there years and years ago."

"I can see why," Slate said, coming to her side. They stood that way for a couple of minutes, the silence and the sunrise rendering them both silent.

Once the sun had fully crested the horizon and was painting Jill's face with warmth, she sighed and turned toward Slate. "What are you doing the rest of the day?"

"Working this morning," he said, slipping his arm around her waist. She leaned into him and rested her head against his chest as they both faced into the sun again. "I'm going to the shelter this afternoon with the boys. Then dinner tonight."

"Who's going to take care of your dog during dinner?"

"Connor is currently fighting with Thomas over who'll get to play with him." Slate chuckled, the sound deep and delicious inside his chest.

Jill smiled to herself, beyond glad she'd orchestrated this moment for the two of them.

He shifted beside her, taking a step to stand almost fully behind her now. He encompassed her in his arms, and they breathed in together. "You're wearing something nice tonight, right?" he murmured, his mouth right against her ear. She shivered in his arms as she nodded.

"Because we're goin' somewhere nice, Jill."

Oh, he was pulling out her name again. And using that soft, sexy voice? He definitely wasn't playing fair.

She wanted to turn in his arms and kiss him. In her mind, it seemed like an easy move to make, but she didn't do

it. Her heart pounded in her chest, and the seconds
ticked by.

Slate finally pressed his lips to her neck, just below her
ear, and Jill naturally leaned her head back so he could have
better access. "We better get goin'," he said. "I promised
Ginger and Luke I'd be on-site by seven."

Surely they hadn't been standing there that long, but as
he dropped his arms and Jill looked at her phone, it was
already six-forty-five. She sighed, because she'd missed
another opportunity to kiss him.

He glanced at her. "Thank you for this," he said, taking
both sets of reins in his hand. He started walking with the
horses, adding, "Will you grab the cinnamon rolls?"

She bent down to get them, and when she straightened
and started toward him, he turned suddenly and came back
toward her. He wore something in his eyes she hadn't seen
before, and he haphazardly tossed the reins toward the post.

"Just a second." He took the cinnamon rolls from her
and put them back on the ground. "Jill, you're amazing," he
said. "No one's ever done something like this for my
birthday."

"It was a sunrise," she said.

He gathered her into his arms. "It is so much more than
that." He swept his cowboy hat off his head and lowered his
mouth toward hers. Her eyes drifted closed as her heartbeat
turned to hummingbird wings. He paused, seeking permis-
sion, and Jill closed the distance between them.

She acted a little too quickly, though, and she hadn't antici-pated that he was already so close. She sort of mashed her mouth against his, but she adjusted quickly. He took the kiss from awkward to sweet to passionate with each new stroke of his lips against hers, and Jill's heart grew wings and started to fly.

Kissing Slate was far better than anything she'd ever imagined and vastly superior to any other man she'd ever kissed.

"Thank you," he murmured, removing his lips from hers for the breath of time it took to speak the words. He kissed her again. "Thank you." And again. "Thank you." And again.

Jill threaded her fingers through his hair and hoped he knew that she'd do all of this and more for him, because he meant a lot to her. Now, she just needed to figure out how to tell him that and make sure he knew she didn't want him to leave Hope Eternal Ranch when the construction work ran out.

CHAPTER ELEVEN

Slate could not stop kissing Jill. He'd been thinking about this moment for a solid week, and now that the moment had started and was going on and on... and on, he'd severely underestimated how amazing a kiss could be.

Her fingers in his hair sent pops of electricity down his spine. The taste of her mouth was almost like the cream cheese frosting on the cinnamon rolls, but with more strawberry from her lip gloss. His heartbeat sprinted through his whole body, beating and beating and beating with every stroke of her lips against his.

You've got to stop, he told himself, but he just kept kissing her. She didn't stop kissing him either, and Slate finally pulled away when he needed to breathe deeper than kissing her allowed.

"You're going to be late," she whispered.

Slate opened his eyes and found Jill's face lifted toward his, her eyes still closed. He couldn't believe he'd caught the attention of a woman like her. She was so kind, and so...good.

"Worth it," he said, smiling at her.

She opened her eyes, and Slate turned shy. He bent to pick up his cowboy hat and settled it low on his head to cover his eyes. He cleared his throat, and didn't dare to look at her.

"Oh, are you embarrassed now?" Jill put her hand in Slate's and led him to get the reins. "That was an amazing kiss. I actually think it was about ten kisses in one, which is probably why it was so spectacular."

Slate's heartbeat still hadn't settled, but he managed to say, "Amazing? Spectacular?"

"Great," she said in a deadpan as she started to lead both horses. "You didn't like it as much as I did."

"I don't think that's possible," Slate said, and when Jill didn't answer, he finally looked at her.

She grinned up at him with all the wattage of the sun they'd just watched come up. "So amazing and spectacular fit."

He smiled back at her, all of his embarrassment and shyness gone. "They fit."

She laughed and passed his reins to him. "It's ten minutes on a horse, but at least twenty with human feet. Let's ride, cowboy." She put her foot in the stirrup and got on her horse, and Slate marveled at her.

"I didn't know you rode a lot," he said.

"I don't," she said. "I'm just grateful I managed to get on and off of this beast without embarrassing myself."

He chuckled and realized he'd left the cinnamon rolls back on the pole. "My breakfast," he said. He swung into the saddle and turned the pretty brown and white horse back toward the tree line. "I'll be right back." He urged the horse to go back to get his cinnamon rolls, and once he'd retrieved them, he returned to Jill.

"Are you getting ready for your trip?" Jill asked as they got moving back toward the homestead.

"Yeah," Slate said. "As much as I can, at least."

"What can I help you with?"

He exhaled heavily, trying to think about what he even needed to prepare. He could gas up his truck and drive all the way to Austin in about three hours. A flicker of fear touched his pulse. It didn't seem far enough away from the man he'd once been—and the people he'd known in Austin.

He'd spoken to his mom several times in the past couple of weeks since calling her, and she really wanted him to come visit for his birthday. But the timing hadn't worked out, and he wasn't going for another week and a half. He'd call her later today, if she didn't call him first. He rarely talked to his father, but he'd been getting texts from their phone with quotes about being a good person and how to work hard.

Those definitely came from his father, and Slate hadn't figured out how to respond to the messages. He knew what

he'd done wrong. He'd paid the penalty. He knew what difficult situations looked like, sounded like, and smelled like on
a level most people didn't.

"The truth is, I don't want to go back," he said.

"Why not?" Jill asked. "You want to see your parents.
Well, your mom, at least."

"Yeah, that's going to be fine," he said, though he had
doubts about that too. "But I don't want to go to the restaurant, and I don't want to run into anyone I used to know."

"You'll only be gone for a weekend," she said. "Just stick
to your parents' house."

"We're not staying there," he said. "It's not a very big
house, and...I mentioned how difficult my father is, right?"

"You may have said so a time or two," she teased.

Slate wished he could be as cavalier about his father's
stubborn and standoffish personality. He could weather his
dad's storms. He didn't want to expose Luke or Dallas to
them, but both of his friends had insisted they come
with him.

Secretly, Slate was glad they were coming. Beyond glad.
Grateful. He'd be protected from himself if they accompanied him. He hated that he needed that protection, but the
truth was, he still did.

"I just need to gather myself together," he said. "No one
can help with that."

"Gather yourself?"

"All the bits of myself that I want to be," he said. "Put
some defenses in place against the person I used to be in

Austin." He glanced at her. "You know those are two completely different men, right?"

"You've said that," she said. "I suppose I can imagine it, but no, I don't really understand it."

Slate couldn't expect her to. "People change, Jill. That's all I'm saying. Sometimes the change is so drastic that the person from before is completely unrecognizable from the person they are now."

"Okay," Jill said. "I once had a friend who was Little Miss Sunshine. She was always dressed in the most fashionable clothes, and her hair was always done just right, and she got straight As. A couple of years ago, I saw her on social media, and she was decked out from head to toe in black clothes, with this gothic makeup, and at least four or five piercings in her ears. One in her nose. She was unrecognizable. Like that?"

"Yes," he said. "Like that."

"Do you have any pictures of yourself from before?"

"No," he said, his voice almost a bark. He tried to tame it into niceness when he added, "Even if I did, Jill, I wouldn't show them to you. I don't want you to know that man. Ever."

He didn't want to be that man ever again. He could handle going to Austin, because he wasn't the Slate Sanders he'd been before. He wasn't going to be that Slate again. He wasn't. He knew better now, and he'd been through a lifetime of experiences in the four years he'd been in prison. He wasn't a junkie anymore.

"Okay," Jill said, her voice a little quieter than normal.

Slate looked out over the ranch, illuminated by the sun. "I'm sorry," he said. "I didn't mean to snap at you."

"You didn't." She looked at him, and Slate looked at her. The moment stretched, and he was glad he didn't have to explain any further. She didn't go on either, and he guided his horse closer to the deck so he could put down his cinnamon rolls.

"I'll help you put the horses away," he said.

"No," she said. "I can do it. You have work to do." As if on cue, Luke came out the back door, his gloves in his hands.

"There you are," Luke said, slowing down. "You're on a horse."

"Birthday breakfast," Slate said, extending the pan of cinnamon rolls toward Luke.

"I stole him for a birthday sunrise," Jill said. "But he's back right on time." She grinned at Luke and then Slate. "Go on, cowboy. Hand me the reins, and I'll get Scalloped Potato all fixed up with a big bag of oats for having to haul you around."

Luke laughed as he took the pan of baked goods from Slate.

Slate wanted to kiss Jill again, but he reminded himself that was why he'd turned back when they were leaving the first time. He'd wanted to kiss her in private, and he wouldn't make out with her in front of Luke, that was for dang sure. Luke already asked him endless questions about Jill as it was. He didn't even want to tell Luke he'd kissed her.

At the same time, Slate knew he would, because he needed Luke's help and advice when it came to women as much as Luke needed to know how Slate was feeling about Jill and how those feelings would impact Slate's future plans.

The cabinetry apprenticeship hadn't panned out, and Slate had tried to be sympathetic to Luke. In reality, he was sympathetic, because Luke was almost done with his re-entry program, and his desperation to find "the next stage of his life" was palpable if Slate spent more than five minutes with him.

He handed his reins to Jill and said, "Six tonight, right, sweets?"

Jill grinned down at him. "I'll be ready at six. Good luck with your dog adoption this afternoon."

"Thanks." He watched her start to plod away on her horse, leading his a head or two behind.

"You've got it bad for her," Luke said, a cinnamon roll in one hand and his gloves discarded on the deck railing.

"Yeah," Slate said, still watching her and the horses. "I kissed her this morning."

"Thatta boy," Luke said with a grin.

Slate finally looked at him. "What? I didn't think you wanted me to do that."

"It was inevitable." Luke shrugged. "As soon as I realized that, I stopped worrying about it." He stuffed another bite of cinnamon roll in his mouth. After he finished chewing and swallowing, he added, "The boys and I put a friendly wager on when you'd kiss her. Nate said yesterday. I said your birthday, but Dallas and Ted wanted that day too. So we narrowed it down by time. I said before noon. Ted took after nine p.m., because he knew you guys were going out tonight. Dallas said sometime in the afternoon— maybe after you get the puppy and before the end of the date."

Luke grinned even wider. "I won. So thanks, friend." He slapped Slate's shoulder with laughter dancing in his eyes.

"You bet on when I'd kiss her?"

"I get extra if she kissed you," Luke said. "So? Did you kiss her, or did she kiss you?"

"I'm not even answering that," Slate said, huffing as he turned toward the house. "I need to get my tool belt and my gloves." He walked away, bristling at Luke's chuckles.

"I'm going to take that as she kissed you," he called after him.

"You're wrong," Slate said, not even deigning to turn and face him. "Too bad, Luke. Nothing extra for you." He nearly yanked the door off its hinges he pulled on it so hard, but he didn't care.

His friends had bet on when he'd kiss Jill? Not only that, they'd bet if she'd kiss him. How humiliating. He went into his bedroom to get his equipment, and he paused, his anger simmering. Finally deciding, he pulled out his phone and sent a message to the group.

You guys are so annoying, he typed. *I've been nothing*

but supportive of all of you and your relationships and you bet against me?

He wanted to say how pinched his heart felt in his chest, but he couldn't find the words. He sent the text, hoping they'd be able to feel the hurt in his text.

His breathing increased until his chest was rising and falling almost violently, and he found he couldn't leave his bedroom. The door stood open, and he heard Luke coming before he appeared in the doorway, his phone at his ear.

"Yeah," he said. "He's upset."

Slate didn't want to talk to anyone right now. This birthday had started so great, and now he just felt...small and insignificant. "Leave me alone," he said, stepping toward the door. Luke fell back, and Slate closed the door in his stunned face. He heard him say something on the other side of the door, but the wood garbled the words.

Slate turned around and pressed his back into the door. He hated overreacting, and he hated how his feelings were so raw now that he wasn't numb all the time. That had been the hardest adjustment once the drugs had been physically cleared from his system. The emotional aftermath was still too much for him sometimes.

If he just kept breathing, he could contain the emotions, stuffing them back down where he could manage them and where they couldn't injure him.

"Slate," Luke said through the door. "I'm sorry. It was just innocent fun."

"Yeah," Ted said. "We didn't mean to make you feel

bad." He knocked, his big bear paw hands recognizable even through sound.

Slate especially didn't want to face them right now. He closed his eyes, which burned so badly. *Please just let them go away*, he thought. At the same time, he didn't want to be alone. He'd counted his role in the group in River Bay as one of the biggest blessings of his life. If he hadn't had Nate, Ted, Dallas, and Luke, he'd be even more lost than he was right now.

They'd provided him with support and friendship at a crucial time of his life, and he hoped he'd done the same for them.

"Slate," Nate said through the door. "I'm sorry. Please open the door."

It wasn't locked, but none of them had tried to open it. They respected him and his privacy, something none of them had had in prison. Living in a dormitory with fifteen other men didn't allow for many private conversations.

Slate's phone rang, and as he still held it in his hand, he looked down at it. Dallas's name sat on the screen. Slate wouldn't be able to ignore them, or avoid them, and he found he didn't want to.

They were all trying to apologize, and he should let them. He swiped on the call and tapped the speaker button.

"Slate?" Dallas said.

"Yeah." Slate turned and opened the door.

"I didn't mean to make you feel bad. I'm sorry," Dallas said.

Slate faced Luke, Ted, and Nate, all of them looking very vulnerable and apologetic too. His chest heaved again, because he hated making other people feel bad. A quote his father had sent him a couple of days ago ran through his mind. *It costs nothing to be kind.*

"Don't be sorry," Slate said. "I'm oversensitive sometimes. It's fine."

"It's obviously not fine," Nate said, glancing at the others. He leaned forward and said louder, "I would've been mad if I found out my friends were betting against me too."

"Me too," Ted said. "It started out as something fun, but I can see that it's hurtful."

"You have been supportive of us," Dallas said, his voice tinny and far away.

Luke said nothing, a frown forming between his eyebrows.

"It's okay," Slate said. "Really."

"So..." Ted glanced at Nate. "I'm assuming you and Jill..."

"Do I ask you what you do with your wife?" Slate asked, quirking his eyebrows.

"Let's get to work, boys," Nate said, putting a hand on Ted's chest as he turned around. "Slate will tell us what Slate wants to tell us about his relationship with Jill."

"Sorry," Ted said, hesitating for another moment. "Really, Slate."

"I know," Slate said. "Dallas, thanks for calling."

"See you in a bit," he said.

With Nate and Ted gone, and the call from Dallas over, Slate simply faced Luke.

"I hate that I'm being left behind," Luke said. "There. I said it. I'm happy for you. I am. I know you like Jill, and she likes you, and you seem really happy together. I'm just..." He shrugged, because he probably didn't have words to explain adequately.

Slate understood that on a deep level. "You're not being left behind," he said quietly. "You can stay here on the ranch for as long as you want. Ginger loves you, and I know she offered you a full-time job once the cabins are built."

"Yeah." Luke looked lost though, and Slate disliked that.

"Let's get out to the site," Slate said. "If you'd just tell me who you've been eyeing, I could maybe distract you with a girlfriend of your own."

"At least you're admitting she's your girlfriend now," Luke said with a grin.

Slate turned to get his tool belt and gloves. "Now that I've finally kissed her, I suppose the label is okay to use." He met Luke at the door, but Luke took another step in, not out.

"I don't want the others to know," he said.

"Of course not," Slate said. "I know how to keep a secret, Luke."

"She has a boyfriend."

"That does complicate things."

"He lives in our basement." Luke delivered that sentence in a whisper.

Slate cocked his head, thinking through the four men

who lived downstairs. Bill was the only one with a girlfriend, and that woman was Hannah Otto.

"She's gorgeous," Slate said. "I'll give you that."

"Why am I always trying to get things I can't have?" Luke asked. He sighed and shook his head. "It doesn't matter. Let's go build a cabin." He turned and walked away, and Slate hurried to follow him.

He didn't need to say anything right now, but he'd keep Luke in his prayers, because he wanted Luke to be just as happy as possible. As he stepped outside, he got a text, and he glanced at it.

If I could come with you to the dog adoption, would that be acceptable?

A smile burst onto his face at Jill's text. *Absolutely*, he typed out quickly. *And I need some major help with someone you live with...*

Intriguing, she sent back. *Can't wait to hear more about that.*

He just couldn't wait to see her again, and it was Jill's blue eyes, quick laugh, and incredible kiss that helped him get through the backbreaking labor of building a cabin in hundred-degree Texas heat.

CHAPTER TWELVE

J ill smiled around at all the dogs that had been brought outside to the shaded tents. The grass was green, and the sky blue, and Mother Nature had even sent along a little bit of a breeze. The dogs ran around in the shade, with plenty of water nearby.

Only a few people could go in at a time, and she, Slate, and Luke currently waited for their turn. Thankfully, the animal shelter had anticipated a lot of people to their afternoon adoption event, and they'd set up tents and water stations for the humans too.

"I like that brown one," Slate said.

"That's so specific," Luke said dryly.

Jill looked away from the dogs to see where Slate was looking. He pointed to a medium-sized dog that could use a haircut who stood near the closest corner of the fenced-off area. He barked and looked around to see if anyone was watching. Barked again. Every few seconds, he seemed to think he could join the fray, and he'd take a step or two forward, only to fall back again.

"He looks like you," Jill said, causing Slate to turn toward her. "You know, the shaggy hair."

"We can trim him up," Slate said.

"Oh yeah?" Jill reached for his hand, not embarrassed to do so in front of Luke. "Are you going to cut your hair soon too?"

"I was thinking about it," he said, reaching up to run his hand along his beard. Jill grinned at him, wishing they were alone so she could kiss him again. That beard had been soft against her skin. "My mother would die if she saw me like this." He smiled like he wouldn't mind that.

Luke chuckled and said, "I found a great barber. He'll make you look respectable."

"Hmm." Slate took a step forward as the line moved, and Jill went with him.

Her phone buzzed in her shoulder bag, and she took it out. Hannah had texted, and Jill's heart stopped cold with the short message.

First, she'd sent a crying emoji. *Need ice cream. Can you stop on the way back to the ranch?* The last emoji was a broken heart.

Ice cream, combined with those particular emojis could only mean one thing. Boyfriend trouble. *I can,* Jill said. *But why do I need to? Is this butter pecan level? Or are we talking vanilla bean?*

Butter pecan.

The air left Jill's lungs, and she groaned.

"What's wrong?" Slate asked, peering over her arm at her phone.

She tilted it toward him so he could see it better. "Bill broke up with Hannah."

She saw the way Luke turned toward her immediately, about the same time she witnessed the confusion roll across Slate's face. "How do you know that?" He pointed to her screen. "From that?"

"Butter pecan level is a break up," Jill said. "Ice cream is what we binge on when we have boyfriend trouble."

He met her eyes. "So you're telling me that if we break up, you're going to binge butter pecan ice cream with Hannah?"

Jill searched his face, not liking the turn this conversation had taken at all. "No," she said slowly. "Hannah's kryptonite is butter pecan. Mine is peanut butter cookie dough. There are *levels*, Slate."

"Oh, levels." His eyes crinkled as he smiled. "What kind did you eat when you broke up with your last boyfriend? Mike, right?"

"First off, he broke up with me," Jill said. "Usually, when a woman breaks up with a man, it's not an ice cream level event. Now, there might have been copious amounts of ice cream consumed *before* the break up, while we're trying to decide if we should end the relationship or not."

"Maybe that's what happened here," Luke said, having

pressed in very close to Slate to read the texts on Jill's phone. "Maybe she needs butter pecan to decide if she's going to break up with Bill."

Jill shook her head. "It's cute how you guys think you can figure out what's going on." She looked back at the screen and tapped out a quick reply. *I'll get a gallon. Hot fudge?*

She showed it to Slate and Luke. "Now, see, if she says yes, we're in real trouble. Like, major. She's probably sequestered in her room right now crying kind of major trouble." She glanced toward the parking lot, worrying filling her chest. "I should go if she says yes."

She hoped Hannah wouldn't say yes, but she had been dating Bill for a while now. Six or seven months at least, and Jill knew they'd started to talk about their future together.

"You should?" Slate asked.

"If she wants hot fudge with butter pecan, we're in crisis mode."

"What do you have in crisis mode?" he asked. "And you never said what you ate when Mike broke up with you."

"I had mint chocolate chip," she said. "It's a level or two down from peanut butter cookie dough."

"Oh, so you weren't that into Mike." Slate wrapped her up in his arms, and Jill giggled as she shook her head.

"I'm not answering that."

"Well, he didn't get peanut butter cookie dough." Slate released her and moved forward with the line. It was almost their turn, and Hannah hadn't answered yet. Jill sent her another message, needing to know if she should head to the grocery store now and then get back to the ranch as fast as possible.

No hot fudge, Hannah said. *I saw it coming a couple of weeks ago.*

I'm so sorry, sweetie. You're going to find the right guy. Jill tapped to send the message and looked at Luke. He wasn't watching her, but he'd moved up with Slate. He glanced back to Jill, and she gave Luke a smile.

"Is she okay?" he asked, and the concern in his voice could've melted the polar ice caps. "I can stop and get the ice cream. Drive your car back to the ranch so you can go with Slate." He actually looked hopeful too, like he wanted to do it.

Slate elbowed him, and Jill didn't miss that, though she dropped her eyes back to her phone as if she hadn't seen it. Smiles and sunshine sang in her soul, because she now knew that Luke liked Hannah. Of course, Hannah wouldn't be ready for a new relationship right away, but Luke had time left at the ranch before the cabins would be done. Maybe if he started dating Hannah, he'd stay. Then Slate would stay. Then she and Slate would fall in love and get married...

Her thoughts ran away from her as they tended to do. She couldn't help her feelings though. She did move from relationship to relationship fairly quickly, because she hadn't had a peanut butter cookie dough man in a long, long time.

The last time had been a year or two after she'd come to

Hope Eternal Ranch, actually. She'd come to the ranch because of a man like that, and she'd promptly fallen in love with another cowboy who'd stolen her heart, stomped on it, and spit it back in her face.

Since then, she'd been flitting from boyfriend to boyfriend, looking for a good time without too many strings. Now, she wanted all the strings. All the fun, too, but the kind that came with commitment.

"Our turn," Slate said, and he entered the pen first. Luke went after him, and Jill put her phone back in her bag before she went inside too. A few of the overly friendly pups came right up to her and started sniffing. She smiled down at them and let them.

"That's right," she said. "Can you smell Ursula? The horses?" No matter what, the dogs liked her and kept sniffing and sniffing at her legs and shorts and boots.

Slate had gone over to the dog in the corner of the pen and crouched down in front of it. The dog had laid down and was currently stretching forward to greet him. He held very still, his hand out for the pup to smell. He did, and then he licked Slate's palm. Jill knew that was the dog Slate would get, and she found herself wishing she had a few more minutes with all the canines in the pen.

But Slate straightened, caught the attention of one of the shelter workers, and indicated he wanted the shaggy brown dog he'd chosen from the line. Turned out, the dog was a five-year-old male that had been abandoned in the parking lot of an apartment complex last month. No collar. No tags.

No microchip. No one had seen who'd left him, and the pet rescue arm of the shelter had picked him up.

"He's a Briard," the woman helping them said. She wore a name tag that said Bernice on it. "He needs to run a lot, and he's very sensitive." She looked at Slate with doubt in her eyes. "What do you do?"

"I work on a ranch," he said. "He'll have plenty of time to run and work. There are several other dogs on the ranch."

Bernice nodded, but she didn't smile and she didn't put down the dog either. "His name is Axle, but you can change it if you'd like."

"Do most people change the name of their rescue dog?" Slate asked.

"That's personal," Bernice said, grinning at Axle. "I have to be honest and say he's been adopted out twice in the past month and brought back. He his very high energy, and he'll do anything to please you. He's very sensitive to loud noises and children. He's nervous, basically."

Slate nodded and reached out to pat Axle again. "Okay."

"We ask that if you don't want him for whatever reason, please bring him back to us. We won't ask any questions, and we'll even refund your adoption fee. We just want him to find his forever home, with his forever human." She looked doubtful that that human would be Slate, but he looked just as determined to make sure it was.

"Okay," he said again.

"Okay," Bernice said. "We need you to fill out the paperwork and pay the fee. And you can't take him unless he's in a kennel."

"I'll get it," Luke said, already moving toward the truck they'd arrived in together. Jill had driven her own car, because she'd stopped by the elementary school to drop off their fall flyers for distribution on her way here.

She stayed out of the way while Slate got all the details taken care of. They gave him a leash and a collar for Axle, and the pair of them walked side-by-side over to Slate's truck.

"He likes you," Jill said.

"He's going to be great," Slate said, herding the dog into the kennel. He bent down and grinned at Axle. "Isn't that right, bud? We're going to get along just fine." He stood up, his smile still stuck in place. "I have a dog."

"You sure do," Jill said, glad he was so happy about it.

"Thanks for coming." Slate hugged her, and Jill did love the feeling of being enveloped in his strength.

"I did nothing," she said. "You picked him out while we waited in line."

"Yeah, but I got to learn about the ice cream levels." He stepped back and smiled at her. "I'll see you back at the ranch in a bit, I assume. Gotta stop at the store?"

"Yeah." She drew in a deep breath and released it. "Do you need anything? Anything for Axle or anything?"

"I just like chocolate ice cream with brownies in it," he said. "No break up needed."

Jill rolled her eyes and swatted at his bicep as he laughed at her.

"Leave her alone," Luke said. "And get in the truck. I'm melting out here." He gave Slate a glare, but his look softened when he met Jill's eyes. She smiled and nodded at him, and he returned the gestures. She wondered how long he'd wait to make his move, and as she walked to her car, she tapped out a quick message to him too.

She won't need long to recover. Give her a couple of weeks. Then sweep her off her feet with something amazing and sweet.

She hadn't even started her car yet when his response came in. *Like what?*

Jill turned the key in the ignition as she grinned. *I'll think of something,* she promised him. And she'd start working on Hannah that very afternoon, as she ate too much butter pecan ice cream and lamented that her relationship with Bill hadn't worked out.

"Wow, Slate," Jill said when she opened the front door of the West Wing. "Look at you."

He whistled, his eyes dropping down the length of her body too. "No, look at you."

She lifted her arms and did a turn for him, the long, black dress almost glued to her body like a second skin. Sure, she had a few extra pounds on her curves, and she had to buy cowgirl boots in the wide width to accommodate her thick calves, but she knew she looked good tonight.

The hunger and desire in his eyes testified of it. He moved right into the doorway, though he didn't fit there, and took her into his arms. "You are stunning in every way." He lowered his head toward hers and kissed her, and Jill fell more in love with him right there half-in and half-out of the house.

"Thank you," she said when he pulled away. This kiss had been much shorter than the one that morning. "You look amazing as well."

He reseated his hat on his head, and it looked like a new one. "New hat?" she asked, taking his hand in hers.

"Yes," he said.

"I like it." She smiled up at him, and they went down the steps together. "How's Axle settling in?"

Slate looked toward the Annex. "Good. He's good. I'm not sure why she said he was nervous around kids. He seems to love Connor and Missy. Remmy even picked him up, though I think he weighs more than she does, and he was fine." He smiled toward the house and then at her. "He laid down flat when Ursula came around."

"She's got a big personality," Jill said.

"Yeah. He was fine after a few minutes with her. Ted's got the cattle dogs with him too, and he's doing good." He sounded a bit nervous, but he didn't detour off the path toward his truck.

Once inside, she asked, "Where are we going tonight?"

"Riverfront," he said, glancing at her.

Jill's breath caught in her throat. "Slate," she managed to say past the blockage there. "That's...insane. You need a reservation for like, six months to get into Riverfront."

"Nah," he said, backing out. "Only about six weeks."

"You called and got a reservation for two at Riverfront six weeks ago?"

"I wanted to go there for my birthday," he said. "I figured someone would go with me. Luke's pretty mad I started dating you." He laughed, and Jill wanted to join in but found she couldn't.

He noticed and sobered as he turned onto the highway. "Relax, Jill," he said. "It's going to be amazing. I've heard the food is like nothing you've ever had before, and you're the only person I want to spend my birthday meal with."

"Okay," she said, wondering what kind of prices the menu would bear at Riverfront. And how Slate had the money to pay for that. She didn't question him, because it was rude, and instead, she asked, "So, are you going to book somewhere for Christmas right now too? Maybe a banquet hall or something?"

He burst out laughing again and shook his head. His laughter wasn't as bright this time, and it didn't last nearly as long. "Not at all."

"Why's that?" she asked. "You don't like Christmas?"

"As a matter of fact," he said. "No, I don't like Christmas."

Jill gaped at him again. "What? I mean...who doesn't like Christmas."

"I not only dislike Christmas, I abhor Christmas. I hate it. I haven't celebrated it in four years, and I'm not planning to do so this year."

Jill blinked at him. "But you go to church every week. That's like saying you believe in God, but you don't want to celebrate His holiday."

"First off," Slate said, shooting her a glance. "It's Christ's birthday, not God's. Second, Jesus Christ was actually born sometime in the spring. Christmas means nothing."

"It's a celebration of the Savior," Jill argued. She didn't normally spend all of her time and energy celebrating Him; she rather loved the pine trees, the ivy, the colored lights, and the mistletoe. Oh, and the gifts. Jill loved buying, giving, and receiving gifts.

"I can celebrate the Savior any time," Slate said.

Jill didn't know what else to say. She and Slate weren't exactly opposites, but the things they seemed to be on other ends of the spectrum on were big things. And the distance between them on those things was very wide.

"Great," he said. "I've ruined this date with my distaste of Christmas."

"No," Jill said. "You haven't. I'm just processing."

"Can you process while you hold my hand?" he asked, some of the darkness and bite that had been in his tone now gone.

Jill reached over and slipped her hand into his. So he

didn't like Christmas. Big deal. She didn't like chocolate ice cream with brownies in it all that much. The difference was, it wouldn't require a major life change to buy a different kind of ice cream. Cutting an entire beloved holiday out of her future certainly felt like a pretty major thing.

CHAPTER THIRTEEN

The Christmas conversation hung over Slate's head as he continued to drive to Riverfront. The restaurant was a sprawling building that looked more like someone's estate house than a commercial building. It was warm and cozy and inviting—and it sat right on the river that carved its way toward the Gulf of Mexico.

Jill held his hand on the way into the restaurant too, and he'd never felt as lucky as he did in those few minutes with her on his arm. She was stunning in every way, not just how she looked. She was stunning to him in her kindness. Stunning to him in her faith. Stunning to him in her loyalty and friendships.

He knew she'd been struggling with the Lord recently, but he also knew she loved Him. In the end, Slate knew Jill would come out of her mother's illness a better person, with stronger faith than before. Everyone dealt with doubts sometimes, himself included.

Maybe it's time you let go of your Christmas hatred, he thought as he gave the hostess his name. She smiled like he was the governor of Texas, and she led them to a beautiful booth that was shaped like a semi-circle. It faced the huge, tall and long, wall of windows that overlooked the river.

"Oh my goodness," Jill said, her voice made mostly of air. "This is amazing." She looked at Slate with those wide, blue eyes, clearly enjoying this experience.

He was too, and he knew a large part of that was because of her. He slid into the booth from the left while she did on the right, and the hostess handed them their menus. "Your server will be Lorenzo, and he's right here."

Sure enough, Lorenzo appeared, and he held a bottle of wine in one hand and a slice of chocolate cake in the other. "I heard it's your birthday," he said with a smile as wide as the sky.

"It is his birthday." Jill beamed at him, and if Slate was seeing clearly, she held a little bit of love in her expression. Could that be right?

Shocked, he looked away from her as Lorenzo put the cake in front of him. "We encourage you to enjoy dessert before dinner on your birthday," he said. "Would you like some too, ma'am?"

"Yes, please," Jill said, a smile blooming across her whole face.

"I'll be right back, but first, anything to drink?"

"Diet Coke," Slate said, as alcohol for him was one short step away from drugs. Jill said the same thing, and Lorenzo left.

He picked up his fork and handed it to her. "You test it out."

"No way." She refused to take the fork, her smile bright and her spirit strong. Slate simply gazed at her, wondering what it felt like to be in love. Could he have fallen for her already? He'd been at Hope Eternal for over three months now, but he'd only been dating Jill for five or six weeks.

He sure did like spending time with her. He enjoyed talking to her, both through text and in person. When he woke up in the morning, he thought of her first, and then what he had to get done that day second. He wanted to be a better man because of her.

"Stop staring at me," she said with a giggle. "Eat your cake. Look, here's mine."

Lorenzo arrived with her piece of chocolate cake and both of their colas. "Happy birthday," he said, and Slate was grateful the whole waiting staff didn't come sing to him.

"Happy birthday to you," Jill sang quietly. She hadn't that morning, and no one had that day yet. When he was younger, and his mother called for his birthday, she'd sing to him. Today, she hadn't. She'd simply said how much she loved him and could remember the day he'd been born.

Jill sang the whole song though, almost under her breath

so as to not make a scene, and then she dipped her fork into her cake and took a bite. Slate copied her, his heart flinging itself against his ribcage. He might be in love with her...

"This is divine," Jill said, moaning. "I've never had a chocolate cake this good."

"No kidding," Slate said, plenty of cake still in his mouth. He finished his and grinned at Jill, who had the tiniest bit of frosting riding her top lip. "You've got a little..." He leaned forward and kissed her, effectively removing that chocolate frosting from her mouth. She tasted amazing, because she'd just eaten cake too, and Slate felt himself slipping in his resolve not to kiss her until he couldn't breathe once they were alone.

He'd done that already today, but he suddenly wanted to do it again, and again, and again.

Thankfully, Jill had the good sense to remember they were in public—and a very expensive, very fancy restaurant at that—and she pulled away after only a few seconds. "We better look at the menu," she said with some grinding in her throat. "What have you heard is good here?"

Slate enjoyed their four-course birthday dinner together. He kept the conversation light, though it was about deep topics. He thoroughly enjoyed himself, and as he helped Jill into his truck a couple of hours later, he realized he hadn't once thought he shouldn't be there with her.

As he rounded the front of the truck, he took a moment to close his eyes and breathe out, "Thank you, Lord, for this good woman in my life." He opened his door and got behind the wheel, casting a quick look at Jill. "That was amazing, right?"

"I'm going to call in the morning and schedule another reservation," she said. "I want that fried shrimp again, and I want to try the fried potato skins, and did you see that triple layer carrot cheesecake?" She spoke with animation and delight, and that made Slate's heart happy.

They chatted on the way back to the ranch, with Jill asking, "So what is Luke going to do now?"

"Now?" Slate asked.

"Yeah, now. He likes Hannah, right?"

"Yeah, I'm pretty sure he does." Slate glanced at her. "He said you texted him today."

"I did," Jill said. "I know Hannah really well, and if he just gives her a couple of weeks, I'm sure he could then ask her, and she'd go out with him in a heartbeat."

"He'll be done with the cabins in another couple of months. He doesn't want to stay at the ranch."

"I've heard that too," Jill said. "So maybe he won't want to ask her out."

"Maybe he will, and maybe he'll fall for her fast, and then he won't want to leave the ranch." That was what Slate was hoping for actually, because he didn't want to tell Luke *he* didn't want to leave the ranch. Luke knew already, but actually having to make the choice would be very difficult.

He pulled up to the fence and killed the engine. "This has been the single best birthday of my life."

"It's not over yet, cowboy," she said, giggling as she opened her door. 'I haven't given you my gift yet."

Slate stared after her, watching her slip from the truck and disappear into the darkness. "Jill," he said, joining her outside. "Yes, you have. You gave me the sunrise this morning. Those amazing cinnamon rolls. The best kiss of my life. And a fantastic evening together."

"The best kiss of your life, huh?" Jill prowled toward him, something in her hands. He had no idea where she'd gotten that box so fast.

"I know that wasn't hiding in your dress," he said, taking the box from her when she met him near the fencepost.

"It's been in your truck all this time," she said. "I put it there this afternoon when I got to the animal shelter."

"Sly," he said. "And it's not something that will melt...so..."

"Just open it," she said, leaning one hip into the post.

Slate did, taking the blue bow off the box. The lid lifted easily, and a brand-new pair of leather gloves rested inside. "I ordered them from the best western wear website in Texas," she said. "They're perfect for wrangling cattle, or horseback riding, or building houses."

"Thank you," he said, taking out the gloves. They felt like rich butter in his fingers. "These are beautiful." He looked at her. "You're beautiful."

"Happy birthday, Slate Sanders," she said, pressing into him and lifting up onto her toes to kiss him. Slate held the gloves in one hand but dropped the box so he could take Jill into his arms. And this time, he didn't have to stop kissing her because they weren't in public.

So he didn't.

THE AUSTIN SKYLINE BROUGHT ANXIETY TO SLATE'S soul. He wasn't driving, because Dallas had offered to take the last leg of the journey from Sweet Water Falls to Austin, and Slate hadn't wanted to be behind the wheel as the city approached.

He thought he might drive the truck into the most solid object he came across. As it was, his fingers gripped the door arm rest to the point of aching.

"You're okay," Luke said from the back seat. "Take a breath, Slate."

Slate did what he said, drawing in the air through his nose slowly. He counted slowly as he did, trying to quiet his pulse. That didn't work, but at least he didn't feel like reaching over and grabbing the steering wheel.

"I don't want to be here," Slate said.

No one responded, and Dallas's GPS kept directing him where to go, though Slate could've gotten him to his parents' house from the road they were on. His brain was functioning, but he couldn't seem to put any thoughts together.

Dallas got off the highway and started navigating

through the suburbs. Slate's throat was so dry. "You guys, he's not going to be—"

"We know," Luke said. "We can handle it."

Slate swallowed and reached for his energy drink in the console between him and Dallas. He needed the burst of caffeine, though his heart was racing around his whole body.

The dark gray house where he'd grown up came into view, with the pair of large trees out front. Slate had climbed them both multiple times, and his brother had fallen once as he'd tried to go after Slate. He'd broken his arm—and then Daddy had dang near broken Slate's as he interrogated him as to what had happened and what he'd been thinking.

Slate hadn't been thinking anything. He'd been thirteen, and climbing a tree had sounded fun. Ryan was only ten at the time, and he wasn't as tall or as strong as Slate, and he'd missed a handhold. Down he'd gone. It had been an accident.

Dallas put on his blinker as they arrived in front of the house, and Slate looked across the cab and found the driveway already stuffed to capacity with cars and trucks, at least half of them in various states of disrepair. "He's still trying to be a mechanic."

"I'm in heaven," Dallas said, his voice awed.

"Don't you dare let him bully you into fixing one of his disasters," Slate said, his tone full of fire. "And Luke, you are not going to give any pointers on boxing techniques."

"All right," Luke said easily as a woman came out onto the front porch.

"That's my older sister," Slate said. "She's like Mary Poppins." Practically perfect in every way.

"Cindi," Dallas said. "Married with two children, right?"

"There's her husband," Slate said miserably. "Winthrop, if you can believe that."

"He looks like a Winthrop," Dallas said with a slightly sarcastic tone that somehow made Slate laugh. So much negativity went with the laughter, and somewhere in the back of his mind he heard Luke say, "At least he's not punching stuff."

That was more Luke's specialty, but Slate didn't say so. He had raised his fists a couple of times in prison, especially at the beginning. Neither Dallas nor Luke had been there then—only Ted and Nate—and Slate had settled into his life at River Bay by the time the other two had joined them.

Dallas made the left turn, barely squeezing the truck into the last available space in the driveway. They sat in the truck until he said, "We can't sit here forever."

"No," Slate said, sighing. "We can't." No one had come down off the porch to greet him, and he led the way from the truck, past the other vehicles, and up the sidewalk that looked like someone had swept it recently. The lawn was mowed, which also seemed to have been done very recently, with a few things out in the grass that hadn't been picked up beforehand.

The whole place had a general air of neglect clinging to it, which was so different from Hope Eternal Ranch and the vibrant energy there. Old, broken down lawn chairs leaned against the porch in the half-empty flower bed. Weeds choked the other half of the bed, and Slate ignored it all as he went up the steps.

He'd been ignoring the state of his home for decades; he could keep doing it.

The crowd on the porch had swelled to include his sister, her husband, and their two kids. His brother and his girlfriend. His mother. Uncle Sam, his father's brother, and his wife, Aunt Gail.

Slate noticed his father had not joined the initial festivities.

"Slate, my son," Momma said, and she stepped past everyone and wrapped him in the hug he'd missed for so, so long. Even before he'd been indicted and gone to prison, he hadn't come to visit his parents very often. They'd lived in the same city, but Slate had been consumed with the drugs, the partying, and then trying to get sober enough to go to work in the morning. There wasn't room to visit a house and a family he'd purposely separated himself from.

"Momma," he whispered when she started to cry. "Don't cry, okay?" He cleared his throat and squeezed her tight before stepping back. "These are my friends, Luke Holt and Dallas Dreyer. Guys, my momma."

Dallas stepped right into her and hugged her too, saying something Slate couldn't hear. Luke opted to shake her hand and tip his cowboy hat at her, saying, "Nice to meet you, ma'am."

"My uncle Sam and his wife, Gail," Slate said. He went around and introduced everyone verbally, and then the handshakes and hugs began.

Cindi said, "Guys, this is Uncle Slate." She smiled at him with all the warmth and charm of the PTA President, which she probably was. His mom had told him a lot about his siblings, and he knew the name of Ryan's girlfriend and his niece and nephew.

"Hey, Uncle Slate," Cora said, wrapping her arms around Slate's upper thighs and waist. She peered up at him with dark brown Sanders eyes. "Do you like rabbits?"

"Rabbits?" Slate asked, a smile starting to move through him. "Sure, I like rabbits."

"We have so many rabbits at our house. You have to come see them."

"Another time, Cora," Cindi said gently. "Remember how Uncle Slate is here to visit Grams and Gramps? We're having dinner, and then we're going to do that marshmallow roast." She smiled at her daughter and then Slate. "Momma's bought everything you like." She turned toward the house first. "C'mon in. We don't need to bake out here on the porch."

Everyone started the migration into the house, which didn't have central air conditioning. The swamp cooler had been working hard though, and the air was definitely cooler than outside. To his left, he heard Cora asking Luke about rabbits, and he looked at his nephew, who was a few years older than Cora.

"I heard you can do some skateboarding tricks," he said. "Grams says you're on a...team or something?"

"Yeah," John said. "It's not really a team. It's just a skate park I go to. They have classes for tricks on Saturday mornings."

"You goin' tomorrow?" Slate asked.

"Maybe," he said. "Daddy says he's not sure what's goin' on 'round here tomorrow."

"Yeah," Slate said. "I probably ruined it for you." He looked at Winthrop. "We're not even staying here. He can go to the class."

"We'll see," Winthrop said, and Slate found him so pretentious. He worked not to roll his eyes, and that was a great improvement over wanting to aim his truck into oncoming traffic.

Slate had just arrived in the kitchen when Daddy came through the back door. Everyone froze, including Slate. He couldn't look away from his father, and he stood there as feelings washed over him, through him, and around him.

He experienced anger, sadness, love, hope, joy, regret, loss, and most of all forgiveness. His father wasn't perfect; far from it, in fact. They hadn't been rich growing up, and they weren't rich right now. But he'd worked hard, and he'd raised three kids, and he currently wore an apron and carried a pair of tongs.

"The meat is done," he said, and that broke the spell. Everyone seemed to have moved to the edges of the room at some point, which left a clear path for Slate to walk to his dad. He did, each step landing quicker than the last until he reached him and swept the shorter man into his arms.

"Daddy," he said, his voice half his and half covered with emotion. "I'm so sorry. I'm doing so good now, and I'm working so hard, and I hope you can forgive me someday."

His dad held him too, the tongs pressing into Slate's back. He didn't care, because this was a powerful moment. "I love you. I'm sorry."

"Don't be sorry anymore," Daddy said. "You've done enough of that." He pulled back and gripped Slate by the shoulders, the metal tongs digging into his bicep. "Not another minute of it, Slate. You've paid your debt."

Slate pressed his teeth together and nodded.

"Okay," Momma chirped. "Daddy said the meat is ready, so we're eating in the back yard. Cindi, will you get that potato salad out of the fridge? Cora, we need the punch." She continued giving people things to bring outside, including Dallas and Luke.

Slate went back outside with his dad, carrying nothing in his hands. The back yard was cleaner than the front, with less stuff in the lawn or leaning against the house. A huge picnic table spanned the length of almost half the house, and as everyone spilled out of the house behind him, they put bowls and pans and plates of food on the table.

Three shade flies had been set up, and Daddy had an enormous tray full of meat resting on the covered fire pit.

"What in the world is happening here?" Luke asked Daddy, stepping next to him.

"That's a pig," Daddy said. "I bought him from one of my hog farm suppliers, wrapped him all up in spices and banana leaves, and buried him with really hot coals this morning. He's been slow-roasting all day."

"It smells amazing," Luke said, leaning forward. "Do you serve this at the restaurant?"

"Every day," Daddy said, a hint of pride entering his voice.

"Time to say grace," Momma said, and Slate turned toward her. He slipped his arm around her and smiled at her as he removed his cowboy hat with his other hand.

"I'll say it," he said. Her eyes widened, and then a smile bloomed across her face.

"All right, baby," she said. "Slate's gonna say it. Everyone hush up now."

Slate hadn't wanted to come to Austin, no. But now that he was here, he knew he was in the exact right place. Not to stay, but he could visit for a couple of days and not lose the man he'd become.

"Dear Lord," he started. "We're so thankful for this amazing evening Thou has blessed us with." He continued to pour out his heart and soul to the Lord, finally ending with, "Bless the food. Amen."

A rousing chorus of, "Amen," went up, and Cora said, "Wow, Uncle Slate. That was a long prayer."

Behind him, Dallas stifled a laugh, but Luke didn't hold back at all. Slate didn't care. He settled his cowboy hat back on his head and said, "All right, Cora. What's the best thing on the table?"

CHAPTER FOURTEEN

J ill laid down her blue seven and a red one. "I think that's it," she said, looking at her father. "Your turn, Daddy."

"Yeah, I see," he said, looking at his tiles and then out to the board where he could play. "You really messed me up with that play."

"I laid out two tiles," Jill said, not sure how her innocent red one on the front of a run would impact him at all.

He sighed and shook his head. "I have to draw." He picked up a new tile and put it on the tray in front of him. He smiled at her, and Jill grinned back, both of them looking at Mama next.

She'd wrapped her head with a colorful scarf this afternoon, though Jill wasn't sure why. She'd finished her chemotherapy treatments almost a month ago, and her hair had been growing in nicely. Jill eyed the rainbow-colored fabric, sure there was a story there she needed to hear before she left the farm.

"Mama," she said.

"Hmm?" She glanced up from her tray. "Oh, my turn?"

"Yep." Jill exchanged a glance with Daddy, but neither of them said anything.

"Let's see. What did you do, Harry?"

"I drew," Daddy said.

"Hmm."

Jill had been visiting for a couple of hours now, and Mama had had lunch ready when she'd arrived. The food had been delicious, as always, and they'd spent some time talking about the farm, the new men Daddy had hired to help now that he was getting older, Mama's treatment moving forward, and Slate.

They'd pulled out this tile rummy game that Jill had loved as a child, but her mother seemed ultra-distracted now.

"Is Kenna coming today?" Jill asked, her voice light.

"Not that I've heard," her mom said, placing a green seven and an orange seven in the playing area. She took a blue seven from another group to complete the set and added, "That's it for me."

Jill had just reached for her next tile when the front door opened and a voice called, "Hello! We're here, Mama."

Haven.

Jill's stomach twisted, flipped, and fell to her cowgirl boots. Haven would hate them, and Jill would bet everything she owned that her sister would comment on them in the first five minutes.

"Oh, Haven's here," Mama said, abandoning the game instantly. She stood up and started into the living room, already laughing before she left the kitchen and dining room.

More voices joined the fray, which meant Haven had brought her whole family. Daddy patted Jill's hand and said, "I had fun, Jilly."

"Me too," she murmured as her father got to his feet and headed out to greet Haven too. Jill picked up her red twelve and put it on the end of the run, then placed another blue seven on the group where her mom had taken it. She still had two tiles left that she couldn't play, but Daddy had seven, and Mama had five, so Jill was going to count herself the winner of this game.

She certainly wouldn't be winning anything once she came face-to-face with Haven.

Sighing, she got up and went out into the living room too. Haven stood with her two kids and was currently detailing what they were wearing. "So the school is requiring navy blue for the kids this year." She shook her head as if navy blue was the most heinous color on the planet.

"We like the black better, but we were out-voted. Turn around Peter, and show Grandma the back."

Her son turned dutifully, and Jill had no idea what she was supposed to be looking at. Of course, she didn't have to wonder, because Haven could talk the ear off a dead man. "Look at the cut of that shirt. Isn't it awful?" She brushed her hand down her son's back. "I suggested a different brand, but it was too expensive to be approved." She pursed her lips. "The girls don't have to wear skirts this year, but Quinn's got hers on." She turned her attention to her daughter, who was a couple of years older than Peter.

Never Pete. Haven would never shorten her son's name. Jill had heard her say on multiple occasions, "If I wanted to call him Pete, I would've just named him that," as if nicknames were something only the devil's spawn abided by.

"It's cute," Mama said.

"It's cute enough," Haven said. "The girls wear the same shirts as the boys, and I think that's ridiculous, but I'm not on the clothing panel. So." She looked back and forth between her kids and then to their parents. Only then did she realize Jill had come into the room, and Haven's face lit up.

"Jill," she said in a falsely bright tone. "I didn't know you'd be here today."

"Where do you want these?" Gil, Haven's husband, came through the front door carrying five covered baking dishes.

"Oh, Mama, these are for your freezer. Put them in the kitchen, Gil."

"Haven," Mama said. "I don't need meals. I'm cooking every night now."

"Nonsense," Haven said. "You can always use something from the freezer." She pasted a smile on her face, because it was always Haven-knows-best.

Jill gave Gil a terse smile as he passed, wondering for at least the hundredth time how he put up with her sister. Somehow, they'd made things work, and Jill suspected it was because Gil just did whatever he was told. He had no opinions of his own. *Naturally*, he thought the same thing Haven did. He had no plans for his own hobbies and spare time. *Of course* he wanted to spend his weekends shopping or picking out new rocks for the garden.

Haven continued to babble about this and that, and then she sent her children off to change out of their school uniforms. She approached Jill with the largest, most fake smile Jill had ever seen.

"Jilly," she said, scanning her. "I *love* those...boots." She returned her gaze to Jill's and it held even more falseness than before. "What are you doing here?"

"Visiting Mama and Daddy," she said, giving herself mental energy points for being right about the boots. "We didn't know you were coming. I'm sure Mama would've made a dessert."

"I've got some frozen tarts in the freezer in the basement," Mama said, heading for the door that led down there.

"Mama," Haven said. "You can't go down those steps."

"Of course I can," Mama said, moving that way without a hitch in her steps. "Who do you think put the tarts down there?" She opened the door just as Haven caught up to her.

"I'll do it." She glanced at Jill, who hadn't moved from

her position just inside the doorway leading from the kitchen. "Or Jill will."

"Sure," Jill said. "I will." She took a few steps and joined the crowd in front of the basement door.

"I can do it," Mama said, that stubborn tone entering her voice.

Jill backed off immediately, because Mama had always been a fiercely independent woman. The cancer and treatments had slowed her down, sure, but they had not knocked her out. She glared at Haven, who frowned at her.

"I don't understand why you can't accept help."

"I accept plenty of help," Mama said. "I'm fine, Haven. I can go downstairs and get tarts."

"Let her do it," Jill said.

Haven swung her attention to Jill, her displeasure like a scent on the air. "Easy for you to say. You're not the one here when she can't even get off the couch."

Jill swallowed and folded her arms. She rarely engaged with Haven, because every argument was a loser when it came to her older sister. "I was here when that happened, actually," Jill said. "I sat with Mama after several of her treatments too, Haven. You don't own the market on that." She noticed her mother slipping through the door and going down into the basement.

"In fact," Jill said, feeling sure of herself and brave in a way she hadn't before. "You were so busy in the kitchen, or doing laundry, or making sure the sheets on the bed were just right, that you missed just being with Mama. I did that. Me and Kenna."

"Someone has to do all of that," Haven said, her voice haughty.

"No, they don't," Jill said. "Mama doesn't need five pans of food, Haven. She didn't need you to change her sheets— she had done it the day before. Daddy knows how to run a washing machine."

"Girls," Daddy said, and Jill turned toward him. She'd forgotten he was even there. "Don't do this."

Jill held up both hands. "Sorry, Daddy." She took a deep breath and faced Haven. "Sorry, Haven."

Her sister did not apologize to her, and Jill rolled her eyes and stepped past her to go into the basement. "I'm going to go see if Mama has any ice cream down there."

"Bring up the rocky road," Daddy called after her, and Jill made her escape. The steps leading into the basement were sturdy and strong, made of thick wood. Her boots plunked against the steps, and she slowed as she reached the bottom and heard sniffling.

"Mama?" she asked.

Her mother turned from a built-in desk, a picture frame clutched in her hand. Her tears ran down her cheeks in fat threads, and Jill's whole world narrowed to that image. She'd only seen her mom cry a few times in her life, and both had been terrible events. The first time was when her daddy had died. Mama had adored her daddy, and Jill had loved her grandfather too.

Mama had cried when she'd spent eight hours making a wedding cake only to have one of the feral cats get into the house and eat through the top tier. She'd stayed up almost all night to recreate it, and Jill had helped as she'd been living at home during that time.

She'd cried when Jill had come home after dropping out of college and accruing so much debt she was still paying it back. Jill could still hear her mother saying, *Oh my baby, look at you.*

Jill hadn't known then what her mother had seen, but she'd let her nurse her back to full health—mentally, spiritually, and physically.

"Mama," she said, hurrying toward her. "What's wrong?" She scanned her from head to foot, trying to find the root of her tears.

The last time Jill had seen her mother cry was the day she'd told McKenna, Haven, and Jill about the cancer. Their brother, Louis, had been on the computer, and Mama and Daddy had sat them all down at once to break the news.

That day, Jill had yelled at the Lord and tried to show Him that she could change the course of the tide with a few rocks.

She couldn't, of course. No one could.

"Look at this picture," Mama said, thrusting it toward Jill. "Look at my hair."

Jill took the picture frame, because she had no other choice. Her mother's hair flowed over her shoulders in soft waves, the color of fall grass that had turned brown and yellow. "It's beautiful, Mama," she said, lifting her eyes back to the scarf. "But your hair is beautiful now, too. Remember how you were going to do it all spunky and short?" She tried to smile, but the gesture wobbled on her face.

"It's not beautiful," Mama said, weeping. "It's hideous."

Jill's pulse bounced in her neck. "Can I see, Mama?" She reached up as if she'd take the scarf off, moving slowly so her mother could stop her. She didn't, and Jill gently pulled on the end of the scarf that was tucked in. It came loose in Jill's hands, revealing her mother's hair and scalp, and her eyes widened. "Oh, dear."

Mama lifted her chin, her courage never-ending though tears tracked down her cheeks. "See?"

Jill could see. Mama's hair had not grown in evenly. It was patchy at best, with some parts thick with hair and whole swatches with none at all. Some parts had hair growing close together, with plenty of space between each individual strand. It was darker in some places than others, and almost like peach fuzz in others.

She looked into her mother's eyes. "It doesn't matter. Who are you trying to impress? Mister Rogers?"

Mama smiled and laughed, because they both knew she didn't care about impressing Daddy's favorite horse. But the sound came out like a scoff and then a choke. Jill smiled too and took her mother into her arms. She'd never thought she was a very tall or very big woman, but her mother felt very slight in her embrace in that moment. For maybe the first time in her life, Jill felt strong enough to do what needed to be done.

"I hate it," Mama said into Jill's shoulder, her breath hot and her tears wet against her skin.

"I know you do, Mama," Jill whispered. So much tore loose inside her, and for some reason, she seized onto a memory that floated near the front of her mind. "Remember when I got asked to the prom only four days before the dance?"

"Yes."

"And you were mad, because that wasn't enough time to get a proper dress, especially if it needed to be altered." And everything Jill wore needed to be altered, especially fancy party dresses. Her torso was too short, and her legs too long. Her shoulders too bony, and her chest too big.

"So you made me wear one of Haven's old dresses that you'd worked day and night to make fit, and I hated it. Like, I *hated* it."

"I remember." Mama stepped back and wiped her eyes. "I'm sorry I made you wear that dress." Fresh tears leaked out of her eyes. "It was all the wrong color for your complexion."

Jill giggled. "Everyone has to wear a dress they hate at some point in their life. Right?" She had hated the purple monstrosity with everything inside her, and she still didn't wear purple to this day.

"You *really* hated it."

"I really did." Jill laughed again and started to re-wrap

her mother's head with the scarf. "Do you remember what you told me?"

Her mom sighed as she sat down so Jill wouldn't have to reach up so high. "Yes."

"You said, 'Jilly, God is the only one who can look at the whole picture and decide who deserves what. Not you, and not me. God didn't give us enough time to get a better dress. This is the dress we have, and you're going to go to that prom with that silly boy, and you're going to be beautiful.'" She tucked the end of the scarf in firmly, so her mother's hair was covered again.

She crouched down in front of her. "So God decided you didn't need a full head of hair, Mama. He didn't give this one thing back to you, but your last scan was clear. You don't have to have surgery. Those are huge blessings."

Jill gave her another wavering smile. "This is the life you have, and it's amazing and beautiful and filled with *many* good things—just not a beautiful head of hair. Daddy loves you. We all love you. Even Mister Rogers loves you."

Her mother reached out and took her face in both of her hands. "How did I get such an amazing daughter?"

Jill just smiled. "I think that one is upstairs, Mama." She stood up, her knees too old to crouch for long.

"No, she's not." Mama stood up too. "She brings me food I don't need and makes me feel like I'm too old and too frail to do anything." She frowned toward the steps, and Jill could only stare at her.

"Mama," she chastised.

Mama looked at her, and Jill searched her face. So much was said without any words, and the two of them burst out laughing simultaneously. Jill grabbed onto her mom, who latched onto her, and they laughed and laughed and laughed.

"What's goin' on down there?" Daddy finally called from the top of the steps. "Are we out of rocky road?"

"Oh, that man and his rocky road," Mama grumbled as she moved over to the chest freezer. "I'll show him a rocky road."

Jill continued to giggle as she took the gallon of ice cream for her father while Mama took out a container of frozen lemon tarts. Together, they went upstairs, Jill's steps and her heart lighter than they'd been in years.

Thank you, Lord, she thought as she handed Daddy his treat. *Thank you.*

She managed to eat a couple of tarts and answer a few questions about Slate for Haven before she could make an excuse for why she needed to leave. As she got behind the wheel of her car, her phone rang, and Luke's name sat on the screen.

"Hey," she said cheerfully. "Did you guys make it back to the ranch?"

"No," Luke said, his voice full of panic. "You haven't heard from Slate in the past ten or fifteen minutes, have you?"

"No." Jill frowned, all kinds of alarms going off in her head. "Why?"

"We can't find him," Luke said. "We were at his parents' place, and he went inside with his brother, and now he's gone."

"Gone?" Jill asked, starting her car. "What do you mean, gone?"

"I mean, he's gone," Luke said, something rustling on his end of the line. "His phone's right here, Dallas."

"Luke," Jill practically yelled. "Tell me what's going on." She heard Dallas's voice talking, and Luke said something else too, but he'd covered up the speaker. "Luke," she said again, desperation making her voice pitchy.

"He's bailed, Jill," Luke said, equal parts misery and anxiousness now. "He's in the wind. Gone. AWOL. In Austin."

Horror struck Jill right behind the heart. It slid around every rib, crushing them as it brought them closer together. "He hates Austin," she whispered.

"I know," Luke said. "We'll find him, Jill, okay? I promise you, we'll find him." The call ended, and Jill could only stare at her phone for several long moments.

Then she put both hands on the wheel and looked up at the ceiling of her car. "Dear Lord," she prayed. "Thou can see the whole picture. Please bring him back to Sweet Water Falls. Please protect him. Please."

She breathed in.

"Please."

And out.

"Please."

CHAPTER FIFTEEN

S late's muscles screamed at him, but he couldn't relax. He had to get out of Austin right now.

Right now, right now, right now.

The city wasn't fading fast enough in his rearview mirror, and he pressed harder on the gas pedal. The problem was, a lot of people seemed to have the idea to leave the city on Sunday afternoon, and the freeway was packed.

"Come on," he muttered, his desire to lay on the horn to get the ridiculously small white car in front of him to *go*.

He yanked the wheel to the right and got off on the exit there, coming to a jerky stop at the end of the ramp. "What are you doing?" he asked himself, trying to find a coherent thought that wasn't full of cheap cologne and a leering smile.

He could practically smell the marijuana that had been on Jackson MacBride's breath. Slate closed his eyes and took a deep breath. "He's not here. He's gone. He's not going to bother you."

A horn sounded behind him, and he opened his eyes to find his light had turned green. After making the right turn, he pulled into the gas station down the block and got out to fill up. He patted his back pockets for his wallet and didn't find it. His heart sunk to the tips of his boots when he didn't find his phone either.

His first thought was that Jackson had stolen them. The man obviously needed money for his next fix. Slate knew, because he'd been in that exact same position dozens of times before. He knew the stench of desperation. He understood the call of the substances that would make him forget everything hard in his life. He craved a release from his thoughts, from time taking forever to pass, from having to be *so good* all the time.

He got behind the wheel again and flexed his fingers. As he rolled out his shoulders, he mentally coached himself to return to the house he'd just fled fifteen minutes before. "You have to," he told himself. "Dallas and Luke are there, and they have no other way to get back to Sweet Water Falls."

He'd have to explain what had happened at the house, and Slate didn't know how to do that. He wasn't entirely sure what had happened. His mother had asked him to go inside and get more bottled water. He had, and while he was in the kitchen, someone had knocked on the front door.

Slate had answered it, only to come face-to-face with the

one person from his past that could drag him back to hell speedily. Jackson MacBride.

Jackson had been the very first person Slate had bought drugs from. He knew everyone on the street and in the underground, and he could get whatever anyone wanted—for the right price. Slate had been willing to give him anything for these little pink pills that worked like wildfire in cleansing his mind from all the unpleasantries of life.

When Slate had seen the man standing on the front porch, he'd blacked out for a moment. The next thing he knew, Jackson was in the house, asking Slate where he was now, and if he had any money. He'd opened a couple of Slate's mother's books, like twenty-dollar bills would be carefully pressed between the pages.

Slate had fled the house without looking back. He'd swiped his keys from the front table and left everything else. "Stupid," he muttered. Surely someone would've noticed he was gone by now.

"Go back," he said. "Just say you went to fill up but forgot your wallet." It wasn't entirely a lie. He had tried to fill up the truck and hadn't had his wallet.

Before he could move, someone knocked on his window. Yelping, Slate jumped away from it as he looked over.

Jackson stood there, his greasy black hair drifting lazily into his eyes. The smile that formed on his face was calculating, and Slate had seen him use it on others before.

His heart pounded, and an instant prayer streamed

through his mind. *Help me*, he thought. *Help me get out of this.*

Jackson's dark eyes glittered like the tips of black water in the moonlight, and he slowly raised his hand to reveal he was holding Slate's wallet.

Anger roared through Slate, and he opened his door and pushed it out in one swift movement. "Give me that," he snarled, snatching the wallet from Jackson as the man stumbled backward. That was one thing Slate did not miss about being high all the time—the complete lack of reaction time. He didn't bumble around anymore. He didn't stutter or trip over his words. He didn't have to use eyedrops all the time. He didn't lose his balance very easily.

Jackson did, though, and he fell after stumbling backward for several steps.

Slate gripped his wallet in his hand and glared at the man, his chest heaving. "Leave me alone."

"Come on," Jackson said with a goofy smile on his face. Slate blinked, realizing the person he was looking at used to be him. He used to grin like a fool all the time too. He used to scramble to his feet, his next words a plea for money.

"No," Slate said, opening his wallet. "If you've taken even one penny from me, I'm calling the cops." Just the idea of dealing with the police made Slate break out in a sweat. But he'd do it, because he was not going back to prison. He was *not*.

"Where are you now?" Jackson asked.

"Far away," Slate said.

"You were home." Jackson's brow furrowed as if he really didn't understand the idea of visiting.

Slate wasn't going to explain it to him. All of his credit and debit cards seemed to be in their pockets, but he didn't trust Jackson at all. He'd have to cancel everything inside and get new cards, because Jackson could've taken pictures of the fronts and backs of them.

"Give me your phone," he said, holding out his hand.

"Tell me where you live first."

"Down in the Coastal Bend," Slate said. He wasn't stupid enough to name the town. Jackson would never leave Austin, not unless properly propelled, the way Slate had been.

Jackson gave Slate his phone, and Slate looked at the gallery. Sure enough, Jackson had taken pictures of every one of Slate's cards...and his driver's license. That listed his address at the ranch, because he'd had to get brand new identification, and new bank accounts, and new everything once he'd been released from prison.

He deleted all of the pictures and thrust the phone back into Jackson's chest. "Don't ever go to my parents' house again. I'm leaving, and you will not follow me." He stared into Jackson's dead eyes, wondering if he'd looked like this too. Lifeless. Almost non-human.

"Do you understand?"

"Yes," Jackson said. "Don't follow you."

"You shouldn't be driving at all," Slate said. "It's danger-ous. You're going to kill someone." He turned back to his truck. "Don't go to my parents' house ever again. They don't have any money."

"They own a restaurant."

"A failing one," Slate said, getting behind the wheel. "I mean it, Jackson. If I find out you've been there, you'll wish you were dead." He slammed his door and jammed his foot on the accelerator. He had to get out of there before he did something he'd regret.

He drove back to his parents' house, where he found his mom on the phone on the front porch and his sister talking to a neighbor. When they saw him, pure relief washed over their features, and Slate realized then how much they cared about him.

"I'm okay," he said as he got out of the truck.

"Thank the Lord," Cindi said as she reached him. She enveloped him in a tight hug and held on. "You left your phone and Mrs. Jacobs said she saw someone in a black sedan leave about the same time you did." Cindi stepped back and searched his face. "No one here has a black sedan. Who was it?"

"Just some loser who came to the door asking for money," Slate said. That was the truth too, just not the entirety of it. "Where are Luke and Dallas? We need to get going."

"They left to search the neighborhood for you." Cindi turned back to the road. "I think they went...toward that, uh, tavern where you used to hang out."

Slate's throat closed. He couldn't go there. So many bad

memories assaulted him, and he just wanted to take a couple of pills and fall asleep.

No more pills, he thought. Everything had started with pills, and Slate felt like throwing up. If only he hadn't gotten that concussion in college. But he'd loved playing football, and he'd have done anything to stay on the team. In the end, his concussion had been so severe, he'd lost his spot on the team, and gained a brand-new addiction —painkillers.

Those led to harder stuff. Stuff that would erase pain in a heartbeat. Pills that could make him feel like he was flying. Pills that made him laugh for hours. Pills that made everything swirl in pinks and reds and purples.

Slate didn't care what they were, as long as they provided the escape he needed and wanted.

"You don't have to go there," he said aloud. "Just call Luke."

Cindi cocked her head at him. "Are you okay?"

"No," he said through a tight throat. "Is my phone inside?"

"Momma has it." Cindi backed up, and Slate saw his mother holding his phone at the top of the steps. He took them two at a time and asked her for it.

"You okay, baby?" She reached up and brushed his hair from his forehead. He had gotten it cut a couple of days ago, and he didn't entirely hate it.

"Yes," Slate said, maybe the first lie he'd told since being in Austin. "I need to call Luke."

"I was on the line with him when you pulled up," she said. "They're on their way back now."

As if on cue, a truck pulled into the driveway, with Luke behind the wheel. He and Dallas both got out almost before the truck had come to a complete stop, and they both strode toward Slate.

"I'm fine," he said as a way to try to appease them. But by the swirling storm on Luke's face, there would be no appeasement.

"Where did you go?" he barked. "You left your phone behind. We didn't know where you went. You said nothing to no one." His fists curled, and he raged silently for another moment before he broke. He grabbed onto Slate and hugged him fiercely. "You scared me," he said in a much quieter voice.

"I'm sorry," Slate said, grateful for such a good friend. "I'll explain once we're out of this city." He stepped back. "Okay? We need to go. It's three hours back to Sweet Water Falls." He turned back to his momma, determined to get these goodbyes done in record time.

"Thanks for having me, Momma." He drew her into a hug too. "I love you."

"Please come back soon," she said, her voice full of tears. He found them in her eyes when he stepped back.

"I will," he promised, though if it were truly up to him, he'd never come back to Austin again. "I'm gonna go say goodbye to Daddy." He practically jogged through the house to the back yard, where he said all of his goodbyes with a few words and a wave before he hugged his father.

"Thank you for feeding us so well," he said. "I love you, Daddy."

"I love you too, son."

Slate stood in his dad's arms, soaking in those words, for as long as he dared. Then he stepped back, nodded, and went back out front. He hugged his sister and got in the back seat of the truck. "Drive, please," he said, his voice quiet but deadly.

Luke backed out of the driveway and got the truck headed away from Slate's childhood home. With every mile that passed, another memory got tucked away behind the closed door in Slate's mind. The problem was, he didn't think he could contain them all before they returned to the ranch. There wasn't enough miles for that.

"Okay," Luke said twenty minutes later. "We're officially out of the city. Tell us what happened back there."

Slate stared out the window, not focused on anything. "I was getting the water when the doorbell rang," he said, his tone flat now. "It was someone I knew from...back then. He somehow got inside the house. He was asking all these questions." Slate pressed both palms to his eyes. Images of who he'd been flashed through his mind's eye, and he wanted to pluck them all out by the root and rid himself of them completely.

How can I get rid of this? he begged to know.

"I'm not that man anymore."

"Of course you're not," Dallas said, but Slate hadn't realized he'd even spoken out loud.

"You came back," Luke said. "You're clean."

"He followed me to this gas station and taunted me with my wallet. He'd taken pictures of all of my cards, my ID, everything." Pure exhaustion came over him. He just wanted to be in the big bed in the roomy bedroom in the Annex. It would be cool and dark, and he could get Axle to curl up at his side. The two of them would breathe together, and there would be no threat of past mistakes threatening to pull him under dark water again.

"I erased them all," he said. "And came back."

"We do need gas," Luke said.

"Pull over in the next town," Dallas said. "I'll pay."

"I can pay," Slate said. "I got my wallet and all the cards back."

"Did you empty the trash on his phone?" Dallas asked, turning around to look at Slate. He met his friend's eyes, pure dread filling his chest with lead bricks.

"No," he said.

"Then he'll still have those pictures," Dallas said. "You better start calling and canceling them right now."

Another round of fury burned through Slate, but he simply clenched his teeth and nodded his head. Then he pulled out his phone and his wallet and started making calls to protect himself.

Halfway through the second one, his phone rang, and Jill's name sat on the screen. He swiped it to voicemail, finished his call, and frowned. "Jill called. She knew I wasn't going to be back until seven or eight." They weren't that far behind schedule. In fact, they'd left a few minutes early, because Slate couldn't stand to be in Austin for another moment.

"Oh, uh, I called her," Luke said, meeting Slate's eye in the rearview mirror. "I thought maybe you'd called her or something..."

"Great," Slate said with a sigh. Anything he'd been hoping to hide about his trip to Austin would be impossible now. She'd want to know everything from what had happened to how he'd felt about it—and why he'd run from his parents' house without a phone or a wallet or telling anyone where he was going.

His phone rang again. Jill for a second time.

"Just great."

CHAPTER SIXTEEN

After talking to Slate and getting the reassurance she needed, Jill sat down in her bedroom, her laptop open to her banking portal. She had to face the disaster that was her finances a couple of times a month, and she did her best to make the process as enjoyable as possible.

She put on her favorite pop music playlist and let the heavy bass beat pump through her blood. "All right," she said, only knowing she'd spoken because of the vibrations in her throat. "Let's do this."

She looked at the amount she'd been paid from the ranch on Friday, and then switched over to the spreadsheet she'd already opened that listed what needed to be paid. She tried to plan what her next payment would be two weeks in advance, and today, she quickly took the figures she'd written down two weeks ago and put them in her bill pay portal.

Before she submitted it, she checked her math to make sure she'd have enough to buy groceries and put gas in her truck for the next couple of weeks. She could live on very little if she had to, and she did have some protein shakes in the pantry, as well as several boxed mixes.

She had a place to live, and she would be fine for another two weeks. Then two more. Then two more. She'd been doing this for years, and finally, the weight of that settled on her shoulders and clawed its way toward her neck.

She leaned away from the laptop, a sigh hissing from between her lips. Her eyes drifted closed and she murmured, "How much longer do I have to pay for the mistakes of the past?"

She knew how much longer—she had it all planned out in the spreadsheet. A couple more years, if she could stay on track. Drawing in a deep breath, she felt her shoulders straighten and strengthen, throwing off the weight. "You can do this."

The laptop made a slapping sound when she closed it, and the music silenced. She basked in the stillness and quiet atmosphere of the homestead on a Sunday afternoon. Without Emma, Jess, or Ginger in the house anymore, slow summer afternoons were definitely quieter than they'd been previously.

Emma sometimes still came to use the huge kitchen in the West Wing to make a feast that would feed the remaining women in the house for a week. Today, though, when Jill went into the kitchen, she only found Hannah and Michelle sitting at the bar. They had bowls of something that smelled like pasta in front of them, and Jill put a smile on her face.

"What did you make?" she asked. She found the pot of cheesy orzo and sausage on the stovetop. It was one of Hannah's favorite foods, and Jill could admit it brought comfort in times where there wasn't much to be found.

Jill turned to the fridge and took out a bottle of water. Ginger likely kept the Hope Springs bottled water company in business singlehandedly, because she made sure every fridge around the ranch always had water in it.

She stocked the mini-fridges in the stables herself, as well as the large fridge in the equipment shed, the West Wing, and the Annex. In the storage shed, half of it was filled with cases of the bottled water, and anyone could take what they wanted.

"You're not going to have any?" Hannah asked.

"I ate at my mother's," Jill said. She did take a seat at the bar beside Michelle and added, "You cut your hair."

"Yeah." Michelle smiled and reached up to her shorter, dirty blonde hair. "I think I went too far."

"No, I don't think so," Jill said. "It's great."

"It's a touch too short to pull into a ponytail," she said, pushing her fork through her orzo without taking a bite. A sigh accompanied the motion, and Jill realized there was something going on here.

"All right," she said. "Talk to me."

"Nothing to talk about," Michelle said at the same time Hannah said, "Charles said he wanted to 'talk' when Michelle gets back to town."

"No." Jill said, surprise darting through her. "You guys have been dating forever."

"Exactly," Michelle said. "If he hasn't asked me to marry him by now, he's not going to."

"You don't know that," Hannah said. "He could be planning to ask you when you get back."

"He's not," Michelle said. "You two have met Charles. He's the most unimaginative man there is. He wouldn't plan anything for a proposal. He'd simply show up for dinner and show me the ring."

"Well, maybe that's what he'll do," Jill said, looking past Michelle to Hannah. She shook her head almost imperceptibly, and Jill's heart squeezed too tight.

"No one's asking me either," Hannah said, getting up from the counter. She scooped more orzo into her bowl and kept her back to the others. Her dark hair cascaded down her back, and Jill couldn't believe no one had snatched her up years ago. She was so positive, and so kind, so smart, so resourceful, and so beautiful.

"You haven't been off the ranch since Bill broke up with you," Jill said.

"I signed up for that dating app," Hannah said, turning back to Jill.

"You did?"

"Five days ago. Not one date."

"Maybe people haven't seen you yet."

"I've been getting matches," Hannah said. "But when I message the men, they don't respond. Well." She shrugged one shoulder. "One guy did, but we've just been talking. He doesn't seem interested in actually going out."

"Hannah," Jill said. "You don't message the men."

"What do you mean?"

"I told her that," Michelle said, exchanging a glance with Jill.

Jill got up and took the full bowl of pasta from Hannah. "Sweetie, you wait for the men to message you."

"I don't want to wait," Hannah said.

"That's the game." Jill put the orzo back in the pot. "Now, come on. If we're going to eat too much, shouldn't it be something with a lot of chocolate in it?"

"This is pasta and cheese," Hannah said. "It's almost the same."

"It's hardly the same," Jill said. "I should've brought home some of my mother's tarts. They were lemon, though, not chocolate." She leaned her hip into the counter, thinking. "Maybe I could—"

"Hello," Emma called, and Jill grinned.

"God has provided for us," she said with a giggle as she went to greet Emma at the end of the hall that led to the garage entrance. Emma led the way with a large plate of cookies.

"Chocolate chip oatmeal," she said, smiling at Jill. "How are you?" Anxiety rode in her expression, and Jill sobered.

Ted came right behind her, with Missy behind him. They had barely cleared the hallway when Ginger, Nate, and Connor arrived. Ginger stepped right into Jill and hugged her, and Jill felt like she was missing something.

"What's going on?" she asked.

"We just came for support," Ginger said. "The boys will be back soon, right?"

"I think so," Jill said. "I talked to Slate. He seemed okay."

"He's not okay," Nate said, and while he was normally pretty serious, tonight, he wore a level of darkness in his gaze that Jill had only seen a couple of times. Her heartbeat turned shallow as he paused in front of her.

"Why isn't he okay?" she asked, her voice quiet.

Nate met her eye, and Jill actually shivered. "I know Slate. He was in with me for three years, and he, Ted, and I nursed Dallas back to health together. He worries more than any of us, and he's so concerned about falling back into the life he had before prison."

"He's mentioned that," Jill said. He had, several times. He enjoyed going to visit his grandparents in Short Tail, but he really hadn't wanted to go home to Austin.

"He ran into someone he knew before," Nate said.

"He did?" Jill hated that Nate knew details she didn't. "He didn't tell me that." She dropped her head, trying to find how she felt about this situation.

"He doesn't want to worry you," Nate said. "He's trying to be kind." He slowly took Jill into his arms, and Jill leaned against Nate for a few moments, letting his strength seep into her. She finally cleared her throat and stepped back.

"Thanks, Nate," she said.

Shouts came from the front of the house, and Thomas and Remmy came flying into the family room. Connor ran toward them, and Missy followed a little slower though she wore a wide smile too. The four kids clamored for cookies and then Connor looked at Nate. "Can we go out front with the dogs, Daddy?"

"Yeah, go ahead," Nate said.

Jill suddenly remembered Axle, and she turned to find Ted, who'd been taking care of Slate's dog.

"He's out front," Ted said, as if reading her thoughts. "He's great, Jill."

Jess entered the family room, and she too carried treats in her hand in the form of two boxes of doughnuts. "I brought all the favorites," she said.

"Bless you," Nate said.

"Be sure to leave one of the maple long johns for Dallas," Jess said, reaching the counter. "Everything else is fair game." She lifted the lid on one box and took out two doughnuts. She approached Jill, who still stood near the hall that led to the garage.

"Tiger tail for you." Jess handed her the doughnut, her eyes huge. "How is he?"

"I thought he was fine," Jill said. "But apparently, I don't have all the information." She frowned at the doughnut, but half of the twisted, glazed doughnut was made with chocolate dough, so she took a bite. The crispy, sugary glaze combined with the soft dough made her moan. "Oh, I love these." She chewed and swallowed, and then she drew Jess into a hug. "Thank you for coming."

She hadn't even realized she needed her friends here, but now that they had all gathered in the West Wing, Jill knew she did. She needed them. She loved them—and they loved her.

They chatted and ate cookies and doughnuts. Hannah got out milk and napkins, and after about a half an hour, Ginger raised both hands and called in a loud voice, "All right, everyone. I need a minute of your attention. Then Nate wants to go sit on the front porch and wait for his boys." She gave her husband a knowing, loving smile, and he returned it.

She took his hand, and the two of them held everyone's attention effortlessly, the way they always had.

"Nate and I are expecting a baby," Ginger said, her voice breaking on the last word. Her face crumpled as her emotion flowed over it, and then she smiled through the tears.

A brief moment of silence filled the West Wing, and then a chaotic eruption filled the air as congratulations and squeals came from all of the women, Jill included.

She waited her turn to hug Ginger and Nate, but when she did, she clung to them with every fiber of strength inside her. "Congratulations, you two," she said, smiling at her. "When are you due?"

"May first," she said. "So not for a while."

"It's so exciting."

"Connor's already got names picked out," Nate said, and he wore such joy on his face that Jill could hardly believe he was the same man as the one she'd embraced a half an hour ago, stealing his strength as he practically glowered with unrest.

Jill went outside first and took a spot on the bottom step, reaching out for Axle. "Hey, boy," she said, glad and comforted when the dog came right over to her and sat on her feet. He leaned his head back and looked up at her with his beautiful, puppy-dog eyes. She leaned down and hugged him. "I'm okay," she said, though she wasn't sure if she was.

She just wanted Slate to get back so she could look him in the eyes and *see* for herself how he was.

She craved the stability she'd found at the ranch. She wanted the husband, the family, the cabin on the edge of the lawn. She'd lived the life where she didn't know where she'd sleep that night, and where she didn't know where her next meal would come from. She'd thought she was happy then, but she hadn't been.

She just wanted a quiet life, right here on this ranch. She wanted what Emma and Ginger had. She'd live in town near Jess—that would be amazing too.

Jess came to sit beside her, and she pressed her knee to Jill's. "I know you're not okay."

Jill couldn't bring herself to look at Jess. If she did, she'd cry, and she'd really rather not. She looked out at the children playing with the four blue heelers and each other, and though it was hot, the sun was going down. The soft glow coming from the west made everything seem plated in gold, and Jill wanted it all.

"I just want...certain things so badly," she said, tucking her hands between her knees.

Jess put her arm around Jill's shoulders. "I know you do."

"I'm falling in love with him," she whispered.

"You're already in love with him," Jess amended.

Jill tried to laugh or scoff, but what happened was actually a sob. She leaned into Jess's shoulder and let her friend comfort her. She pulled back on her emotions when the front door opened and more people came outside.

Hannah took the spot on Jill's other side, handing her a cookie with a knowing look.

"Thank you," Jill murmured. She looked at Hannah fully, not embarrassed by the tears, not with Hannah. "Luke really likes you, Hannah. I've been helping him plan a way to ask you out."

Her eyes widened. "What? You have?"

"I thought you needed a couple of weeks, and it's only been ten days since Bill broke up with you. I didn't want him to seem too eager, and I wanted you to have some time and distance from Bill."

Hannah's shock melted off her face, and she leaned over and hugged Jill. "You are a very good friend."

"I love you and want you to be happy," Jill said. "He's meeting with his parole officer on Tuesday. I think he wanted to be free before he asked you out."

"I love you and want you to be happy too," Hannah said.

"I am happy,' Jill said.

"No, you're scared," Hannah said.

"And worried," Jess added.

Ginger and Nate sat behind them, and Jill couldn't argue with her friends. She listened to them talk to Emma and Ted about babies, cribs, strollers, and all of the things it required to be a parents of a newborn.

Her chest squeezed, and her stomach twisted. "Maybe I am," she conceded.

"Dallas said he's okay," Jess said quietly. She handed Jill her phone. "You can read our texts."

Jill looked at the dark screen on the device. "I'm okay," she said. "I'm glad Dallas and Luke were with him. Can you imagine what might've happened if they hadn't been?" Jill's gratitude reached a new level, and she thought of the conversation she'd had with her mother in the basement only a few hours ago.

She believed what her mom had said to her all those years ago, before the prom. Maybe she'd lost her way from time to time over the years. Maybe she'd been angry with the Lord a few months ago when she'd learned about her mother's cancer. Maybe she struggled with her faith from time to time.

But it was still there. She still had it, and she clung to it now with every ounce of strength she had.

Lord, she thought. *Only You know the whole picture. Only You know what I deserve, and what Slate deserves. I want us to deserve each other, just so You know. Please help me to accept whatever I have to...*

She couldn't continue, because she didn't want to accept that she might not be able to have Slate in her life for good.

She had fallen in love with him, and she linked arms with Hannah and handed Jess's phone back to her, the texts unread. She just had to wait until the boys got back, and then she'd see Slate for herself.

CHAPTER SEVENTEEN

"Oh, boy," Luke muttered. "They're all on the steps."

Slate found the crowd of people easily, and he drank them in—especially Jill. She sat on the bottom step, and Axle lay right in front of her. She looked at Hannah, who said something to her, and everyone swung their attention toward the truck as the tires crunched over the gravel.

Slate hated drawing attention to himself, but such a sense of love accompanied the group of people who were now standing up to greet the three of them. He swallowed and said, "I feel like an idiot."

"Don't," Dallas said. "They care about you. That's all." He put the truck in park and neither he nor Luke hesitated to get out of the truck. Slate let them go first, and he took an extra moment to breathe in deeply and center himself.

He'd done the right thing. He hadn't stayed and argued

with Jackson. He'd gotten out of the situation. Maybe not in the best way possible, but he hadn't immediately fallen back in with his old crowd at the first sign that he could.

He got out too, and Axle had beat everyone over to the truck. "Hey, bud," he said, crouching down and keeping his head low to use the brim on his hat to conceal his face. He smiled at the dog, who licked his face and made him laugh. "Yeah, I'm okay. Are you okay? How was your weekend with the *American Idol* dogs? Good, right? Ted said he gave you some steak."

Axle didn't respond, but Slate felt accepted by him. Straightening, he realized all of these people accepted him, and that was why they'd gathered in the darkness to wait for his return. Sure, Jess and Dallas's kids had come for him, but still.

Nate and Ted approached him first, and he embraced them both at the same time. "I'm fine," he murmured.

"Of course you are," Nate said, his voice gruff. "But are you okay?"

Slate stepped back. "I'm worried he's going to bother my parents."

"I'll make some calls," Nate said. Slate wasn't sure what that meant, but Nate had a lot of money, and he knew people Slate couldn't even begin to imagine. "You missed the news too. Ginger's pregnant."

"That's great," Slate said, a smile stretching across his face.

"She's worried," Ted said quietly.

"I told her you ran into someone you knew," Nate said. "I didn't realize she didn't know."

Slate nodded, a silent sigh moving through his body. "I didn't want her to worry. She has enough to worry about." He certainly didn't want to add to that, and he didn't want to be the cause of it for her.

"Sorry," Nate said.

"It's fine." Slate smiled at his friends and stepped around them. He hugged Ginger and Emma, who said there were cookies and doughnuts inside.

"Both of those sound amazing," he said, his gaze sliding to Jill.

She reached up and tucked her hair behind her ear. She looked toward the house, and Slate got the message. She went up the steps, and he accepted a hug from Connor and Remmy, the youngest of the children in Slate's life, and he told Axle he'd be right back. Then he followed Jill up the steps and into the house.

It was much quieter inside, and he found her in the kitchen, wearing a pair of jeans that made her legs look twice as long as they really were. He drank in her curves as he approached, his throat suddenly so dry. "Hey," he said, standing beside her. "I'm sorry I made you worry."

"Cookie or doughnut?" she asked.

"Both," he said. "Want to go to the sunrise spot?"

"Walking?"

"Yes."

"All right." She picked up a couple of cookies and a

couple of doughnuts and put them on a paper plate. "Ready."

She finally met his eye, and Slate slipped his arm around her waist. "I missed you," he said, his mouth barely moving. "How was the afternoon at the farm?"

"It was actually really good," she said. "Even though Haven showed up."

"I can't wait to hear this story," he said with a smile.

She smiled at him too, and the sense of love and forgiveness he could feel between them made everything in the world just right. "I hear you have some stories too."

"So many," he said with a chuckle. He sobered and met her gaze, the fire and electricity between them light liquid lightning. "Kiss me first?"

Jill closed her eyes and closed the distance between them. Their kiss was sweet and hot at the same time, and she pulled away when the noise level from out front grew because someone opened the front door.

"Let's go," he said, and he took her hand and led her toward the hallway that would get them out of the house. Axle met them at the bottom of the steps in the garage, and Slate said, "Come on, boy. Let's go for a walk."

Together, the three of them set off for the spot next to the river, and Slate could see his whole future in the few minutes it took to cross the grass and get on the path that led to the river. He wanted this woman to be in his future, and this dog, and this ranch.

"Okay, first, my mama's hair is not growing in great," Jill started, and Slate could listen to her talk all day and all night, her voice soothing and feminine in the best of ways. He'd have to tell his stories too, but he knew she wouldn't judge him, and that was one of the most amazing feelings in the world.

"UNCLE SLATE!" CONNOR YELLED FOR SLATE FROM somewhere in the house, and Slate hurried to finish the last stroke to shave his face. Before he could wipe his face and splash on some aftershave, the little boy appeared in the doorway leading to the bathroom.

"Wow, look at you," Slate said, leaning against the counter. "Your hair is all swept nicely." He grinned at the towheaded boy who had some of Nate's facial features, but the wrong color of hair. "New shirt, too. Fancy."

"I'm not fancy, Uncle Slate," Connor said, coming into the bathroom. He patted Axle, who never got more than ten feet away from Slate. "It's the first day of school, remember?"

"How could I forget?" Slate swept Connor into his arms. He was starting second grade today, and Slate couldn't remember ever being as excited to start school as Connor was. He did like it when he had to go to school, because then he didn't have to deal with his dad or work at the restaurant. But school was no picnic either.

"Daddy sent me to ask if you or Uncle Luke want breakfast from town."

"I do," Luke yelled from his bedroom.

Slate grinned at Connor. "He does." They laughed together, and Slate added, "I do too, bud. Tell your daddy to get whatever he's getting for me."

"Okey doke." Connor wiggled down, and he ran into Luke's bedroom too. The child didn't seem to do anything without running, and Slate wondered how he sat in a desk and did math or reading all day long. He listened to Luke and Connor laughing as he put on his aftershave and pulled on his cowboy boots.

The last cabin would be done by Friday. Luke had interviewed with a construction firm in town, one in Fish Lake, a town about an hour north of Sweet Water Falls, and one out of San Antonio. He'd decided he wanted to work construction for a living—at least right now. That was what he said. "At least right now."

Slate understood Luke's dreams to explore the world and find his place inside it. He simply thought he'd already found his—right here at Hope Eternal Ranch.

"Come on, Connor," he called. "You too, Axle." The three of them went outside, where Nate was just coming toward the Annex.

"There you are," he said to Connor. "We have to go, bud. School starts soon." He touched his hat. "Morning, Slate."

"Morning." Slate went down the steps with Connor and

Axle, and went with them to the driveway. Connor started to climb into the truck and then turned back to Axle, who'd trotted right behind him as if the dog would go to school with the boy.

"You have to stay here, buddy," Connor said, grabbing the dog that stood almost as tall as him right around the neck. "I'll be gone for a little bit, but I'll be back this afternoon." He hugged him tight and turned back to get in the truck.

Nate shook his head and went around to the driver's side.

"That boy needs a dog," Slate called to him.

"Nope," Nate said. "He's good with yours." He smiled and they left the ranch, Missy in the back seat of the truck.

They'd survived the heat of August, but September wasn't much better. Slate worked with Luke on the cabin that week, and he saw Jill whenever he could. He rode Scalloped Potato every chance he got.

In the couple of months since he'd gone to Austin, his life had normalized. He went to church, and he felt like he was in the right place, with the right people.

Friday came, and Slate went with Luke to the cabin for the last time. They'd technically finished yesterday, but Luke went inside and picked up a broom. They worked in silence to get the place swept clean and wiped down, as construction had a way of dropping sawdust and debris in the oddest of places.

Only an hour later, Luke replaced the broom in the closet and sighed.

"Well," Slate said. "You're done here."

Luke nodded, but he didn't look happy about it. As the cabins had been finished—Luke and Slate had worked on a total of eight of them, a few bigger than the others. Ginger and Nate had moved into one of those. Ted and Emma had too, vacating two of the smaller ones. Ginger had been hiring more and more people and filling the cabins, but Slate knew there were still three empty ones, including this bigger one.

He had a meeting with Ginger on Monday, and he was planning to ask her if he could have this cabin. He'd pay rent or take a pay reduction. Whatever it took to get it. He wanted one of the larger cabins so he could raise a family in it the way Ted and Nate were going to do.

"You sure you don't want to come with me?" Luke asked, piercing Slate with one of his harder looks.

Slate didn't want to have this conversation again. "I want to, Luke," he said. "I do." He shook his head. "I just feel like this is where I should be."

"I know." Luke sighed and went out the back door. He sat down on the top step on the deck he'd built with his bare hands and looked out over the ranch. This particular cabin sat right at the end of a road that led due north, many tall trees lining the west side of it to protect the field on the left from the harsh winds.

Slate followed him and sat beside him. He didn't know

what to say that he hadn't said before. Luke had an entire tornado inside him that blew with ideas and emotions, and Slate knew to sometimes just let them swirl until they settled.

"We should go get some lunch," he said. "Then I can help you pack."

"I'm packed," Luke said, glancing at him.

Slate's eyebrows went up. "Really?"

"How hard is it? I have one suitcase with some clothes in it. Once I shower on Monday morning, all I need to do is put in my deodorant and my razor, and that's it. I'm ready."

One suitcase. Slate wondered how long it would take him to pack. Probably about the same amount of time it had taken Luke—ten minutes. If that.

They gazed over the hay field in front of them, which had just been mowed. Nick and Spencer oversaw a lot of the agriculture at Hope Eternal, and Slate had gotten to know them better over the past several weeks. He did live with them, after all.

Luke had not asked Hannah for a date, despite his crush on her. He'd told Slate and Jill that he wasn't planning on staying at the ranch, and he didn't think it was fair to start a relationship that would end when autumn arrived. Slate had let the topic drop, but Jill had kept at Luke for a week or two until she finally backed down too.

"I'm going to miss you," Slate said. "When you get to your new apartment, you'll have to do a video tour for us."

"It's not an apartment," Luke said.

"What do you mean?" Slate looked at him. "You said you got an apartment."

"It fell through." Luke looked left, a tactic Slate had seen many times. He didn't want Slate to be able to see his expression.

"So where are you going to live?"

"I found a place," he said. "But I don't want to do a video tour."

"Why not?"

Luke exhaled heavily and turned to glare at Slate. "You're relentless, you know that?"

"I am not," Slate said. "I'm your best friend, and I'm concerned about where you'll be living in three days."

"It's a little place in someone's back yard," he said. He pulled out his phone and started swiping. "It's not nice, but I keep telling myself it's not permanent."

"That's what we told ourselves every day in prison," Slate said, not enthused by Luke repeating that mantra again. He took the phone from Luke and looked at the "shack" on the screen. "This is...small," he said.

"It's four hundred square feet total," he said. "Big enough for a bed and a couch and a bathroom. There's a row of counter space and a fridge," he said. "I'll survive."

Slate swiped to see the interior pictures, and they weren't terrible. "It looks clean at least."

"Yeah."

Slate handed the phone back. "You don't have to go."

"Yes, I do," he said.

Slate nodded, because that was true too. Luke did have to go, just like Slate needed to stay. "You're still going to see your family first, right?"

"Yes," he said. "So I don't have to be there until next Monday. Ten days, not three."

"I stand corrected," Slate said dryly, and they both laughed. They sobered quickly though, and finally Luke stood up. Slate did too, and they embraced.

"I'll miss you too," Luke said. "I can call you whenever, right?"

"Whenever," Slate said. "Absolutely."

"And you won't go to Austin without me, right?"

"Never," Slate promised.

Luke nodded and looked out over the field again. "All right," he said. "That's that. Let's go to lunch if you have time. I'm officially unemployed, so I'm free."

"I have time," Slate said. "I'll always have time for you, Luke."

"Let's see if we can get all the boys to go," Luke said. "I'll text them." He did, and within ten minutes, the five of them piled into Nate's luxury pickup truck and started toward Sweet Water Falls.

Slate let his happiness wash over him, through him, and around him, beyond grateful for a loving Lord who'd brought him to this tiny corner of Texas and allowed him to find a second chance at life, love, and joy.

A FEW NIGHTS LATER, SLATE WAS AWAKENED FROM A deep sleep by Axle's barking. The dog jumped up on Slate's bed and gave several loud, overbearing barks in his face.

"What in the world?" he asked. "Shush."

Axle jumped down and ran to the closed bedroom door. He turned, and barking constantly, ran through the bathroom to Luke's room.

Slate got out of bed at the same time a light snapped on in Luke's room. His bedroom door had obviously been open, because Axle's bark had moved down the hall.

"What is his problem?" Luke asked, appearing in the bathroom doorway.

"I don't know." Slate opened his bedroom door and followed Axle. The dog came running back, his barks getting deeper and more urgent. He wasn't stopping, and Slate had never seen the dog act like this before. He barked at prairie dogs and the rabbits he saw. He barked at the chickens sometimes, but he never barked at people, and never when someone came to the door.

He was usually nervous around new people, but he knew everyone in the house. Footsteps started up the steps, and Spencer joined Slate in the foyer. "What's goin' on?" he asked.

"I don't know," Slate said as Axle ran around him in a circle. "He's going crazy."

Axle put himself between the two men and the door and faced them, barking, barking, barking.

"I don't think he wants us to go out there," Luke said.

"I'll see what's out there," Slate said, moving into the half-bath that sat right off the front entrance. Besides the office to the right, it was the only room with a window that faced the front yard.

"I'll check over here," Spencer said.

"What's happening?" someone else asked, but Slate had already gone into the bathroom. He opened the window, as it had frosted glass that didn't let him see outside. The air had cooled slightly, but Slate's chest filled with ice when he saw the figure standing on the sidewalk in front of the West Wing.

A truck had been parked in the gravel lot where most of the cowboys parked, and the headlights illuminated the path toward the West Wing.

In the distance, Slate heard another dog barking, and he recognized Ursula's voice. Hers got louder in the next moment, and Slate wasn't surprised to see the German shepherd come tearing around the Annex and toward the West Wing.

The figure turned toward Ursula, and Slate sucked in a breath at the sight of the man's face.

He blinked, sure he was hallucinating.

He hurried back into the foyer, where Luke stood with Nick, Bill, and Jack—all the cowboys from the Annex. "It's Jackson MacBride," he said.

Luke frowned. "What?"

"It's Jackson MacBride," Slate repeated. The same fear that had hit him in Austin threatened to debilitate him again, but then Ursula yelped in pain, and that made anger fill him in less time than it took to breathe.

He marched over to the door and opened it. Axle shot outside, joining his voice to Ursula's. Slate followed the dog a little slower, Luke right behind him. The rest of the men came with them too, though they were all only in pajamas.

Ted's four blue heelers joined the fray in the front yard, and Jackson finally lifted both hands in surrender.

"Get out of here," Slate said, striding toward him. The dogs backed him against the fence, but Slate kept going. He heard other people talking, but he couldn't distinguish what they were saying.

"You are here," Jackson said with a smile. His hair had been cut, and he clearly wasn't intoxicated now, the way he'd been last time Slate had encountered him. "I found you."

Those three words struck fear right behind Slate's lungs. They got him to stop. "What do you want?"

"This is what you're doing now? Living on a ranch?"

Slate didn't answer.

"It's two o'clock in the morning," Luke growled. "What are you doing here?"

"I came for him," Jackson said, a horrible smile on his face as he continued to stare at Slate.

Horrible thoughts streamed through Slate's head, and he realized in that moment that he would never be free from his past.

At least here, he thought, and as Ginger and Nate

entered the front yard and took control of the situation, Slate found himself retreating to the Annex and pulling that single suitcase out of his closet.

He couldn't stay here if Jackson was able to find him. He had to go somewhere where no one would ever find him again, and he had to go now.

CHAPTER EIGHTEEN

J ill watched the scene from behind the safety of the glass in the West Wing. Only Hannah was at her side, as everyone else had moved out, and Michelle hadn't come to the ranch this weekend.

When Nate and Ginger arrived, things broke up quickly, and the stranger got in his truck and left the ranch.

She'd texted Slate, but he hadn't read the message nor responded.

"Looks like it's over," Hannah said. "Should we go back to bed?"

"Yeah," Jill said, though she didn't think she'd be able to go back to sleep after such a fright. Still, she followed Hannah through the kitchen to the hallway that led to the bedrooms, and she went inside hers. She sat on the bed and looked at her phone, willing Slate to call or text.

When he didn't, she slipped a pair of sandals on her feet

and quickly left the West Wing. They never locked the door that led to the garage, and she thought they better start. The back door to the Annex was also open, and all the lights on inside. Spencer and Nick stood in the kitchen, coffee mugs in their hands.

"Hey," she said, suddenly nervous. "Is Slate here?"

"Yeah," Spencer said. "In his room." He sipped his coffee as Jill strode through the kitchen.

"...you have to talk to her," she heard Luke say as she approached Slate's room. The door stood open, and she filled the doorway, taking in the scene as quickly as she could.

Slate, with bare feet and a bare torso, had an open suitcase on the bed.

He was putting clothes into it as quickly as he could.

Luke, also shirtless, sat in the armchair in the corner, and he jumped to his feet when he saw Jill. "Jill," he said.

Slate spun around, his eyes wide. She rarely saw him without his cowboy hat, and she hadn't realized how long his hair had gotten again. Her eyes slipped down his body to those well-defined muscles in his chest and abdomen, and she quickly yanked her gaze back to his.

"What are you doing?" she asked.

"I'm leaving," he said, his voice as cold as ice and as hard as flint.

"Leaving?" she repeated, not understanding the word in this context.

"I can't stay here," he said. "He knows where I am."

"Who was that?"

"My drug supplier from Austin," Slate said. "I'm not putting you or anyone else on this ranch in danger."

Axle licked Jill's hand, and she yanked it back, her adrenaline spiking. The dog backed up a step at her reaction, but Jill was having a hard time thinking at the moment.

"You can't leave."

"I can," he said. "And I am."

"I'll give you two some privacy," Luke said, striding in front of her. "Come on, Axle. Come with me." He took the dog into the bathroom and closed the door.

Slate sighed, but Jill's heartbeat kept getting faster and faster. Tears were imminent, and she hated the way the back of her nose was already burning.

"Luke got on with a construction crew," he said. "He was leaving in the morning anyway, and I'm going with him. Me and Axle are going with him."

Jill shook her head, her eyes filling with tears. "You're coming back, right?"

Slate ducked his head, but he didn't have his hat to hide behind this time. "No, sweetheart."

Fury roared through her. "Don't you dare call me that." Her fingers clenched into fists. She sucked at the air then, finding it an inadequate source of oxygen.

"I'm sorry, Jill," he said, his face still turned down. "I really can't explain more than I have already. I don't want to put you in danger, or the two pregnant ladies who marched out onto the lawn in the middle of the night."

Jill exhaled and pulled in another breath, her determination still strong. "You can't go, because I love you." Her chest tightened when he still didn't look up at her. "If you go, you have to come back, Slate, because I'm in *love with you*."

A new idea occurred to her. "When are you leaving? I'll come with you."

That got him to meet her gaze. "You can't come with me."

"Why not?" He couldn't leave her here. She would wither and die without him.

"You love this ranch. This is where you belong. Your family is close, and..." He shook his head and looked at something over her shoulder.

She hated it when he did that, and she clung to that anger still swirling within her. "You're just going to run away."

"Yes," he said.

"When does that stop?" she asked.

"Doesn't matter," he said.

"Your family is close too," she said, seizing onto anything she could. "You can't just abandon your grandparents."

His jaw jumped as he pressed his teeth together, and he shook his head.

"Look at me," she said. "Look at me and tell me you don't love me."

It seemed to take an extraordinary amount of time for him to switch his gaze to meet hers. Storms rolled through his eyes, and all the muscles in his face twitched.

"You can't say it," Jill said, letting the tears spill down her face. "Please don't go. At least wait to think about it. Or let me come with you. I can be ready in thirty minutes."

Slate shook his head. "How I feel about you or how you feel about me is irrelevant."

"I don't know what that means," she said, desperation clawing up her throat. She took a step toward him, but the look on his face stopped her.

"I'm no good for you," he said. "That's the honest truth." He turned around and slowly put another pair of jeans in his suitcase.

"Slate," she said, his name choking her.

"I'm no good for you, Jill," he said, louder now. "I'm sorry, but I'm not. You deserve someone a thousand times better than some loser ex-con who got addicted to pain pills in college and couldn't stop as an adult." He was yelling by the end, and Jill fell back a couple of steps, exiting his bedroom.

He turned to face her, his anger and disgust plain to see. "Please, just go back to your beautiful life. I will never fit into it."

A door opened somewhere, and Luke came between her and Slate. He wore pure agony on his face as he came toward her. "Come on, Jill," he whispered. "This isn't helping anyone."

She let him put his arm around her and guide her down the hall. Then through the kitchen, where Nick and Spencer gaped at her now.

Outside, under the wide, black expanse of the universe, she shrugged off Luke's arm. "Tell me you didn't ask him to come with you."

"I didn't," he said, frowning. "I swear, I didn't."

Jill believed him, but it would be so much easier to direct her anger and hatred at him than Slate—or herself.

"Let me talk to him," Luke said. "He just needs some time and distance."

Jill sobbed as she walked away. What was she supposed to do? Slate had obviously made his choice.

"Jill, wait," Luke said, following her. He caught her arm just as she reached the bottom of the steps. She spun back to him, and with him still on the stairs, he was much taller than her.

"What?" she demanded. "You've always wanted to leave the ranch, so just go already."

"You don't know what prison is like," he said, his voice quiet but strong. Deadly. "I understand that you *can't* know what it's like. You don't know what it does to a man like Slate Sanders. I've known him for a very long time, and I know that makes you angry. But I think it should make you trust me when I say he just needs some time and distance. He will come back to you."

"You don't know that." She'd had plenty of conversations with Slate about his tortured past, his time in prison, and the man he was terrified he'd become again.

"Yes, I do," Luke said. "Because I know he loves you too."

Jill opened her mouth to retort, but her voice faltered.

Luke pulled her into a hug, which would've been awkward in any other situation. "Let him go for now," he whispered, which caused her sobs to renew. "Give him time and distance, and I promise you, he'll come back to you."

She clung to him as she cried, and Luke showed her a great kindness by holding her, stroking her hair, and staying silent until the storm inside her subsided.

She stepped back and wiped her face, humiliation making her hot from head to toe. Without another word, she turned and went back to the single bedroom in the West Wing where she'd lived alone for the past eight years.

Always alone, she thought as she threw herself onto the bed and started crying again.

THE NEXT EVENING, SHE PULLED UP TO THE FARMHOUSE where she'd grown up, already crying. She wondered when she'd run out of tears, because they'd been showing up at random times all day.

Mama came out onto the porch, and Jill leapt from her car. "Mama," she said, her vision blurry as she ran up the sidewalk and mounted the steps to the porch. "He's gone, Mama."

"Oh, my poor dear," Mama said, receiving her into her arms. This embrace was the opposite of the one they'd shared in the basement when her mother had seemed so small and Jill had felt so big.

Now she was the tiny one. The one who couldn't stand without her mother's support. The one who had never felt so lost, even though she'd literally lost everything before. Now, she still had a home, she still had a car, she still had a job, and yet it felt like she'd lost more than she'd ever be able to get back.

"Come inside," Mama murmured. "I have things that will help."

"Nothing is going to help this," Jill said miserably. "I thought I'd hit rock bottom before, Mama, but this is...this is *awful*."

She thought she'd been in love before too, but she knew now that she hadn't loved as deeply as she loved Slate.

"How is losing him worse than losing my apartment, my friends, and all my money?" She only made it inside because Mama was holding her hand. "How is losing him worse than embarrassing you and Daddy?"

"Hey, sugar," Daddy said, rising from his favorite armchair in the living room. "I see why Mama's been baking all day."

"Hush, Harry," Mama scolded. "Her one true love broke up with her. What I've been baking won't fix that, but I'm hoping it'll help a little bit." She led the two of them into the kitchen, where the entire dining room table was covered with baked goods.

Chocolate cake, and chocolate chip cookies, and caramel

oat bars dipped in chocolate ganache. Chocolate milk, and chocolate almonds lacies, and chocolate covered Twinkies.

"You made the mousse pie," Jill said, her eyes filling with tears again.

"Is that where you want to start?" Mama asked. "I'll get the forks."

The three of them sat down at the table, and Mama put the whole pie in front of Jill before handing her a fork. "All right, baby. Let's talk as we eat."

JILL SMILED AT MISSY AS SHE LEANED TOWARD HER again. "Those lashes look amazing," she said. "Now, hold still so I can get this wing just right."

The twelve-year-old didn't move a muscle as Jill swept the eyeliner onto her face. She barely blinked, and when Jill finished the first eye, she sat up straight. "You can relax for a minute."

Missy exhaled, and Jill looked down at her makeup palette. "Thanks for doing this, Jill," she said. "My mom says she's hopeless with makeup."

"Oh, your momma's hopeless at getting up early when she doesn't have to." Jill grinned at Missy. "Because I've seen her with some pretty flawless makeup before."

"She's just extra-tired right now," Missy said. "You should see her ankles. They're like..." She looked past Jill as if Emma would be standing there. She wouldn't be, so Jill didn't look. It was barely six a.m., and Jill was driving Missy to the junior high today too. She had a hair appointment at eight o'clock, as it was Halloween, and no one wanted to work once school got out.

Jill had been moved to horse care now that the honeybee programs had ended, but she'd taken the whole morning off today. She normally loved Halloween, but this year, she hadn't been able to get into the spirit of things.

She hated that Slate had stolen an entire month from her as it was, but now she'd given him her love of holidays too. He'd never said specifically that he didn't like Halloween, but none of the cowboys around the ranch did, so she assumed he wouldn't either.

She wasn't planning to celebrate Christmas either. Or maybe she would. She would celebrate the heck out of Christmas, decorating the West Wing from top to bottom. That would show Slate.

In the first couple of weeks after he'd left Hope Eternal Ranch, she'd tried calling and texting him. He'd responded a couple of times via text, but she hadn't heard his voice in almost two months now.

A sigh came out of her mouth, and Missy said, "We're almost done, Jill. Sorry the makeup is so intense for this costume."

"Not at all," Jill said. Missy would put on the wig they'd found online, and she'd be transformed into the perfect Morticia from *The Addams Family*. She leaned forward again. "Now, one more eye, and we can get the wig on."

Missy turned into a statue again, and Jill finished the makeup with utmost precision. She helped set the wig in the exact right place, and Missy stood up and did a little twirl.

"It's perfect," Jill said. "Go stand right over there with your momma's piglet."

Missy obeyed, scooping Petunia into her arms and grinning.

"No smiles," Jill said. "Remember how serious she is."

"That's going to be so hard for me," Missy said, trying to straighten her smile. She managed it, and Jill snapped a couple of pictures with her phone. She studied them, her heart swelling with love for the almost-teen.

She looked up, her eyes filling with tears. "Thank you for letting me do this with you." She drew Missy into a hug, and the girl held her tight. Jill let go before things got too awkward, though Missy was the most amazing child, and she would've let Jill hug her for a long time.

"Did you ever figure out what you wanted to be for Halloween?" Missy asked.

Slate's girlfriend, Jill thought, but she just shook her head. "I think I'm going to skip it this year. I'll go to my parents' after work and eat sloppy Joes and potato chips with them. My mama makes these amazing 'spiders' out of these Chinese noodles and this butterscotch-peanut-butter mixture. She puts mini chocolate chips on for eyes and everything." She smiled warmly at Missy. "She's a lot like your mom. Amazing in the kitchen, and she always knows just how to make me happier."

"I'm glad, Jill," Missy said, hugging her again. "I know my mom has been worried about you."

"I know." Jill said, her voice tightening. "Sometimes I worry about me too."

"How's it going?" Emma asked, and Jill stepped back.

"Good." She pulled in a long breath. "Look at her."

Emma waddled forward and Missy handed her the piglet. "Wow, Jill is a master with those false lashes." Emma peered at her daughter's face. "And that eyeliner. Flawless."

Missy grinned and struck a very stoic pose that had everyone laughing.

Emma groaned as she set Petunia on the floor. "I think I'm going to wear all white and say I'm a marshmallow." She went to the couch and sighed as she sank onto it. "You did not afflict me like this, Missy, just so you know." She rested her hands on her pregnant belly. She was about six months along now, and things had started to swell in many places in the past week or so.

Emma was actually worried about it and she had a doctor's appointment tomorrow. Ted came whistling into the kitchen, fully dressed and ready for work. He stopped short when he saw Missy. "Wow," he said. "That is the best costume I've seen in...ever."

"Thanks, Teddy," Missy said, hugging him. "You're not dressing up either, are you?"

He reached up and pushed his cowboy hat forward so it hid his face. "Sure I am. I'm a cowboy Rockstar."

"That is not a thing," Missy said, giggling.

"It is on Halloween," Ted said, straightening. He stepped over to the back door and opened it. All four blue heelers trotted inside, two of them pausing to get a drink from the bowls Ted kept by the back door for them, and the other two going over to Missy. One went right up to her and the other stopped and stretched out, his nose working double-time.

"It's just me, Ryan," she said. After all four of them had inspected her and deemed her safe, they jumped up onto the couch with Emma, who chastised them at the same time she patted them.

Jill basked in the healthy, beautiful spirit of family and love that existed in this house. Her emotions surged, but thankfully, no tears appeared. Since Slate's departure from the ranch, she'd spent an astronomical amount of time on her knees. The Lord had reassured her over and over that she was deserving of love and family, and that one day, she would get it.

Whether that was with Slate or not, she didn't know. God hadn't been as forthcoming about that, and Slate hadn't come back to the ranch yet, despite Luke's promise that he would.

Jill had no idea where either of them were, as she'd asked Ted, Nate, Dallas, and anyone else who might hear or know not to tell her. For the first month, she hadn't trusted herself not to get in the car and drive straight to him, begging him again not to leave her behind.

Now, she thought she could probably resist that temptation.

"Happy Halloween," she said. "I'll see y'all later." She left the cabin and went back to the homestead. Half an hour later, she loaded up with Missy and drove to town. She dropped the girl off to join the streams of teens entering the junior high in various forms of someone or something else.

When she arrived at Lana's for her hair appointment, she sat down in the salon chair and said, "I'm ready for a huge change. Let's dye it black."

"You want to dye your hair black?" Lana looked at her with wide eyes. She had nearly orange hair today, as she'd dressed up as Lucille ball.

"Yes," Jill said, determined to make a new future for herself. Maybe Slate would return. Maybe he wouldn't. It was time for Jill to figure out how to be happy by herself, something she'd never really achieved in her life. "Time for a change. Make it black."

CHAPTER NINETEEN

Slate had never lived anywhere but Texas, and he was completely unprepared for the chill that came with winter in Colorado. He marveled at the first snowfall, and his toes froze on the job site for three days before he made it a priority to go to the store and get hand warmers to put in his boots.

He didn't love construction as much as Luke, but he did love the man for passing up the opportunities they had to work in a warmer state. They'd visited his family for a week as planned, all while looking for other jobs in other states.

They'd come to Vail together, and Slate had loved the Rocky Mountains in the fall. Now, though, he hadn't seen the tops of them in over a week, as the clouds had settled in and started dumping rain and then snow as the temperature plummeted.

"You ready for this?" Luke asked as he entered the kitchen.

Slate could only grunt. He didn't get on social media, and he didn't have anyone to connect with other than Nate, Ted, and Dallas in Texas. He texted with them regularly, but the only people he actually spoke with were Luke, his boss, a couple of other guys on the crew, and his mother.

His heart felt like a black stone in his chest, and he told himself every day—sometimes every hour—to learn to live with it. Jackson had not shown up in Vail, and Slate had started to relax a little bit.

At the same time, he knew that meant he was still in Texas, and he worried constantly that his parents would be contacted, or that Jackson would show up at Hope Eternal again and hurt someone. He couldn't carry that around for the rest of his life if it happened, and Nate had assured him over and over that Jackson would not be returning to the ranch. How he knew that, Slate didn't know. He'd asked, and all Nate had said was, "I took care of it."

Right after that text, Ted had said, *You could come back, Slate.*

Slate hadn't answered that, and Dallas had moved them to a different topic a few minutes later.

"What are my chances of calling out today?" Slate asked.

"Bad," Luke said as he pulled on his coat. "Matt already did, and Jude wasn't very happy about it."

"All right." Slate left his half-drunk coffee on the table

and stood up to start getting dressed to face the weather outside. "You owe me dinner for this."

"We'll stop at Rib Roost after work."

"Deal." Slate pulled on a beanie and a pair of gloves and followed Luke out of the apartment they'd rented together. They drove Slate's truck, and they arrived at the construction home base in only five minutes. That was a bonus of living in the same small town where all the work was.

Slate wasn't even sure what day it was. He got up every day. He went to work. He showered to get warm. Luke ordered food or made something simple for them. They both fell asleep on the couch as darkness fell, and they did it all again the next day.

One afternoon, Jude said, "Thanks, everyone. See you in a week." The group broke up, and Slate blinked around at everyone.

"A week?" he asked Luke as they went to his truck. The snow had melted a bit in the past couple of days—or a week? Slate wasn't sure—and everything was a muddy mess.

"Yeah." Luke looked at Slate. "It's Thanksgiving next week, Slate. We're not working for the next ten days." He peered at Slate. "We're leaving for Vegas in the morning, remember?"

"Of course," Slate said, but he hadn't remembered. He didn't allow himself to think farther ahead than the next five minutes. The next task.

Luke sighed, the sound of it extra loud and extra long. Slate didn't ask what he really wanted to say, because Luke wouldn't hold back. They got in the truck, and Luke kept his eyes out his window as Slate adjusted the heater settings.

"When are you going to admit you're miserable and just go back?" Luke finally asked.

"I'm fine," Slate said.

"You're the opposite of fine," Luke said. "It's time to stop lying to yourself."

"I won't put any of them in danger."

"You won't," Luke said. "Nate said—"

"I'm sick of relying on Nathaniel to take care of my problems," Slate said, glaring at Luke until he turned to look at him. He wore surprise in his expression. "Aren't you?"

"No," Luke said. "I grew up fighting, Slate. Physically and mentally and spiritually. If someone else can fight a battle for me, I'm all for that." He glared right back at Slate. "I don't like my life either. This sucks. I don't like working in the snow and mud and muck and cold. I hate it here." His chest heaved as he pulled in breath after breath. "I'm going to look for something in Vegas while I'm there."

"Great," Slate said. "Let's do that."

"No," Luke said. "You're not invited to stay with me. You need to go back to Austin and see your parents. I heard your mom begging you last week. You were *cold* to her, Slate. Like, ice cold."

Slate didn't know what to say. He didn't feel anything. That wasn't entirely true. He experienced plenty of self-loathing and plenty of regret. He suffered with plenty of misery and plenty of depression. Coupled with the desperation, Slate considered it a miracle that he could get out of bed at all.

"After that, you need to do whatever it is you need to do to close the door on your past once and for all. Then you better drive as fast as you can to that beautiful woman you love at that ranch you love."

"I'm no good for her," Slate said quietly.

"Another lie you need to stop perpetuating," Luke said. "Besides, it's not up to you, Slate. It's up to her, and I was there while she stood in front of you and said how much she loved you."

"No, you weren't." Slate practically slammed the truck into drive. "You'd gone into your bedroom by then."

"I could hear everything," Luke said. He looked away again, and Slate drove back to their apartment. He started to unbuckle to get out of the truck, but Luke didn't move.

"What do you want for dinner?" Slate asked. He just wanted to curl into the couch with Axle against his chest and fall asleep.

"Listen," Luke said. "I'm going to rent a car for the drive to Vegas. Then you can go to Texas."

"Luke," Slate said.

"I've made up my mind," he said. "You're uninvited to my family Thanksgiving dinner." He got out of the truck and slammed the door.

Slate followed him, his anger finally making him feel alive. "Who's being cold now?"

"If I have to be to get you to open your eyes and stop

lying to yourself, I'll do it," Luke called over his shoulder. "And if you could order from that bread company, that would be great. I want the Thanksgiving feast on rye."

Slate wanted to yell at him to order his own sandwich. Instead, he marched back to the truck and got behind the wheel again. With the heater blowing, Slate breathed in and out, out and in. "He's wrong," he said, but the words felt false in his mouth.

"He's wrong, right, Lord? I can't go back to Texas." An impossible balloon of hope inflated instantly. He recognized his misery, and he realized how unhappy he'd made Luke at the same time.

"I thought this was what I needed to do," he said, hanging his head. "How do I fix this?" He put the truck in gear again, this time more gently, and drove to the bread company to order sandwiches. He got the one Luke wanted, as well as a roast beef sandwich with sauerkraut and spicy mustard that he really liked.

Armed with dinner, he prayed the whole way back to the apartment. When he walked in, he found a suitcase by the door and Luke nowhere to be found. He called his friend, who said, "I'll be back in twenty minutes."

Double that amount of time passed before Luke walked in, a jangling set of car keys in his hand. "Thank you for dinner," he said.

"You really rented a car," Slate said.

"Yes."

"Luke," Slate said, unwrapping his sandwich. "I'm sorry I've made your life so miserable."

"I know."

"I hate it here too."

"I know."

"I really can't come to Vegas?"

"You really can't." Luke sat at the table too and started unwrapping his sandwich.

"All right." Slate nodded and took a bite of his sandwich. He would miss this combination of flavors, but he wasn't going to stay in Vail for a sandwich. "Then I need your help to come up with a plan for what things will look like in Texas."

Luke looked at him, his eyes wide. "Really?"

"Really," Slate said. "I'm beyond miserable, Luke."

"You're in love with Jill."

"I'm in love with Jill," Slate said. "I miss the ranch. I miss my grandparents' farm. I want you to come back with me, but I get it if you can't." He reached over and clutched Luke's hand. "I'm sorry I've ruined your first grand adventure out in the world."

"I think I can forgive you," Luke said, grinning. "Okay, so first things first. We should call Ginger and talk to her. See what's going on at the ranch and all of that."

Slate nodded. "That's a good idea."

"Second," Luke said. "You call your mother and say you'll be there for Thanksgiving."

Slate nodded, though the thought of going to Austin

alone didn't sit well with him. "I didn't think I should go to Austin alone."

"I think...I think you need to *know* you're not the man you were before. And I don't think you'll *know* that until you go alone."

Slate nodded, because he'd spent a lot of time hiding behind things. First, it was the concussion he'd suffered from in college. That had caused him to start with the prescription pain medication.

That had led to his drug addiction. He'd hidden behind his job, with the suit and tie and professional bank setting. Once he'd been exposed and gone to prison, he'd hidden behind Ted and Nate. When he got out, he hid behind the fear of becoming the person he'd been in Austin.

You're just going to run away.

Jill had said those words to him, and he'd admitted that he was.

"It's time to stop running," he said. "Stop hiding."

"Yes," Luke said. "I know that terrifies you. I understand it, Slate. I do. But it's time. You can't be happy when you're running."

They finished their dinner in silence, and as Slate crumpled up the paper their sandwiches had come in, he looked at Luke. "What are you doing, then? You're not running?"

Luke shrugged. "I'm searching for myself. There's a difference."

"I hope you find him," Slate said, standing up. "I know you will. You're smart and resourceful."

"I'm going to tell my dad you said that," Luke said, following the statement with a laugh.

"Maybe college," Slate suggested. "You never did that, and I don't know. Maybe you'd find yourself there."

"I'm not ruling anything out," Luke said. He grabbed onto Slate as he passed and clapped him loudly on the back. "You can do this, Slate. It's time to take control of the reins of your life and leave everything else behind."

"Yeah," Slate said. "It is time for that."

A few days later, Slate pulled into the driveway at his parents' house. Crossing into the city of Austin had required some steel nerves, but he'd done it. He took a few moments in the truck to get everything together after driving for a few hours, and then he faced the house.

No one came out onto the porch today, but he found them inside in the kitchen, elbow-deep in fixing Thanksgiving dinner.

"Oh, Slate's here," his mother said, a genuine smile on her face. Slate wished he could do the same, but as he hugged his mom, he felt happier than he had in months.

She laughed as she brushed breadcrumbs off his shoulder. "We're maybe an hour out."

"What can I do to help?" he asked.

"Go see what Daddy's doing in the back yard," Cindi said. "He's been out there tinkering with the turkey for about ten minutes, and that usually means we're seconds away from calling the fire department."

"You're cooking a turkey in the back yard?" Slate asked.

"He's frying it," Momma said. "It's actually really good, even if we did have to call the fire department a couple of years ago."

"I'll check on him," Slate said, already walking toward the sliding glass door. Outside, he found his father hovering around a steaming fryer while Cindi's husband loitered nearby. They both turned toward Slate as his footsteps hit the stairs, and he lifted his hand to say hello.

His father actually smiled, and Slate returned it. "How are things out here?"

"Your mother sent you to check on me, didn't she?"

"She did," Slate said, not trying to hide it. "She doesn't want to call nine-one-one today."

"Oh, we're not going to do that." Daddy took Slate into a hug. "She's so happy you're here. Thanks for coming."

Slate's throat narrowed. "I'm glad to be here." He cleared his throat. "Dad, there hasn't been anyone coming by, has there?"

"Coming by?"

"The house," Slate said. "Asking for things. Or at the restaurant, looking for money or anything." He watched his dad to make sure he didn't miss any signs of trying to keep a secret.

"There's a guy who comes every day," he said. "Right

around four. He stays 'till we start to get busy, and then he leaves."

"Does he order anything?"

"Same thing every time," Daddy said. "The brisket platter. Pays in cash—down to the penny. Eats in a few minutes and just watches out the window. No one's ever with him. He chats up Peggy, and he leaves her a couple of dollars."

"Is he, uh, intoxicated?" Slate asked.

Daddy turned toward him, his eyes full of curiosity. "Doesn't seem to be." He searched Slate's face. "What's going on? Do you know him?"

"I think I do," Slate said. "And I don't want him hanging around there." Slate's mind moved along several dark paths, and he hated that he knew the horrors that existed on those roads. He suspected Jackson was watching a drop spot, and once he saw one of his thugs leave the drugs where they'd arranged, he left his two-dollar tip and left the barbecue joint.

Slate did not want him there. He didn't want his family anywhere near a drug drop-off point, and he didn't want cops coming in to talk to his father about the man who ate there every afternoon at four o'clock.

"You'll be open tomorrow?" he asked.

"We open tonight at five," Daddy said.

"Can I go in with you?"

His father's eyes widened, and Slate didn't blame him. He'd said some hurtful things about the restaurant in the past, and he needed to apologize for those. "Of course."

Slate put his arm around his father's shoulders, which had once been so big and so powerful to Slate. Now, he stood a few inches taller than his dad, and his father seemed much frailer than Slate remembered.

"I'm sorry for what I said about you and the restaurant," he said.

"I don't remember what you said," Daddy said, focusing on the turkey happily bubbling away in the hot oil.

"Yes, you do," Slate said quietly. "And it's not true. It wasn't then, and it's not now. You didn't love that restaurant more than you loved us."

Daddy didn't say anything, and they stood there and watched the turkey cook.

"I wasn't the nicest," Daddy said. "I know that. I pray every day that you and your brother and sister will find a way to forgive me—and that you'll do better than I did."

Slate nodded. "I think I've got a long way to go to even be as good as you."

His dad shook his head. "You're wrong, Slate. You're a good man. You made a few bad decisions, that's all. We all make back decisions sometimes."

Slate nodded again, and this time he didn't stop. He had made some bad decisions in his youth that had snowballed out of control. The real problem was, he'd made some pretty poor choices in the past couple of months too, and he still had miles to go before he could stand next to his father and say he was the man he wanted to be.

Thankfully, he knew where to start. A family Thanksgiving dinner.

A barbecue restaurant confrontation.

And then a three-hour drive to Hope Eternal Ranch.

SLATE LOOKED TOWARD THE TWO-WAY, PLASTIC DOOR that led to the dining room as Peggy pushed through it. "He's here," she said, putting a plate on the counter for the dishwasher. She looked nervous, and she had a reason to be.

Slate nodded. "Thanks, Peggy. Remember, everything is normal here." He lifted one hand and put his palm down. "We're calm. You're going to take him the brisket plate and his sweet tea. The end."

Her eyes were as big as the dinner plates they served barbecue from. "Okay."

"You're fine," Slate said, but he wasn't sure if it was for her or for him. His heart beat with the speed of light, and he took a long breath, trying to quiet it. That didn't work, and Slate pushed away from the stainless steel counter where he'd been standing.

He'd come to the restaurant with his father last night, but Jackson hadn't showed up. Slate supposed even drug dealers took Thanksgiving Day off, though he had been surprised. Annoyance had sang through him then, as his trip back to Sweet Water Falls had been postponed.

The delay had given him time to formulate a plan

beyond sitting down in front of Jackson and telling him to clear out of Austin. As he'd laid awake on the couch in the living room, he'd realized he didn't want Jackson MacBride in any city, corrupting any more lives.

He'd risen with the sun and gone somewhere he'd never thought he'd go. Luke would be horrified, as would Ted. Slate had told himself he didn't have to tell them. His business in Austin was exactly that—his.

The woman he'd met with at the police station had listened to him for only ten minutes before she'd stood and said, "Can you give me a minute? I need to bring someone else in here." She'd held out both hands, almost like she needed to placate him into staying.

Slate had almost bolted, and she could probably feel his nervousness. The anxiety bled off him, even now.

He went out the back door, where no less than eight uniformed and armed cops waited. Not just any team of cops either. The special forces team against drugs in Austin.

They'd been looking for Jackson MacBride for over a year, apparently. When Slate came in, saying he knew who he was, and where he'd be, and that there would likely be drugs nearby? The whole team had been mobilized, and Slate had left the police station only forty-five minutes ago.

Everything had been explained to everyone in the restaurant, and Slate met the eyes of the team leader, the same woman he'd spoken to hours ago. "Ready?" she asked.

"Everyone's going to be okay, right?" Slate asked. "My father. My brother. Peggy. There's two receptionists in today, because my daddy thought it would be busy. We were only expecting one."

Lauren took him by the shoulders, though she was easily a foot shorter than him. "Slate," she said. "You're going to lead him away from the restaurant."

"Yeah, but..." Slate looked down the narrow alley behind the restaurant. He'd hated it out here with the fire of a thousand suns. He'd been forced to work at the barbecue joint, and he'd been on garbage duty for almost a year before Daddy would even let him touch a dirty dish.

"There are people on the street," he said. "It's Black Friday."

"It's almost evening," Lauren said. "And besides, everyone on the street is with our team. We've closed the streets leading to this area."

Slate looked at her, surprise in his eyes. "You have?"

"Five minutes ago," she said. "When one of our eagles spotted our man going into the restaurant."

Slate's stomach turned over again. "Okay," he said, reaching up to rub his shoulder where the wire had been sealed to his skin. "I'm free to leave town the minute you arrest him, right?"

"Yes," Lauren said. "We know how to get in touch with you if we need to."

"Lead us to the drop-off, and we won't need to talk to you again," James said, a tall, African-American man that would intimidate anyone on the planet. There was no way he blended in anywhere, so it was no surprise he was in the back alley.

"Okay," Slate said again. "I better go. The brisket plate is just a scoop-and-serve."

He turned to go, but Lauren stopped him. She looked into his eyes with her similarly dark ones. "You can do this, Slate. You survived four years in prison, and this is nothing. You know how to be a junkie."

"Yeah," he said, a certain level of misery accompanying him. He did know how to be a junkie, but he wished he didn't. He went back inside the restaurant, seeing the open, blank, staring eyes of the last guy who'd come back to Austin after his stint in prison. He hadn't had the circle of friends to help him stay off the streets and away from the drugs.

He'd died only thirteen days after his release.

Slate pushed through the black plastic door and kept going. Past the bar and past all the tables until he got to the one where Jackson sat, his food in front of him. It was half-gone already, and Slate pulled out the chair across from him and sat.

Jackson's eyes met his, and no, he was not intoxicated. He was not high. How he managed to move the stuff he did without taking it was a miracle to Slate. His legs shook with the need to run, but he stayed put.

"Well," Jackson said, slathering some butter onto his roll. He loaded one half of it with chopped brisket. "What are you doing here?"

"I need those pink pills. Do you still get those?"

Jackson chuckled and took an enormous bite of his sandwich. He shook his head as his eyes met Slate's. He wore something in his eyes that made Slate want to yell at him, lunge across the table, and start swinging.

He fisted his hands in his lap. His shoulder twitched, and he let it. In fact, he amplified it. "I have money."

Jackson transformed right in front of Slate's eyes. His eyes turned dead, and he actually stopped eating. This was the hard-nosed businessman Slate knew. He was the best friend when a guy needed a fix. He could take care of a man if he just needed a quick hit during lunch. But when it was time to pay...

"Let me see it." He dusted off his hands as he set his roll back on the tray. "You've interrupted my lunch, by the way."

"It's four o'clock," Slate said, digging into his pocket. He pulled out the wad of cash Lauren had given him. Apparently, the bills were marked in some sort of untraceable, electronic way. Slate had questioned her about that plenty, because he didn't believe something electronic could really be untraceable.

She'd shown him cameras he couldn't even see—but his face came up on the computer screen. Technology had advanced while he'd been behind bars, he supposed.

He put the pile of money on the table in front of him, and said, "There it is."

"Are you insane?" Jackson hissed, glancing around. He shoved the money toward Slate. "Hide it, you idiot."

"Sorry, sorry," Slate said, covering the money with both

hands. "I forgot." He gave a nervous laugh that was entirely too real. "I've been out of the game for too long, and I need a pill."

"More than one," Jackson muttered, now playing the salesman. He looked out the window, his eyes narrowing for a moment.

"You have some close by, right?" Slate asked. "My dad says you eat here every day." He too looked out the window. "The drop has to be real close."

Jackson picked up his sandwich and finished it, leaned away, and regarded Slate. Slate held his gaze for only a moment before remembering that junkies didn't stare down their suppliers. It was always, *yes, sir, I have the money, sir, just give me the pills.*

"We better go now, or all the good stuff will be gone." He signaled to Peggy, who came toward the table.

She looked at Slate and then to Jackson. "All done, sugar?" she drawled, seemingly normal to Slate. "You didn't even finish your chips."

"I had an old friend join me today," Jackson said, reaching into his back pocket for his wallet. He dropped a twenty on the table. "Keep the change, Peggy." He stood with a smile and started for the door, his eyes locking onto Slate's as he went behind the waitress.

That was more than a two-dollar tip, and alarms started to wail in Slate's head. He repeated the same mantra that had been streaming through his mind since late last night. *Get him off the streets. Get him off the streets.*

Slate wouldn't wish prison on anyone, but for a man like Jackson MacBride—he deserved it.

Jackson had stopped just outside the door, and he looked both ways down the street. "Walk ten feet behind me," he said as Slate stepped next to him. "I'll double-tap the drop. You pretend like you dropped something, and you bend down. If you can't find it from there, you're a moron."

"I need a fix," Slate said. "I'm not thinking clearly." He tried to make himself sound utterly desperate, and it was almost strange how he felt exactly that way.

"You won't miss it," Jackson said. "Take the box out. Take what you want. Leave the money."

"As much as I want?" Slate looked at him with eager eyes. "Really?"

"One packet per hundred," Jackson said. "Don't get greedy on me now, Slate. You've been off the hard stuff for a long time. You need to start with the yellow pills."

"I want the pink ones."

"Your funeral." Jackson shrugged, and Slate once again felt this primal need to pummel his face into a pulp. How many people had he said those exact, nonchalant words to where it had resulted in exactly their funeral?

Before Slate could unclench his fingers, Jackson took off down the street. He waited until he'd gone a few paces, and then Slate followed. He stuck his hands in his pockets and kept his head down, just in case Jackson turned around. It wouldn't do to have him see Slate scoping out where all the undercover police officers stood.

He watched him touch a parking meter. Just once.

His pulse picked up speed.

Jackson touched a fire hydrant. Just once.

He tapped a light pole once, then actually stepped toward a parked car and touched it once.

Finally, he crossed the street at the light—doing absolutely nothing illegal should anyone be watching—and started back toward the barbecue joint.

Another parking meter. A signpost for the directions to a museum. One tap. One tap.

Almost directly across from the restaurant, he double-tapped a garbage can and kept going.

A garbage can? screamed through Slate's mind. He watched Jackson continue to saunter down the street, randomly tapping poles and posts as if that was just something eccentric he did.

Slate shot his right hand straight into the air, the fingers in a fist, and then he dropped to his knees in front of the garbage can. Knowing Jackson, he'd duck into a doorway or around the corner to watch Slate. He'd check his stash immediately after that, because he'd never leave the goods out when he wasn't there to watch them.

"Did you drop something?" a woman asked, crouching down next to him. "Austin PD," she whispered. "We need him to get the drugs out. Having you do it makes you guilty, not him."

Slate looked at her in horror. "I am not going to jail

again." He'd *known* this was a bad idea, and he couldn't believe he'd gotten himself in this situation again.

"Get him back here," she said, straightening. "Okay," she said loudly. "I was just trying to help."

Slate stared after her and then looked at the garbage can again. It looked like any other he'd seen around the city for most of his life. Plain brown plastic container. Inside, there would be a big, round plastic can with a black liner. The container could be lifted straight up to get the can out, and then the two parts were put back together.

With shaking hands, he felt along the bottom edge of the brown plastic. Panic filled him. He could not be arrested again. What would he tell his mother? How could he ever show his face to Nate and the other boys again?

To Jill?

Get up! his mind screamed at him. *Get up and get out of here!*

He looked in the direction Jackson had continued walking, and sure enough, he loitered in the doorway of a paper goods store, about thirty feet down the block. He gestured for Jackson to come help him, and he could feel the man rolling his eyes as it happened.

Please, Slate prayed. *Dear Lord, if there was ever a time I need You, it's now. Please.*

By some miracle, Jackson stepped out of the doorway and came back toward Slate. "You really are an idiot.'

"There's nothing here," Slate hissed, standing up and moving out of the way. A glance in both directions told him there was really no one on the streets. Those that were had given up pretending like they were talking to friends or window shopping.

Jackson knelt on the ground. "There's a key right here," he said, picking it up. Slate hurried to step back to his side, shielding his view of the now quiet and immobile people on the street. "It fits into the side there," he said, and Slate moved his foot back so Jackson could unlock a compartment on the side of the can.

Slate's nerves vibrated as if he'd been hooked to an electrical supply.

The key turned, creating a click.

"There's a tray here, and you..." Jackson kept talking, but Slate backed away from him, his fist back in the air.

Someone blew a whistle, and someone yelled, "Sir, I need you to freeze right where you are."

The special forces team swarmed across the street. Men came out of the doors right behind Jackson and Slate. Someone grabbed his arm and pulled him down the street, out of the way.

Jackson screamed as he tried to get away and got tackled to the ground. He snarled and spat at the officers as they handcuffed him and arrested him. Though Slate was practically being dragged backward, he couldn't look away.

"Arrest me," he said to the man who had a death grip on his arm. "Pretend to arrest me," he said again. "Like I'm running."

His eyes met Jackson's as he got hauled to his feet, and

Slate wrenched his arm out of the officer's and started to run.

The man yelled—several others did too—and the next thing Slate knew, he'd been knocked to the ground. The yell that came from his mouth was involuntary, and he really hated the cool kiss of metal and the horrifying click of handcuffs as he got arrested.

His heart pounded as he was helped to his feet and led away. Everything inside him shook. "Don't let me go until he's gone," he said. "Please. Make sure he can't see me." He kept the pleadings going all the way to an unmarked black SUV.

The man shoved him in the backseat and went around to the front driver's side as another man got in the passenger seat.

He turned, his eyes wide and somewhat afraid. "Give me two minutes, sir," he said. "And we'll get those cuffs off."

"Is he gone?" Slate asked. "He has to be gone first."

"Laurel's got him," the other man said as he climbed behind the wheel. He too faced Slate, his eyes anxious. "Did I hurt you?"

"I'm fine," Slate said, though his shoulder pulled, and his chest ached. "I'm fine." He took a deep breath and tried to see through the nearly black windows. "I'm fine."

And with Jackson off the streets of Austin, maybe he really would be able to let go of the past and step into the future.

CHAPTER TWENTY

J ill lifted the lid on yet another box, surprised Ginger had accumulated so many Christmas decorations. She'd never paid attention to how many were put up around the West Wing before, but now that she was doing it single-handedly, she knew how much work it was.

She didn't care. With the music playing songs about Santa and reindeer, cups of cheer and chestnuts roasting, she didn't have to think about things she'd rather forget.

She'd put up the main tree in the living room that morning, and tonight, she was going to climb the fence in the front and take a picture of it as it welcomed everyone to the ranch. Hope Eternal had a website, and Jill had volunteered to spruce it up. She'd been learning how to add pictures of happenings around the ranch, and she'd been writing a blog a few times a week, with convenient links to their upcoming programs and events.

Someone had asked if there would be a Santa Claus at the ranch, perhaps wearing a cowboy hat, and that they'd love to have a photo opportunity with a "western Santa."

Jill had immediately taken the idea to Ginger, who'd given her the green light. Jill had slept little for the past week as she researched what she'd need to set up a photo booth of sorts to create the perfect western Santa experience for children.

She knew what they did at the mall, and she may have gone to town a few days in a row to stalk the mall Santa, talk to the elves managing the camera, and learn how much they charged for the photos.

To sit on Santa's lap was free, and she thought she could get Ted to don the red suit and say the ho ho ho's. He was already a big teddy bear, and she could shove a pillow under his coat to make him a bit puffier.

She'd been practicing with her cell phone to get the perfect pictures, and all she needed was the tripod she'd bought to arrive in the mail, and she'd be ready.

It was the day after Thanksgiving, and she'd promised everyone on the ranch blog that she had some exciting news coming the following Monday. Her determination to get the rest of the holiday decorations up ate at her fiercely, and she kept hanging ornaments on the smaller tree in the kitchen. This one was getting treated with various utensils that

Ginger had gotten from somewhere, and Jill was going to finish it with plenty of tinsel.

Then she had clings to put on all the windows, and all the little knick-knacks that she'd arrange on the bannister, the shelves in the living room, and the back of the piano. After that, she was planning to drive all the empty boxes to the equipment shed and swap them out for the bigger lawn ornaments.

Ginger had never bothered with those that Jill could remember. But she wanted the light-up deer in the front yard, and the red-and-green elf to stand guard on the front porch. Her first couple of years at the ranch, Ginger's father had still been in control, and he'd definitely brought out the bigger Christmas décor.

She'd even spied a sleigh and reindeer that could go on the roof. "That's overkill," she murmured to herself as Bing Crosby started singing about a winter wonderland. She shook her head. "There's no such thing as Christmas overkill this year," she said sternly.

She loved Christmas, and she was going to celebrate it in style this year. Since she'd decided to do that a few weeks ago, she'd been doing some online shopping for the men and women she knew around the ranch. She didn't have a lot of expendable income, but she could afford a pair of gloves here, and a chocolate orange there.

Jess loved peppermint candy, and she'd bought her a giant bag at the big box store just yesterday. It was a well-spent ten bucks, and Jill couldn't wait to wrap it in brightly colored paper and put it under one of the trees in the West Wing.

"Something smells good in here," Hannah said as she came down the hall.

"Don't get excited," Jill said. "It's a hot chocolate candle from Haven." She turned to greet her friend and found Hannah with a man Jill had never met. "Oh, hello." She lifted her eyebrows and smiled at Hannah.

Hannah grinned like the cat who'd swallowed the canary. "Jill, this is Chuck Knight. Chuck, my best friend, Jill."

"Nice to meet you, ma'am," Chuck said with a wide, white-toothed smile. He was very good-looking, and Jill returned his grin easily. She turned her gaze to Hannah, her eyebrows refusing to go down.

"How did you two meet?" Jill asked.

"Look at this place," Hannah said. "Oh, it's a baking tree. I remember when Brooke set this up the first time. She put all of her gifts under it, and we all got something for the kitchen that year."

She'd dodged the question, and Jill let her as she walked over to the nearly finished tree.

"I ate dinner with her family yesterday," Chuck said, drawing Jill's attention. "My brother is married to her sister."

"Ah, got it," Jill said, turning back to watch Hannah adjust one of the ceramic whisks. "Well, Hannah is a pretty amazing woman. Have you not met her before now?"

He reached up and swept his cowboy hat off his head, ran his hands through his hair, and put his hat back on. "I've been serving in the military for a few years, so I haven't been around."

"I see." Jill gave him another grin. A military cowboy. He was right up Hannah's alley. In the past, Jill might have experienced a dose of jealousy as she thought a military man combined with a cowboy was pretty sexy. Now, though, she felt nothing. Not for Chuck, and no envy whatsoever. "Well, thank you for your service."

"Ma'am," he said, and Hannah turned back to them.

"I'm still getting used to your hair," she said as she rounded the island. "Should I make no-bake cookies?"

"Yes," Jill said instantly. "And we have all of that ice cream that needs to be eaten. Ginger wants to put those little cups in there for the baby shower, and she said she'll throw it away if we don't clear it out."

"She wouldn't dare," Hannah said, freezing as her eyes widened.

"She didn't seem to be kidding," Jill said with a laugh. "I'll take all of the peanut butter cookie dough." She glanced at Chuck. "Do you want some?"

"I'll take whatever you've got," he said.

Jill joined Hannah in the kitchen as she pulled out a jar of peanut butter and the plastic container with oats. "Hannah's favorite is butter pecan," she said, setting it on the counter. "We've also got mint chocolate chip, the cookie dough, and some cookies 'n cream."

Chuck moved into the kitchen and started opening cupboards. He found the bowls and got down three. "Just us?"

"For all of this ice cream?" Jill said. "I'll text Ted. He can take some for Emma."

"Text Spencer too," Hannah said. "Those cowboys next door can eat more than a herd of wolves."

Chuck burst out laughing, and he had a nice, loud, deep laugh. Hannah grinned too, finally laughing a little with him. "What?" she asked, clearly flirting with him.

"Wolves don't go around in a *herd*, sweetheart," he drawled. "They're a *pack*."

"Fine," she said, nudging him with her hip. "Those cowboys next door can eat more than a *pack* of wolves."

Watching them together made Jill's heart constrict in a weird way. She wasn't jealous. She wasn't hurt. She was so, so happy for Hannah, because she really did want her to be happy, and Chuck seemed to bring out something in her that had been absent for the past several months.

Jill just wished Slate were there. She wished he'd come over to the West Wing from next door and take some of this ice cream off of their hands. Without him, they wouldn't even have three quarts of peanut butter cookie dough ice cream filling their freezer.

She turned away from Hannah and Chuck as she said something to him in a quiet voice. Jill finished the tree while the scent of cocoa and peanut butter filled the air, and she said, "I'm just going to put these boxes in my truck, then I'll be back to eat all of this."

"I'll help," Chuck said, and with two of them, they got the empty boxes out to her truck in record time. When they went back in after the last load, several more voices had joined the party in the kitchen, and Jill's heart sang when she found Spencer, Nick, Jack, and Ted sitting at the bar.

Emma had come too, and she laid on the couch with her feet in Missy's lap. Connor stood at the sink, his cowboy hat so cute on his little head. Jill loved having people around, and she fed off their energy as more than one of them told her how festive and amazing the West Wing looked.

She collected her bowl of ice cream and took a handful of no-bake cookies to the living room, where she gave one to Emma and one to Missy.

"How are your feet?" she asked. She'd been to the doctor, and she definitely had more swelling than normal. She'd been tasked with drinking an impossible amount of water each day, staying off her feet as much as possible, and wearing compression socks.

Now, though, her daughter was rubbing her feet.

"They're actually better," Emma said. "Missy wanted to ask you something."

"Sure," Jill said, scooping up a bite of ice cream with plenty of cookie dough balls in it. "What's up?"

Missy looked at her mom and then Jill. "My birthday is coming up, and Momma said I could have a party. Our cabin is small, and she's so...I don't want to bother her. Could we have it here in the West Wing?"

"I would literally pay you to have it here," Jill said with a smile. "This place is so quiet now."

"Jill hates the quiet," Emma said.

Jill couldn't argue, so she didn't.

Missy smiled and said, "Thanks." She cleared her throat and tucked her hair behind her ear. She focused on her mother's feet like they were the most fascinating things in the world.

Jill looked at Emma, but she'd closed her eyes. Something was afoot though.

"Would you do our makeup?" Missy asked. "There will only be four of us. Everyone loved my makeup at Halloween, and Yancey suggested we could do makeup at the party."

Jill's surprise pulled her mouth down. "Wow, uh, Emma?"

"The girls are thirteen," she said. "Makeup is a thing at thirteen."

"Sure," Jill said, remembering being that age and wanting to shave her legs and wear mascara so badly. "But you have to do something for me."

Missy raised her eyes to Jill's. "What?"

"My roots are starting to grow out, and I need someone to help me touch them up."

"I can do that," Missy said, her eyes shining. "I would *love* to do that." She grinned at Jill. "The party is on

December eleventh."

"I'll put it on my calendar." Jill smiled back at her and took another bite of her favorite ice cream. She looked around at the large room that hosted the kitchen, dining table, and living room. With everyone here and all the decorations, Jill thought this house was starting to feel more like the ranch she'd first come to years ago.

Laughter, life, and love filled the air, and while she didn't have all of those things in her life at the moment, she still clung to the hope that she would one day.

The music played a popular Christmas tune, and all the cowboys started singing at the top of their lungs.

"Oh, boy," Emma said, but Jill loved it. She loved the energy and the noise. Maybe she didn't think Rudolph the Red-Nosed Reindeer was all that exciting, but she liked that they could have good, simple fun without arguments.

Thanksgiving had been a nightmare for Jill—she and her sister had gotten into a fight. Big surprise. Haven just "couldn't fathom" why anyone with blonde hair would dye theirs black. Mama had come to Jill's defense, and the argument hadn't died until Daddy said Haven wouldn't be able to come back to the house if she couldn't be nice.

Jill was grateful for her parents, and that they finally saw Haven for who she really was. She wasn't happy that Haven blamed her for the arguments or that she felt picked on. Jill had wanted to tell her, *Welcome to the last thirty years of my life*, but she'd said nothing.

She yearned for good, for clean, for simple, and the cowboys singing a Christmas song was exactly that.

Someone came into the living room from the foyer, and Jill turned toward the movement. Her heart froze, right there in her chest. Her eyes widened. She lost the ability to hold things, as first her spoon dropped to the floor, and then her bowl of peanut butter cookie dough ice cream.

Slate Sanders stood there, Axle at his side, and the man was the stuff of Jill's dreams. Black leather jacket. Black cowboy hat. Dark-wash jeans. Tall, broad, and brooding—and looking directly at her despite the chaos around them.

His mouth moved, but she couldn't hear him above the now-obnoxious singing. The song ended, and Slate yelled, "...your hair is black," into the resulting silence.

His voice drew everyone's attention, and a literal uproar happened from the ice-cream-intoxicated men in the kitchen. Ted led the charge toward Slate, and he got swept up in hugs and handshakes that separated him from Jill, who still hadn't moved.

Hannah appeared in front of her with a washcloth. "Go on," she said, looking up. "He's obviously here for you."

"What do I say to him?" Jill asked, suddenly scared and desperate for help.

"Honey," Emma said. She'd sat up at some point, and she leaned toward Jill. "You've already said everything that needs to be said. You just let him talk."

Jill swallowed, her lips sticky from the ice cream. She licked them and nodded. "Okay. I can do that." She got to her feet, realizing she wore a casual pair of cotton pants with wide legs and a T-shirt with a pear on the front of it. No shoes.

She ran her fingers through her hair, mussing it up slightly. Then she searched for Slate. The sea of people in the West Wing parted, leaving a clear path for Jill to get to Slate.

He took the first step, and Jill's heart started beating like a big bass drum.

CHAPTER TWENTY-ONE

S late told himself he'd take as many steps as he needed to in order to have Jill Kyle in his life. He'd step first, he'd step last, he'd step sideways.

He didn't want to talk to her in front of everyone, and there was entirely too much jingle and jolly in the West Wing for his liking. She didn't look away from him, and he sure hoped it was because of the magnetic pull that had existed between them since the day he'd found her throwing rocks at the ocean and cursing the Lord.

He now understood that level of desperation, and he'd previously thought he'd descended as far as a man could go.

Four more steps.

This place was huge.

Three more steps.

Would everyone stop staring?

Two more steps.

He was sweltering hot inside this jacket, with the heat on in the house.

One more step, and they met.

Without speaking, he took her hand in his, a thrill moving through every cell in his body simultaneously. Detouring, he led her down the hall and outside, leaving the chaos and the Christmas décor behind inside the house.

Relief struck him behind the ribs, and he drew in a deep breath of the evening air. The sun went down earlier in late November than he remembered it doing when he'd left Texas, and the words he'd been trying to find for days finally appeared beneath his tongue.

"I should've never left this place," he said. He didn't slow or stumble, not in his feet or his words. "Can you ever forgive me?"

"I don't know," she said, her voice deadly calm and quiet.

Slate's pulse pounced at him, and a stream of negative talk assaulted his mind. He pushed against all of it, because he wanted to be here for this moment.

When he'd walked in and seen her eating that ice cream...the very flavor she'd told him she'd eat if he broke up with her...

His heart ached.

So many thoughts had streamed through his mind from, *wow, this music is loud* to *her hair is black* to *how much ice cream has she eaten since September?*

"But I probably already have," Jill said, linking her arm through his. "Wait, no I haven't. But I probably can. I will."

Slate looked at her out of the corner of his eye, and her grin was just as electric and just as bright as he remembered.

"I'm not going to talk," she said, sobering. "You do all the talking."

Slate could barely think because of her touch. He'd missed that so much. He hadn't even realized how much he needed it in his life until he hadn't had it. Even then, he hadn't known how much he loved her, and how much he needed her, and how much he wanted to hold her and kiss her.

"I'm going to lead with the important stuff," he said. "I guess it's all important." The well-organized thoughts had scrambled again. "Uh, let's see." He stopped walking near a tree in the back yard that hadn't been there when he'd left. The scent of horses rode on the air, and a bark sounded from far away.

He glanced toward the West Wing, where he'd left Axle. He was fine, and Ted had picked him up like a baby the moment he'd released Slate, almost as if he was happier to see the dog than he was his friend.

He looked back at Jill. "I love you."

Her eyes widened and filled with tears. Her chin wobbled, and she pulled in a breath and held everything tight.

"That's an important one," he said. "I'm not going to run when things get hard. That's equally as important. I never should've left this place, that's one hundred percent true. I've been miserable for months." Now that his tongue had untangled, the words were just rolling out of his mouth.

"I can go to Austin by myself. Things are great with my family. I confronted my past and made peace with it. And now, all I need to be truly happy is you." He took her other hand in his. "It's always been you, Jill. Always. You make me laugh, and you make me strong, and you make me better. I like who I am when you're with me, and while I'm not so sure about the black hair, if you like it, I like it."

He leaned toward her, glad when she kept her head down, not overly eager to kiss him. He rested his forehead against hers. "I've made mistakes. I know that. But I'm fixing them one by one. None of it will matter if I can't have you. I love you. I love you so much I can't adequately explain it."

"I understand," Jill whispered. She raised her head and looked into his eyes. "That was a pretty perfect speech. Have you been practicing that?"

"A little," he said. "But there was this bit about Colorado, and Luke, and your pretty eyes, and I didn't say any of that." He smiled at her, the moment between them soft and perfect.

"You didn't tell your friends you were coming."

"I didn't come to see them." He bent his head further and traced the tip of his nose down the side of her face. "I did call Ginger last week, and she burst into tears when I asked if there might be something for me to do around the ranch." He smiled again, just before placing a kiss along Jill's jaw.

The night wasn't particularly warm, and she shivered. He pulled her into his body and wrapped his arms around her. "I didn't stop at my grandparents'. I didn't stop for anything. All I could think about once I got things squared away in Austin, was getting to you."

"Well, you got here."

"Mm." He closed his eyes and took a deep breath, getting the scent of her hair in his nose. "I'll do whatever it takes to get you back and prove to you that I'm not going to run again."

Jill pulled away slightly and looked at him. Her eyes danced with a mischievous smile, and Slate's whole world brightened, though he felt sure she was going to make him work for his forgiveness.

"Whatever it takes?" she asked.

"That's right."

"Even wear a Santa suit and that sexy cowboy hat while you hold children on your lap, smile for pictures, and flirt with a pretty elf?"

Confusion raced through him. "What are you talkin' about?"

"It's a yes or no question, Slate," she said, teasing him. At the same time, a distinct river of seriousness accompanied her tone. "Will you wear a Santa suit and a cowboy hat while you hold children on your lap, smile for pictures—and a real smile too. None of this fake business I've seen you do before—and flirt with a pretty elf...with the most amazing short, black hair?" She ran her hands up his chest, and that caused Slate to shiver. "Yes or no?"

"This is a hard question," he said, though it really wasn't. He wasn't entirely sure what she had up her sleeve, but she'd be there. She wanted him to flirt with her. "Can Axle be in the pictures too?"

"I'm counting on it," she said.

"Then yes."

"Then I forgive you." She rose onto her toes and took his face in both of her hands. "And I love you too." She smiled and added, "Now kiss me, cowboy, before I self-combust with all this body heat you're pumping into me."

Slate chuckled and did what she wanted, because it was exactly what he wanted too. He ran his hands through her dark hair and kissed her like it was the first time. In a lot of ways, it was. He wasn't entirely the same man he'd been on his birthday, and he and Jill were in a brand-new place.

A good place.

An amazing place.

Axle barked, louder this time, but Slate couldn't tear himself away from Jill. She carried magic in her lips, and he wanted to taste every last drop.

Unfortunately, Axle wanted to reunite with Jill too, and he jumped up on the pair of them, giving one final bark.

"Okay, okay," Jill said, laughing. "Hey, buddy. Yes, I missed you so much." She scrubbed him down while he wound himself around her in circles, such joy on his canine face. She giggled at the dog one final time and looked at Slate. "You have a lot of stories to tell."

"Do I?"

"Don't play coy with me, Mister." She slapped at his chest. "This leather jacket, for one." She grabbed onto the lapel with both hands. "What is this about?"

"It's cold in the winter, even in Texas," he said.

"Yeah, I think you bought it because you know I'm a sucker for a cowboy in a leather jacket."

"You may have mentioned that once," Slate said, not really admitting to anything.

"You lived in Colorado?"

"I do not want to talk about Colorado," he said.

"Two sentences," she said.

"Luke and I got a job there, on a construction crew in Vail. It was awful—cold and snowy, with long hours. Days would pass, and I didn't even know it. Luke hated it; I hated it. I made him miserable with how unhappy I was. I don't ever want to go back to Colorado."

"That was at least six sentences." She smiled at him and wrapped both arms around him, making him feel steady and strong and like she needed him to stay upright. "You can go to Austin by yourself?"

"Yes." It had been hard, but he had done it, and he could do it again. "I'd like to take you next time I go."

"I'd like that too," she said. "Your family is doing great?"

"Amazing." He had a lot more to say about that, but it didn't all need to be said right now.

"You...what was it? Confronted your past?"

"Face to face. Me and Jackson MacBride, in my father's barbecue restaurant, if you can believe it."

Jill pulled back and looked at him. "My heart is beating really fast," she admitted.

"Let's walk somewhere," he said. "The stables. I miss Scalloped Potato."

Axle started that way as if he knew where Slate wanted to go, and Slate took Jill's hand as they followed the dog.

"You don't need to worry about Jackson," he said. "I sat down and had a little heart-to-heart with him."

"Who is he?" Jill asked.

Slate hadn't realized how much he hadn't told her. "He's the guy who got me hooked on pain meds," he said. "I've known him for years; we were in college together. He was my drug supplier for years after I graduated and started my job. He's still a dealer in Austin, and he's been sniffing around for information on me."

"Why you?"

"I've always been an easy sale for him," Slate said. "Until now." He took a deep breath. "Now, he's in jail and his underground has been exposed."

"Slate," she said. "Is he going to come here again?"

"No, sweetheart," he said, putting his arm around her. "He's not. He's going to go to jail for a very, very long time." They approached the stables, and Slate saw something he'd never seen before. "What is going on here?"

Bales of straw had been set up strategically to form a

throne of sorts. It was easily big enough for two people, and a series of trellises had been erected on three sides. Dried corn stalks, vines, and poinsettias had been woven throughout the holes in the trellis.

A cowboy hat hung on a hook, with a rope next to it, and a false window next to that. A rough-hewn table sat next to the throne, with an oversized, red mug with the name *Santa* on it.

So many things started connecting inside his head.

"This is where you're going to sit," Jill said, pure glee in her voice. "It's a country Christmas scene. We're going to have families out to the ranch every weekend in December for a Christmas corn maze, holiday baking, and pictures with Santa."

She adjusted the mug slightly and turned to look at him. "I'll get a rug for Axle to lay on."

"You have got to be kidding." The scene dripped with small-town cowboy charm, and so much red and green that Slate wanted to gag.

"It's time to start building some new Christmas memories, my cowboy," she said, leaning into him and wrapping her arms around him again. "With me. On this ranch. Will you *please* be my Cowboy Claus?"

"Are you going to be a sexy elf, or just you know, a regular one?" Slate tore his eyes from the horrible scene and looked at Jill just as she burst out laughing.

He thought it was a pretty serious question, but he sure

did enjoy the sound of her laugh. "I've missed that laugh so much," he said, silencing her by kissing her.

She let him for a minute, and then she pulled away. "It's a *family* event, Slate," she said. "I'm going to be a dreary, regular elf."

"You're responsible for the West Wing screaming Christmas, aren't you?"

"Yes," she said, not even trying to look apologetic about it. "I was angry with you, Slate, for a long time. I decided about a month ago that I wasn't going to celebrate Christmas either. Then I was like, no. No. Yes, I am. I'm going to celebrate it so hard, and that will drive him out of my head."

Slate hated that he'd caused her to be angry, to hurt, to doubt herself. "I'm sorry," he said. "Did it work? Hanging all those ornaments? That got me out of your head?"

"For maybe five minutes," she said. "You're really stubborn, and you didn't want to go."

"I love you."

"We're having a real conversation here," she said, sighing. She stepped away from him, and Slate let her go. "So yes, I went overboard on the decorating. I've been updating the website for the ranch, and writing blogs, and I got a great idea from a comment. We're doing the Howdy Holiday Festival thing, and it's going to be great. Ginger is excited about it. So am I."

"Do we have the budget for all of this?" Slate asked, picking up a harness that probably belonged to a horse but that bore the name tag *Prancer*. "I'm in charge of that now, you know."

"Then you should know that I didn't have the funds to hire a professional Santa. I was going to have to use one of the cowboys on the ranch."

"Who were you going to ask?"

"Ted."

"He'd be so much better than me."

"Slate." Jill stepped in front of him, her eyes hard and sparking, but not with the good kind of energy now. "There is no one better than you. Not for this job. Not for this ranch. And not for me."

She spoke with such conviction that Slate actually believed her.

"I love you," Jill said. "I love you so much I don't know how to adequately explain it. I love you so much that I never could get you to leave me alone inside my heart, and inside my mind. I colored my hair. I went Christmas crazy. I ate so much ice cream, I should be forbidden from ever eating it again. And the chocolate. My mama made every chocolate dessert in her recipe book, Slate, and I ate at least one bite of all of them."

His heart tore and bled, and he let it. He wouldn't run from what he'd done. He wouldn't try to pretend like the pain and hurt he'd caused didn't exist.

"No matter what I did, you were still there, and I *wanted* you there. I didn't really want to forget about you. I didn't want to get over you. I've been praying and hoping you'd come back, and we could do exactly what we're doing right now."

He nodded, though he wasn't sure he really wanted to be having this exact conversation. "Your mama is going to take some sweetening, isn't she?"

"No," Jill said. "If I'm happy and in love, she'll be happy too."

"Your daddy?"

"He's been telling me for months to stay strong and keep the hope alive."

"I don't know if I deserve you," Slate said. "But I'm going to work hard every day to try to be the man you love."

"And I will work hard every day to be the woman worthy of your love."

Slate marveled at her. At her strength. At her insight. At her perfectly charitable heart.

"My sister is going to tear you apart," she said with a smile. "Just so you know. But it's going to be awesome, because that's who Haven is. You'll get to see our family fight, because that's what we do." She stepped into his arms again. "None of that matters. All that matters is you and me."

Slate held her close to his heartbeat, feeling the truthfulness of her words. "You and me," he repeated.

"Well, and this Santa thing," she said. "I love you for saying yes to this."

Slate took in the disgustingly charming set, finding a sleigh propped in the corner he hadn't seen before. His thoughts softened as he realized how much this meant to Jill —and how many more steps he still had to take to truly be the man he wanted to be.

"It is time for me to make new memories for Christmas-time," he mused. "I'll always be your Christmas cowboy, Jill. As long as you want me to be."

"Thank you, Slate," she said, and she kissed him, and Slate started making new memories in that very moment, with the straw-scented air, and the hot cocoa cup, and Santa's cowboy hat hanging on the wall.

Oh, and the woman he loved—and who loved him—in his arms. He couldn't ask for a better Christmas gift than that.

CHAPTER TWENTY-TWO

Jill untucked the long piece of black hair, letting it fall from under her pointy elf hat. Even she could admit that she was tired of dressing up and playing a part, and she normally *loved* doing so.

But it had been four long weekends of work to host the Howdy Holiday Festival at the ranch. Profitable, yes. Ginger had given Jill a bonus of a thousand dollars for coming up with and executing the idea that had brought families to the ranch from all over the Coastal Bend region of Texas.

But tiring at the same time. "Ultra tiring," Jill said as she took in the bags under her eyes. And if she was tired, Slate was probably downright exhausted.

He'd said last night that he could ho-ho-ho for one more afternoon. He'd said the he was ten times happier here, doing this, than he'd been in Vail, and Jill believed him. She'd been pretty miserable without him in her life too.

But he was back now, and he'd moved right back into the bedroom he'd been living in before. No one had taken Luke's room either, and Slate said he hated looking through the bathroom and finding a dark bedroom on the other side.

Jill knew he missed Luke powerfully. She knew the five of them texted constantly, though, and she knew Luke would be in town for a few days over Christmas. Or maybe before Christmas? Maybe after.

She wasn't entirely sure; she only knew he was coming. Right now, Jill didn't even know what day it was, other than the last day she had to wear this elf costume.

Turning away from her reflection, she picked up the basket of candy canes and headed outside. Down the lane and near the stables, the festival was already in full swing. Hannah led the class on holiday sweets, and today, they were making fudge in plastic zipper bags.

Jill watched the kids kneading, smiling as she passed them. Jess had a dozen horses out today, and she was currently giving a demonstration on how they could learn to prance and walk sideways. She'd been dressing them up with red flowers and sprigs of ivy for the festival, and today she'd added white ribbons to their manes.

They'd had over fifty new registrations for horseback riding lessons during the month of December, and Ginger had gushed about that too. Jill loved it when an idea came together, and she loved that she'd been able to do something to help the ranch.

Truth be told, she'd never felt very useful around the

ranch, because did it really matter if the honeybees died off? Probably not. It was one of their more popular after-school programs, and their summer camps usually sold out too.

Awareness of the ranch had risen, and they'd been getting sign-ups for all of their programs as more people came to the ranch, and as Jill continued to strengthen their online presence.

"All right," she said in a loud voice as she approached the line of people waiting to meet Cowboy Claus. "Who's ready for Santa to ride in on his horse?"

The kids cheered and the adults wore polite smiles. A few of them clapped, and Jill surveyed the crowd. "Around these parts, we don't just have candy canes." She lifted one of the treats out of the basket. "We have peppermint horse-shoes." She started handing them out, telling the kids that the horses here at Hope Eternal never went anywhere without the proper footwear.

"And neither does Cowboy Claus," she said. "Let's see if we can get him to show up. I know he doesn't like to be late." She turned toward the stable and added, "You have to yell, Giddy up, Cowboy Claus! as loud as you can. If he hears us, he'll come." She faced the children again. "Are you ready?"

One little girl bounced on her feet, her face bright. Jill had seen children like her go from excited to terrified the moment Cowboy Claus appeared, and she hoped there would be no criers today. There had been every other day of the festival, but Slate had handled them all like a champ.

"Here we go," Jill said. "On three. One...two...three!

Giddy up, Cowboy Claus!" she yelled with the kids. They kept at it, calling for him a couple of times before Slate came flying from behind the stable, decked out in the full, furry red Santa suit. He held the reins in one hand while his other pressed his snowy white cowboy hat to his head.

"Yeehaw-haw-haw!" he yelled instead of *ho ho ho!*

The kids and their parents cheered and clapped, and the line grew as more people joined it from the other activities.

"Whoa, there, Prancer," Slate said to Scalloped Potato, and she slowed to a stop. He jumped from her back like he was made of springs, and he swaggered toward the children with a bright smile on his face. "Well, howdy partners. Howdy, little girl. Howdy, my elf." He slipped his arm around her and gave her a quick squeeze.

Jill giggled and moved to the front of the line. She handed out the coded cards that parents could use to buy pictures for the next three days. Each child got a couple of minutes with Slate to tell him all they wanted for Christmas. Jill got a picture. Repeat, repeat, repeat.

She couldn't have said how many times she'd heard Slate say "Yeehaw-haw-haw!" He said it with almost every child, and as the line moved and he pulled little boys and little girls onto his lap, Jill fell more in love with him.

Finally, the event ended—and not a moment too soon, as she only had two peppermint horseshoes left in her basket.

"Well, that's a wrap," she said, starting to take down the tripod.

"Do you have time for one more?"

She looked over at the familiar voice and found Luke standing there, decked out in a red and white vest, jeans, and his cowboy hat.

"Luke," she said, rushing toward him. "It's so good to see you."

He chuckled as he hugged her. "Good to see you too, Jill." He stepped back and ran his hand down his clean-shaven face. "I was right about him, wasn't I?"

"Took forever though," Jill said, giving him a playful swat on the upper arm. "Why no beard?"

"You don't like it?"

"You look twelve," she said, laughing afterward.

Luke rolled his eyes and said, "I need a minute with Santa." He grinned as he walked toward Slate, and he leaned against the bale of straw they used for a table while Slate continued to lounge in the straw throne.

Jill finished taking down her equipment and took it into the stable. Jess came around the corner as Jill closed the closet, and she said, "Thank you, Jess. This was so amazing, and I couldn't have done any of it without you."

"It was fun," Jess said. "I'm just so tired lately. I haven't been sleeping well." She scraped her bangs off her forehead. "Dallas is leaving the kids here with Nate and Ginger tonight, so hopefully, I can sleep as late as I want."

Jill grew concerned as she took in Jess's drawn face. She hadn't noticed her being overly tired during the demo. "Are you okay?"

"Yeah," Jess said. "I think I'm fighting a bug or something." She gave Jill a smile and a hug. "Merry Christmas. I'll see you at our place for lunch, right?"

"Yes," she said. "Slate and I will be there."

Jess nodded and left the stable. Jill watched her go, glad Jess and Dallas were hosting a Christmas Day luncheon at their house. It would be nice to get off the ranch, and it would be a new holiday memory—and a possible new tradition—for both her and Slate.

They were then going to her parents' for the afternoon, where her mother would serve a "light dinner." Jill knew that meant a regular dinner, with pie afterward, and she'd warned Slate accordingly. After that, they were going to his grandparents' to say hello and spend an hour with them on Christmas too.

Jill suddenly wanted a day where she could sleep as late as she wanted too.

Instead, she turned and went back outside. Hannah had finished her fudge-making class long ago, and Spencer and Nick were currently loading the tables onto a trailer to put away. "Thank you," she called to them.

"Anytime," Spencer said, and Jill waved to them. Everything was cleaned up except the picture area, and she and Slate would do it tomorrow. Or the next day. Or next year. She actually wanted to keep it mostly intact, so they didn't have to reassemble everything every year. At the same time, she wanted the Howdy Holiday Festival to be different every year, and that meant they certainly couldn't use the same set they had this year. The straw could rot anyway.

Someone had taken Scalloped Potato back to her stall long ago, and Jill went over to the throne, where Slate still sat. She climbed into the seat with him and draped her legs over his. "Thank you, Slate," she said.

"Sure thing, sweetheart." He smiled at her and closed his eyes. "It was a lot of work, though. We should start looking for a new Cowboy Claus right now so I don't have to do it next year."

"You're so good at the *yeehaw-haw-haw!* though."

They laughed together, and Slate lifted his arm so Jill could curl into his side. "I love you," Jill said. "Those were some pretty great new memories made, right?"

"Yeah," he said, sighing. "I hope those kids get all the things they want for Christmas."

"No one gets everything they want for Christmas," she said.

"I have." He tracked his fingers up her arm and back down.

"Is that right? And what does Cowboy Claus want for Christmas?"

"Hm," he said. "I think he just has one thing on his list."

"Has he been naughty or nice?"

"Cowboy Claus is nothing but nice," Slate said, sliding to the edge of the straw seat. "Come on. I'll show you what I want." He extended his hand toward her, and she put hers in his.

"Is it far? Because I'm tired and can barely walk in these shoes."

"It's not far," he said. "It's right over here." He took the few steps to the rustic cabinet in the corner of the fake country room where Cowboy Claus lived. He opened the drawer, and Jill had just started to peer around his back to see what he held when he turned and dropped to one knee.

"Jill Kyle," he said, and Jill squealed. She clapped one hand over her mouth, and her eyes could not get wider. She could not drink in Slate down on that one knee, holding that dark blue jewelry box, and wearing a ridiculous cowboy Santa suit any faster.

She wanted to freeze time and live in this moment forever.

He grinned at her. "I'm in love with you. I want Christmastime to be a source of joy and happiness for us, and I couldn't think of anything better to do to make that happen than to ask you to be my wife."

He opened the box and a blindingly white diamond sat there, nestled in dark, silky fabric.

Jill's eyes filled with tears as she looked from the ring to her forever love. "Yes," she said.

"I haven't asked yet," he said.

"You did too," she argued.

"No, I said I couldn't think of anything better than to ask you. I haven't actually asked yet." He shook his head, his smile still in place, though. "You're always jumping the gun."

"Sorry," she said, giddiness gathering up inside her. She bounced on the balls of her feet. "Go on, then. Ask me."

He just looked at her, that perma-grin so fake.

"I'm going to say no this time," she said, and he burst out laughing.

When he sobered, he said, "Jill Kyle, will you marry me?"

"Yes," she said, practically shooting the word out of her mouth. "Yes, yes, I'll marry you!" She squealed again and launched herself at Slate, who barely managed to save the ring and catch her at the same time.

She placed a sloppy kiss to his mouth, both of them laughing. Well, Jill was half-laughing and half-crying, but they were both because of something amazing. She found herself kneeling with him as he slid the ring on the appropriate finger, and this time, when their mouths met, it was for a proper Christmas engagement kiss.

He pulled away too soon for her liking, and he helped her to her feet. He turned toward where she normally stood, and asked, "Did you get it?"

"All of it," Luke said, striding forward and handing Slate his phone. "It's pretty epic."

Slate took his phone and held it out in front of both of them, swiping through the pictures Luke had taken. He stalled on one, where he was down on that one knee, the ring box held out in front of him, his face turned up toward her, lit with hope and love.

She had her hands clasped against her breast, her face tilted down toward his, lit with anticipation and joy.

"This one," he said.

"It's perfect," she said. "Though I hate this costume. I'm burning it, and I'm finding one that's not made of felt for next year." She looked up at him. "You'll have to come up with the money in the budget."

"Oh, I'm going to start putting a few dollars away every month for air conditioning for this event," he said. "You can count on that."

She grinned at him, and he grinned at her, and he said, "I was a pretty good Christmas cowboy, wasn't I?"

"The best," Jill agreed. "Will you send me that picture so I can send it to my mama?"

"Absolutely." He did, but Jill didn't take out her phone when it buzzed in her pocket. Instead, she reached up and took off Slate's cowboy hat. She ran her fingers down the side of his face, the moment turning serious and charged in that single movement.

"I love you, cowboy," she said. "Winter, spring, summer, fall, Christmas. I can't wait to be yours for all of them."

"I love you too, Jill." When he spoke her name like that, coated with such care and such love, Jill's whole heart melted. "You're all I need for Christmas, and for forever."

He kissed her, and Jill saw a future of love, hope, and happiness with this tender-hearted cowboy.

Read on for a sneak peek at what's happening with Luke

and Hannah in the next book in the Hope Eternal Ranch series, WISHFUL COWBOY.

WISHFUL COWBOY, CHAPTER ONE

Luke Holt lay in the bed where he'd slept for a few months—the last few months of his prison sentence. Axle lay on his feet, the warmth from the dog's body seeping into Luke and making him sweat. He hadn't gone to bed with the pooch, but the dog wandered back and forth between the two bedrooms connected by the Jack-and-Jill bathroom.

He listened for the sound of Slate's breathing, but he couldn't hear it. It was still odd, even nine months later, to not be in the same room with over a dozen other men and all the noises they made in their sleep.

Luke blew a fan at night, mostly to combat his body's natural furnace tendencies. But also to mask any sounds that might wake him.

He'd slept better here at Hope Eternal Ranch than he had anywhere else since leaving. He frowned, not sure what that meant. He'd never thought he'd stay here the way everyone else had. The problem was, there wasn't much for him out in the world either.

"At least there's no snow in Vegas," he muttered as he rolled over. Axle got up and moved, padding up the length of Luke's body, turning, and leaning right against his back. Luke didn't complain, because it sure was nice to have another living, breathing thing so close to him.

The dark gray light filtering into the room told him it wasn't quite dawn yet. He wasn't getting up yet—and he wouldn't get up when the sun did. He didn't work here anymore, and as today was his last full day in Texas, he and the rest of the boys from River Bay were going fishing.

Fishing.

Such a mundane thing to do. But Nate had requested it as his Christmas gift, and no one in the group could deny Nathaniel Mulbury. Least of all Luke.

With his eyes closed, he thought of the first time he'd met Nate. His first night in prison. He'd been a fighter before, and it was his natural instinct to have conversations with his fists instead of his words. He didn't have to talk to his opponents. He didn't have to care how they felt. All he'd cared about was winning.

He'd done a lot of that, and he believed his prison sentence to be an injustice to him. He still felt that way, and if he dwelt on it for too long, his anger caused his fingers to clench and his jaw to tighten. Then all Luke wanted to do was start swinging.

He deliberately breathed in and pushed the air out. *Can't change the past,* he told himself. *Accept what's happened, and move on.*

He was getting much better at actually doing what he thought. Since seeing Slate overcome the demons in his past, Luke figured it was time for him to practice what he'd been preaching.

Yes, he didn't think he was guilty of any crime. But what he thought didn't matter.

Nate had taught him that, on that very first night in prison. Luke had picked a fight, because he always felt better when the pent-up energy inside of him flowed out through a jab or an uppercut. Nate had pulled him off a guy half his size and barked right in his face.

"That's not what we do here, champ. Get control of yourself."

Luke had gone right after Nate too, shoving him back and taking a swing at that pretty face, but Nate was a bigger man, and had been in prison longer, *and* he had three guys right there willing to take blows for him.

Ted, Dallas, and Slate.

Luke had faced down all four of them, wondering how they'd formed such a strong brotherhood in prison. How they'd formed a bond at all. He wasn't great at that, but he'd been willing to try.

Luke had been the last in the group, and he still wasn't sure how great he fit. The crew had been there for Family

Day for Dallas when his wife had filed for divorce and dropped her kids off at her sister's.

They'd come to visit Luke and Slate when they were the last two left. They'd come and picked them up on their release day.

Ginger had petitioned to have Luke in the re-entry program. He felt a debt of gratitude for her he hadn't for another person other than his friends in prison.

So maybe you should stay here. He pushed the thought away. His family lived in Las Vegas now, and he had enjoyed being closer to them. They'd moved while he was in River Bay, and his Family Days had consisted of Nate's brother and Dallas's wife. Ted never did have much family come to the facility, and neither did Slate.

They both seemed to be thriving now, though. Heck, Nate and Ted had fallen in love by the nine-month mark of their releases, and Luke felt like it was just one more way he was failing.

He tried so hard. Tried and failed, almost all the time.

His mind cleared, and he managed to go back to sleep. He woke when a woman said, "Go on, Axle, you naughty thing. You're not supposed to be in here."

He knew the voice, but his eyes were sluggish to open to see her face. In the next moment, the blanket got torn from his body, and the fan he used blasted cold air across his bare torso.

That got his eyes to snap right open. He grunted too, and that was when Hannah Otto said, "Oh, I'm so sorry."

Luke sat halfway up, his heart pounding in the back of his throat. "Hey," he said.

"I didn't know anyone was in here," she said. "And Slate said he needed a blanket, and..." She trailed off as her eyes moved from his face down his body.

Luke knew he had a lot of muscles. He worked purposely to get them and keep them. He'd loved boxing, and at least half of that was because of the physical conditioning it required.

He liked to run, and he like to lift weights. With all the muscle he had, it was no wonder he was like a walking furnace—or that he only slept in a pair of thin gym shorts.

Hannah stared at him, her mouth hanging open, and the moment turned awkward. Luke reached for the blanket she still held in her hands, and it came loose easily. He covered himself up as she blinked her way back to the land of the living.

He didn't know what to say or do. He'd entertained a pretty massive crush on the woman standing in front of him while he'd lived here at Hope Eternal Ranch.

But Hannah had been dating Bill Buckingham at the time, and Bill was one of Luke's roommates in the Annex. When they'd broken up, Luke had started to form a plan with Jill to ask Hannah to dinner, but in the end, he hadn't.

In the end, he'd gotten a job with a construction crew and knew he wouldn't be staying in town. He didn't think it fair to start a relationship with Hannah that he couldn't finish, and he'd never asked.

He met her eyes and found her face red and getting redder fast. Without a word, she spun and left the bedroom, the slam of the door behind her making him cringe.

He sighed and looked up to the ceiling. "Really?" He didn't have any other words for the Lord. Out of all the people who could've come in and disturbed his sleep, it had to be Hannah?

She was dating someone else now, and Luke wasn't surprised. She was easily the most beautiful woman he'd ever met in his life, and he was honestly surprised she hadn't been taken a long time ago.

He wasn't as surprised that he was still single. He'd never really wanted a girlfriend growing up, because his older brother had had one, and she was so much *work*. Luke had enjoyed wrestling in high school, and then he'd gotten into boxing immediately afterward.

He hadn't gone to college, and he'd never wanted to. He liked working with his hands, and he'd thought construction would be a good career for him. The work was hard, and he had to get up early, but he didn't mind either of those things.

His father was a part-owner in a real estate development firm, and Luke had been working for him since Thanksgiving.

Someone knocked on the door, and Luke said, "Just a sec." He jumped up from the bed, left the blanket behind, and pulled a T-shirt over his head before opening the door.

Slate stood there, looking over his shoulder as he said something to Nick and Connor down the hall. When he turned back to Luke, he said, "I'm an idiot." He stepped past Luke into the bedroom and started pacing.

"Why?" Luke asked. "What happened?" Slate felt like the little brother Luke had never had, though he was technically older than Luke. He closed the door and watched his friend go back and forth.

He'd done this in prison too, when he needed a couple of seconds to work out his thoughts. It was amazing to Luke how much of a person was ingrained in who they were, and also how much a person could change.

"I forgot Jill and I were going to her parents for brunch in the morning."

Luke frowned, the dots not lining up. "Okay."

"I can't drive you to the airport."

"Oh." Luke smiled and ran his hands through his hair. "It's fine. I'm sure one of the other boys can."

"They can't." Slate stopped pacing and faced him. "When Jill reminded me last night, I asked everyone. Ted and Emma are going to San Antonio to see Missy's other mom. Dallas and Jess are leaving for Montana tonight. Ginger has a horse she's taking through a birth, and she wants Nate there, because she's getting bigger, and she's worried she'll need to take a break, and someone has to be there with the horse..."

Slate hung his head as Luke's mind spun. Everyone had such busy lives...except for him.

"There are tons of cowboys here," Luke said. "I'll find someone to take me."

"You don't need to do that," Slate said. "I found someone."

When he wouldn't say who, the unrest in Luke's soul stirred. "It's not Bill, is it?"

"No." Slate scoffed. "Give me some credit."

"Why aren't you saying who it is?" Luke asked, squinting at Slate. "There's no credit, unless you somehow got me a ride on a spaceship or something so the drive will only take five seconds." Luke hated driving in the car. He felt like it was such a waste of time.

"You like this person," he said.

"Is this a guessing game?" Luke's patience was already thin, and he hadn't even showered yet. "Just spit his name out, Slate."

"It's not a him," Slate said. "It's a her. It's Hannah."

Luke opened his mouth to respond and only a guttural squeak came out.

"She seemed really happy and excited to do it," Slate said in a rush.

"That's not happening," Luke growled, the words coming out coated with gruffness and maybe a little distaste. "I can get my own ride to the airport." Heck, he'd call a cab before he rode for an hour with Hannah Otto. The woman had just fled his room without a word; riding in the car together for even five minutes would be akin to torture—for both of them.

No way. Wasn't happening.

WISHFUL COWBOY, CHAPTER TWO

Hannah Otto pressed her palms into her hips as she slid her hands over them. These jeans were amazing, delivering everything they'd promised they would from the ad she'd tapped on. They had some sort of magic material in the waist and hips, and they'd slimmed her by at least five pounds. Probably ten.

The flowery shirt she'd paired with them actually lay mostly flat against her stomach, and she stepped into a fashionable pair of cowgirl boots she'd never wear around the ranch. She was a part-time cowgirl at best, and she was truly happiest curled into the couch with a bowl of caramel popcorn and the largest diet cola someone could bring her.

She loved horses and dogs, goats and chickens. She didn't mind her daily chores of making sure the small animals on the ranch got fed. She even knew how to mend fences, as the goats at Hope Eternal seemed to have a special knack for breaking things. Every morning was an adventure as she walked out to the paddock as the first rays of sun warmed the path beneath her feet.

Hannah had learned to like getting up early, just like she'd learned to like her barrel-sized and shaped midsection and her impossibly thick hair. In high school, she'd shaved the bottom half of her head—everything in the back below her ears—in an attempt to have the same amount of hair as other girls her age.

"All right," she said with a sigh. She turned and picked up the keys to her car, which she'd only gotten a few days ago. She'd only driven it back to the ranch, and she realized as she went into the kitchen that she should've gone out yesterday to practice.

Her nerves needled her, but she managed to pour herself a large amount of coffee into her thermos, add sugar, and a healthy splash of cream. She reached for her purse, which held all of the essentials, and headed outside.

She'd expected to be early, because she was always early. Always ready before everyone else. And yet, she seemed to have fallen behind all of her friends. She put away her jealousy, because it could act like a poison, spreading through her whole system before she even had time to breathe. The antidote worked in a far slower way, and Hannah hated how off-kilter her envy could make her feel.

"Ready?" Luke asked, and Hannah flinched away from him, dropping her keys in the process.

"Oh." Her humiliation had no end, as she was constantly making a fool of herself in front of the man. Things between them had been much easier before Jill had told her Luke was going to ask her out. She'd gone out to the cabin construction site several times and had intelligent—or at least cohesive—conversations with him.

Since her break-up with Bill, though, everything between her and Luke had shifted. He never had asked, and then he'd left the ranch.

"Here you go." Luke had bent and retrieved her keys while Hannah stood there mute. She'd done the same thing yesterday, but at least she'd had a good reason then. The man had muscles everywhere. Muscles on top of muscles, and while she'd never seen him work outside without a shirt on, he obviously went shirtless at some point, because his skin had been golden and beautiful.

The familiar heat that had assaulted her yesterday made a reappearance, and she was grateful she'd thought to double-down on the deodorant.

"Thanks," she said, taking the keys. "Let's see... unlock..." She found the right button the key fob and pressed it. The car made a satisfying clicking noise, and Hannah beamed a Luke like she'd done an amazing thing by unlocking the car.

"Can you pop the trunk?" he asked. "I just have the one bag."

"Sure." Hannah got that job done too, and Luke lifted his bag into the trunk as if it were empty. He met her gaze as he rounded the trunk to the passenger side, and Hannah opened her door to get behind the wheel.

The new car smell filled her nose, and she managed to get the engine started. "Okay." She flexed her fingers on the steering wheel and looked at all the controls. "This is a brand new car for me. I literally got it a few days ago."

"It's nice," Luke said, sliding his seat back to accommodate his longer legs. "Why did you need a new car?"

"Oh, uh." She laughed lightly and wished she'd pulled her hair up for this drive. An hour trapped in the car with this man. What in the world were they going to talk about? "I had a little mishap a week or so before Christmas, and my old car got filled with river water."

"Filled with river water?" Luke chuckled, and Hannah dared to look at him. Their eyes met, and the ice broke into tiny shards. She laughed with him. "That doesn't sound like a little mishap, Hannah."

He drawled her name out like a true Texan, and this time, the warmth filling her body was comfortable and wanted.

"I sense a good story," he said, buckling his seat belt. "You can tell me on the way." He was so calm, and Hannah wondered how he did that. He probably didn't have feelings for her anymore. That was how.

Too bad hers hadn't disappeared, despite her relationship with Chuck Knight. They'd only been seeing each other for a month, but he'd kissed her on the second date, and she could admit that she liked Chuck a whole lot.

They had a decent level of electricity between them, but nothing like the spitting, crackling lightning she felt when Luke got within ten feet of her.

"I want a good story from you too," she said, putting the car in reverse.

"Oh, I can't promise that," he said with a grin.

"You've been gone for four months," she said. "Surely you've had at least one interesting thing happen in that time." She eased past the cars and trucks parked in the gravel lot and turned around to leave the ranch and go over the bridge covering the river.

She turned toward town and reached for her coffee. "I'm assuming you want me to go first."

"Hmm?" Luke looked up from his phone, clearly distracted. "I hate to say this, but my flight just got delayed."

"Oh." Hannah eased up on the accelerator. "Should we go back? How much of a delay?"

"About ninety minutes," he said. "I was thinking we should go to breakfast." He looked at her, hope in those dark eyes.

"Breakfast?" Hannah squeaked.

"Yeah," he said with a playful smile. "Did you eat already?" He let his eyes drift down her body, though she was sitting, and she could tell he already knew the answer to his question. Of course she hadn't eaten that morning. It was barely light, and she'd showered, curled her hair, put on makeup, and the cutest clothes she owned...for an hour-long drive to an airport.

"I could eat," she said.

"Great," he said. "There's that pancake place that everyone loves."

"You sound like *you* don't love it." She looked at him out of the corner of her eyes and caught a half-shrug. "I'm going to take that as a no," she said. "Okay, I know a place we can go."

"You do?"

"Sure," she said. "I grew up out in the country here. We had to drive forty-five minutes to get to Sweet Water Falls just to get groceries. Well, we did have a tiny country store, but they sold more supplies than groceries. We could get bread and milk and the very essentials there."

"Did you like it?" Luke asked. "Living out in the middle of nowhere?"

"I didn't hate it," Hannah said. "Not sure I liked it either. It's nice only driving a few minutes to town. Our whole family would go one Saturday a month, and the trip took all day long." She sighed as if she'd actually run a marathon not just gone shopping for apples and shoes.

"I grew up in Beeville," he said. "We lived right in town, and I could walk across the street to a store that had everything we could want."

"Stop bragging," she teased, and he laughed. Hannah relaxed even further, and she made the turns that would take them to Madam Croque. She arrived in the parking lot, noting that it wasn't very busy this morning. She loved the old, brick building, all of the vines on the pillars, and the vibrant flowers in the springtime. Now, in the winter, the landscape still held a certain beauty in the form of tall, brown grasses that grew straight up in bundles.

"This place has real food, right?" Luke asked, peering out the windshield.

"I'm offended," Hannah said, putting the car in park. She reached for her purse. "You're going to love this place."

"I'm kind of a diner type of guy," he said. "This looks...fussy."

"I know good food," she said. "And you are not a diner type of guy. You like good food, right?"

"Yeah," he said slowly.

"Put your cowboy hat on then, Luke. You're going to be blown away." She got out of the car, hoping Jared was cooking this morning. He had a way with eggs that no one else did, and Hannah enjoyed his cooking and that he took a few minutes to come out and see how his patrons liked the food.

She reached the door first, but Luke jumped in front of her. "I got it," he said, smiling at her.

"Thank you." She smiled at him, admiring those broad shoulders in that burnt orange shirt. It had a collar and a couple of buttons down the chest, with thick fabric that still seemed to stick to the ripples in his muscles.

He wore jeans and work boots, with a belt and a buckle that indicated his Texan heritage. With the cowboy hat, he almost looked like he belonged at Hope Eternal. The boots gave him away, though Hannah had seen him ride a horse and he certainly knew how.

Inside, Lana said, "Hannah, how are you?" as she grinned and picked up two menus. "Two?" She didn't bat an eyelash as Luke came to her side. "This way."

"You know her?" Luke asked.

"I may or may not eat here a lot," Hannah said. She loved the quaint booths, each one decorated with something unique to Texas. Her favorite one bore a table with pressed bluebonnets under a thick sheet of glass.

"I had no idea you were fussy, Miss Hannah," Luke said, his mouth practically touching her ear.

She shivered and giggled, instantly hating how girlish it made her sound. She sucked in the laugh and followed Lana through the restaurant to the Marble Falls booth. This table had maps and trail guides beneath the glass, and Hannah peered at them.

"Have you been out to the Hill Country?" she asked Luke.

"Couple of times," he said, sliding onto the bench across from her. "Look, I should be honest with you."

Emma picked up her menu but kept her eyes on him. "Okay."

"I'm from Beeville, right?"

"Yes," she said. "You said that."

"My mother is a Bee," he said. "She, uh, owns ninety percent of the town, and well, a couple of the bigger resorts out in Hill Country too."

Hannah didn't know why this made him uncomfortable. "Sounds like a lot of work," she said.

Luke blinked at her and started laughing again, and Hannah didn't know what she was doing. This felt like a date, and he wasn't her boyfriend. At the same time, she didn't want to say goodbye to him in another couple of hours.

"It was a lot of work," he said. "My uncle manages most of it now that my family's moved to Las Vegas."

"She must be a black sheep, your mother. Land-owning Texans don't usually up and leave."

"My father wanted to try real estate development, and Vegas was in a huge boom," he said. "That's what I'm doing there now. Working for him." He reached for his water glass, his eyes flitting all over the place before he finally looked at her again.

She got the feeling talk of his job made him uncomfortable. Perhaps it was the conversation about his family. No matter what, it was something.

"Hannah," a man said, and she looked up at Jared. They laughed, and Hannah launched herself out of the booth to hug him. "How are you? I haven't seen you in at least a week."

"Oh, come on." Hannah stepped back and tucked her hair. "It's been at least nine days. Maybe only eight."

Jared grinned at her. "Whatever you've been doing is working." He whistled as he looked down to her toes and back to her face. "You look amazing."

"Thank you." Hannah cocked one hip and put her hand on it. "Now, we want those special crispy potato nachos that aren't on the menu..." She raised her eyebrows, and Jared laughed.

"You got it, Hannah. What else can I get you guys?" He glanced at Luke, and Hannah did too. He wore an expression of wonder, and the buzz in Hannah's veins made her feel beautiful and charming.

"I want the peach sunrise," she said. "And the spinach and bacon soufflé, with the grapefruit segments."

"Makin' me work this morning," Jared said, grinning. "For you, sir?"

Luke looked like he'd been asked an impossible question. He hadn't picked up the menu, and Hannah just watched him. She was just about to say maybe he needed another minute when he said, "Do you have anything like a western omelet?"

Jared flicked his eyes to Hannah for the briefest of moments. She kept her smile hitched in place. "I have a western omelet breakfast roll," he said. "It comes with a toast cup or fresh fruit."

"I have no idea what a toast cup is," Luke said. "Or a breakfast roll, but it sounds great."

"Comin' up," Jared said, and he walked away.

"He's the chef-owner," Hannah said once he'd gone.

"And you know him personally."

"Yes," Hannah said, smiling at him. She reached for her water glass too, and hid halfway behind it as she added, "I actually dated him for a while." She took a drink immediately afterward, watching Luke.

He looked steadily back at her, and he finally folded his arms and rested them on the table in front of him. "Hannah, if I ever came back to Texas for good, would you...I don't know. Would you consider going out with me?"

Hannah's smile felt like it was made from pure gold. "We're out right now."

"Are we?"

"Aren't we?"

"I thought you were dating someone," he said, leaning back in the booth. He shook his head. "Nah, this can't be a date, because you're not a cheater, and I would never go out with someone who was dating someone else." His eyes sparked with something bright and hot and dangerous.

Hannah swallowed and nodded. "Of course. You're right. I'm seeing Chuck."

"This is just breakfast on the way to the airport with a friend, because his flight got delayed."

Hannah leaned into the table now. "Sounds like a great way to start the day. Now, about these luxury resorts in the Hill Country...can you get, I don't know, discount rooms or passes for your friends?"

A COUPLE OF HOURS LATER, HANNAH PULLED UP TO the curb at the Corpus Christi airport, her face actually aching from how much she'd smiled this morning. Not only that, but her throat was dry and scratchy from all the talking.

"Here we go," Luke said before he got out of the car. She jumped out after him and reached back into the car to open the trunk. He lifted his suitcase out and put it on the sidewalk. He repositioned his cowboy hat and cleared his throat.

Hannah could only watch him war with himself, but she did want to know what he was debating. She was just about to ask when he faced her. With that sexy beard and such a perfectly symmetrical face, he was the definition of handsome.

"Can I tell you a secret?" he asked.

"Yes."

"You can't tell anyone. Not Slate, and definitely not Jill, because she'll tell Slate."

"Okay."

"Not Emma or Ginger or Jess either. No one." He wore a stern expression, and yet Hannah wasn't afraid of him in the slightest. She wanted to know all the intricate sides of Luke Holt, and she really wished he didn't have to go.

"I will not tell a soul," she promised.

Luke drew in a deep breath and blew it out. He looked back toward the doors to the airport and back at her. "I don't really like Las Vegas. I don't like my job there."

"Oh," Hannah said. Whatever she'd been expecting him to say, it wasn't that. "I'm sorry, Luke. Can you do...something about that?"

"I should probably look into it." He reached down to extend the handle on his bag. "Anyway, thank you, Hannah. For the ride and for breakfast." He grinned at her, and Hannah thought he could probably light the whole state of Texas with the brightness of it. He easily drew her into his arms, and she closed her eyes as pure bliss flowed through her.

He smelled like cool water and mint and bacon and pine, and Hannah wanted to bottle him up and take him home with her. Her heart pulsed inside a too-small cage as she thought about him leaving—and she remembered Chuck.

"Anytime," she said, her voice choked and far too low. She stepped back, and Luke adjusted his hat again. He nodded at her once, stepped onto the sidewalk, and headed for the doors.

Hannah stood next to the taillight and watched him go, noting that he never once looked back. When he disappeared, she got behind the wheel of her car and sighed. She had another hour of driving in front of her, and a date with Chuck on the horizon.

Her stomach squeezed, and she knew why.

She didn't want to go out with Chuck now that she knew what she could have with Luke. She knew there was a difference between the two men, and how she felt when she was with each of them.

For the first half-hour, she debated with herself whether she could break-up with Chuck over the phone. They'd only been seeing each other since Thanksgiving, and tomorrow was New Year's Day.

"You can't break-up with him on New Year's Eve," she said, realizing what their date was tonight. But how could she kiss him at the stroke of midnight, knowing she wanted him to be someone else?

"But that someone else doesn't even live here," she said. "You don't even know when you're going to see him again." Could she really ruin what was a good, fun relationship with Chuck for what could be nothing with Luke?

"Nothing," she told herself. Right now, she had nothing with Luke, and something with Chuck. She didn't want to be alone, and she could build off of something. She couldn't work with nothing, and she didn't call Chuck on the way back to the ranch. She could kiss him—she'd enjoyed kissing him previously—that night and continue to get to know him.

Something is better than nothing, she repeated, hoping it wouldn't become a mantra for why she was staying with Chuck.

A reason for not admitting her feelings for Luke.

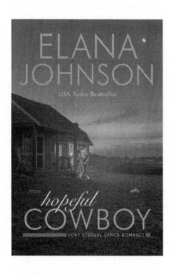

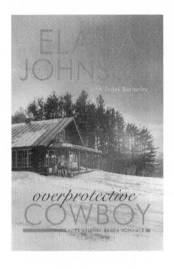

Overprotective Cowboy, Book 2: Can Ted and Emma face their pasts so they can truly be ready to step into the future together? Or will everything between them fall apart once the truth comes out?

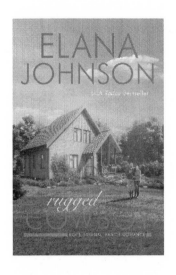

Rugged Cowboy, Book 3:
He's a cowboy mechanic with two kids and an ex-wife on the run. She connects better to horses than humans. Can Dallas and Jess find their way to each other at Hope Eternal Ranch?

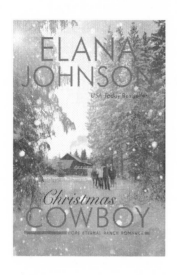

Christmas Cowboy, Book 4: He needs to start a new story for his life. She's dealing with a lot of family issues. This Christmas, can Slate and Jill find solace in each other at Hope Eternal Ranch?

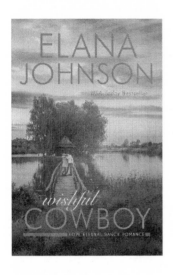

Wishful Cowboy, Book 5:
He needs somewhere to belong. She has a heart as wide as the Texas sky. Can Luke and Hannah find their one true love in each other?

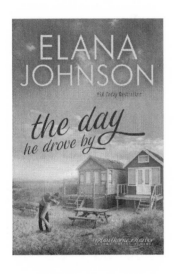

The Day He Drove By (Hawthorne Harbor Second Chance Romance, Book 1): A widowed florist, her ten-year-old daughter, and the paramedic who delivered the girl a decade earlier...

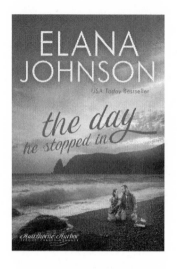

The Day He Stopped In (Hawthorne Harbor Second Chance Romance, Book 2): Janey Germaine is tired of entertaining tourists in Olympic National Park all day and trying to keep her twelve-year-old son occupied at night. When longtime friend and the Chief of Police, Adam Herrin, offers to take the boy on a ride-along one fall evening, Janey starts to see him in a different light. Do they have the courage to take their relationship out of the friend zone?

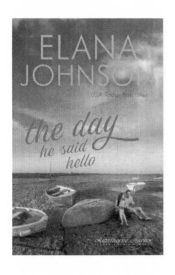

The Day He Said Hello (Hawthorne Harbor Second Chance Romance, Book 3): Bennett Patterson is content with his boring fire-fighting job and his big great dane...until he comes face-toface with his high school girlfriend, Jennie Zimmerman, who swore she'd never return to Hawthorne Harbor. Can they rekindle their old flame? Or will their opposite personalities keep them apart?

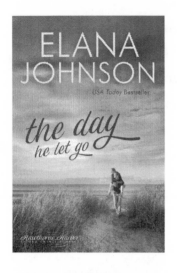

The Day He Let Go (Hawthorne Harbor Second Chance Romance, Book 4): Trent Baker is ready for another relationship, and he's hopeful he can find someone who wants him and to be a mother to his son. Lauren Michaels runs her own general contract company, and she's never thought she has a maternal bone in her body. But when she gets a second chance with the handsome K9 cop who blew her off when she first came to town, she can't say no... Can Trent and Lauren make their differences into strengths and build a family?

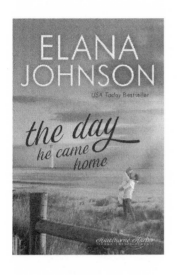

The Day He Came Home (Hawthorne Harbor Second Chance Romance, Book 5): A wounded Marine returns to Hawthorne Harbor years after the woman he was married to for exactly one week before she got an annulment...and then a baby nine months later. Can Hunter and Alice make a family out of past heartache?

The Day He Asked Again (Hawthorne Harbor Second Chance Romance, Book 6): A Coast Guard captain would rather spend his time on the sea...unless he's with the woman he's been crushing on for months. Can Brooklynn and Dave make their second chance stick?

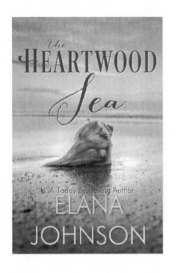

The Heartwood Sea (Book 1): She owns The Heartwood Inn. He needs the land the inn sits on to impress his boss. Neither one of them will give an inch. But will they give each other their hearts?

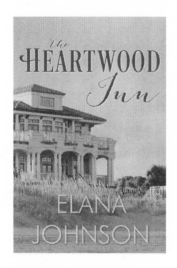

The Heartwood Inn (Book 2): She's excited to have a neighbor across the hall. He's got secrets he can never tell her. Will Olympia find a way to leave her past where it belongs so she can have a future with Chet?

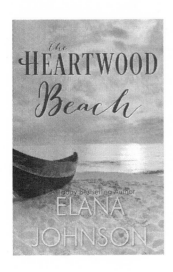

The Heartwood Beach (Book 3): She's got a stalker. He's got a loud bark. Can Sheryl tame her bodyguard into a boyfriend?

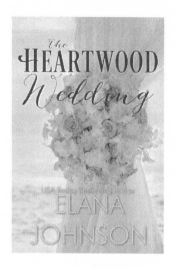

The Heartwood Wedding (Book 4): He needs a reason not to go out with a journalist. She'd like a guaranteed date for the summer. They don't get along, so keeping Brad in the not-her-real-fiancé category should be easy for Celeste. Totally easy.

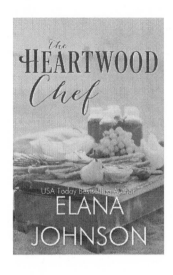

The Heartwood Chef (Book 5): They've been out before, and now they work in the same kitchen at The Heartwood Inn. Gwen isn't interested in getting anything filleted but fish, because Teagan's broken her heart before... Can Teagan and Gwen manage their professional relationship without letting feelings get in the way?

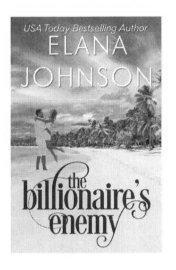

The Billionaire's Enemy (Book 1): A local island B&B owner hates the swanky highrise hotel down the beach...but not the billionaire who owns it. Can she deal with strange summer weather, tourists, and falling in love?

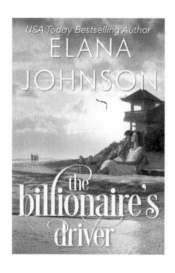

The Billionaire's Driver (Book 2): A car service owner who's been driving the billionaire pineapple plantation owner for years finally gives him a birthday gift that opens his eyes to see her, the woman who's literally been right in front of him all this time. Can he open his heart to the possibility of true love?

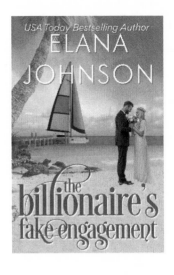

The Billionaire's Fake Engagement (Book 3): A former poker player turned beach bum billionaire needs a date to a hospital gala, so he asks the beach yoga instructor his dog can't seem to stay away from. At the event, they get "engaged" to deter her former boyfriend from pursuing her. Can he move his fake fiancée into a real relationship?

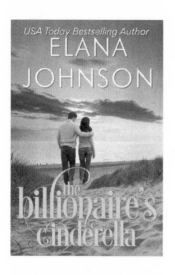

The Billionaire's Cinderella (Book 4): The owner of a beach-side drink stand has taken more bad advice from rich men than humanly possible, which requires her to take a second job cleaning the home of a billionaire and global diamond mine owner. Can she put aside her preconceptions about rich men and make a relationship with him work?

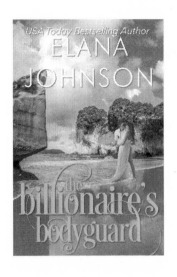

The Billionaire's Body-guard (Book 5): Women can be rich too...and this female billionaire can usually take care of herself just fine, thank you very much. But she has no defense against her past...or the gorgeous man she hires to protect her from it. He's her bodyguard, not her boyfriend. Will she be able to keep those two B-words separate or will she take her second chance to get her tropical happily-ever-after?

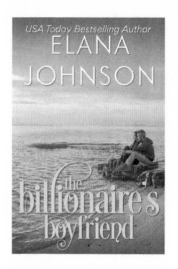

The Billionaire's Boyfriend (Book 6): Can a closet organizer fit herself into a single father's hectic life? Or will this female billionaire choose work over love...again?

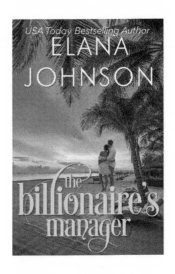

The Billionaire's Manager (Book 7): A billionaire who has a love affair with his job, his new bank manager, and how they bravely navigate the island of Getaway Bay...and their own ideas about each other.

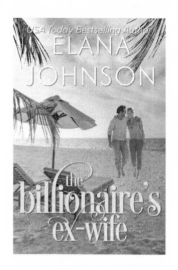

The Billionaire's Ex-Wife (Book 8): A silver fox, a dating app, and the mistaken identity that brings this billionaire faceto-face with his ex-wife...

BOOKS IN THE BRIDES & BEACHES ROMANCE SERIES

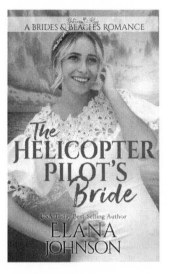

The Helicopter Pilot's Bride (Book 1): Charlotte Madsen's whole world came crashing down six months ago with the words, "I met someone else." Her marriage of eleven years dissolved, and she left one island on the east coast for the island of Getaway Bay. She was not expecting a tall, handsome man to be flat on his back under the kitchen sink when she arrives at the supposedly abandoned house. But former Air Force pilot, Dawson Dane, has a charming devil-may-care personality, and Charlotte could use some happiness in her life.

Can Charlotte navigate the healing process to find love again?

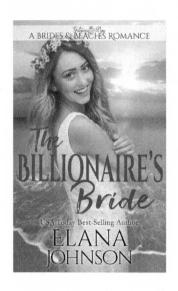

The Billionaire's Bride (Book 2): Two best friends, their hasty agreement, and the fake engagement that has the island of Getaway Bay in a tailspin...

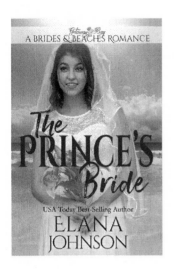

The Prince's Bride (Book 3):

She's a synchronized swimmer looking to make some extra cash. He's a prince in hiding. When they meet in the "empty" mansion she's supposed to be housesitting, sparks fly. Can Noah and Zara stop arguing long enough to realize their feelings for each other might be romantic?

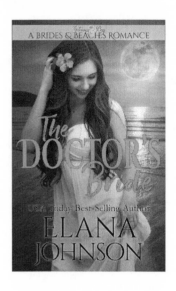

The Doctor's Bride (Book 4): A doctor, a wedding planner, and a flat tire... Can Shannon and Jeremiah make a love connection when they work next door to each other?

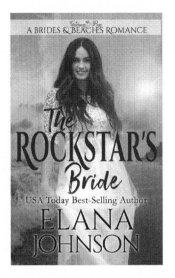

The Rockstar's Bride (Book 5): Riley finds a watch and contacts the owner, only to learn he's the lead singer and guitarist for a hugely popular band. Evan is only on the island of Getaway Bay for a friend's wedding, but he's intrigued by the gorgeous woman who returns his watch. Can they make a relationship work when they're from two different worlds?

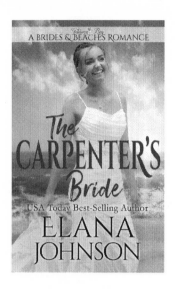

The Carpenter's Bride (Book 6): A wedding planner and the carpenter who's lost his wife... Can Lisa and Cal navigate the mishaps of a relationship in order to find themselves standing at the altar?

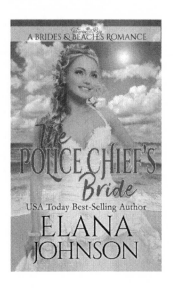

The Police Chief's Bride (Book 7): The Chief of Police and a woman with a restraining order against her... Can Wyatt and Deirdre try for their second chance at love? Or will their pasts keep them apart forever?

BOOKS IN THE STRANDED IN GETAWAY BAY ROMANCE SERIES

Love and Landslides (Book 1): A freak storm has her sliding down the mountain...right into the arms of her ex. As Eden and Holden spend time out in the wilds of Hawaii trying to survive, their old flame is rekindled. But with secrets and old feelings in the way, will Holden be able to take all the broken pieces of his life and put them back together in a way that makes sense? Or will he lose his heart and the reputation of his company because of a single landslide?

Kisses and Killer Whales (Book 2): Friends who ditch her. A pod of killer whales. A limping cruise ship. All reasons Iris finds herself stranded on an deserted island with the handsome Navy SEAL...

Storms and Sentiments (Book 3): He can throw a precision pass, but he's dead in the water in matters of the heart...

USA TODAY BESTSELLING AUTHOR
ELANA JOHNSON

Crushes and Cowboys (Book 4): Tired of the dating scene, a cowboy billionaire puts up an Internet ad to find a woman to come out to a deserted island with him to see if they can make a love connection...

ABOUT ELANA

Elana Johnson is the USA Today bestselling author of dozens of clean and wholesome contemporary romance novels. She lives in Utah, where she mothers two fur babies, taxis her daughter to theater several times a week, and eats a lot of Ferrero Rocher while writing. Find her on her website at elanajohnson.com.

Made in United States
Orlando, FL
17 June 2022

18893947R00217